UNLEASHED

BLAKE BRIER BOOK TWO

L.T. RYAN

with
GREGORY SCOTT

LIQUID MIND MEDIA, LLC

For information contact:

Contact@ltryan.com

https://LTRyan.com

https://www.facebook.com/JackNobleBooks

THE BLAKE BRIER SERIES

Blake Brier Series

Unmasked
Unleashed
Uncharted

1
***

Blake Brier slammed the axe down with one hand. The crack reverberated in his ears as it sunk deep into its target. He tugged downward on the handle. The axe did not budge. He inhaled deeply, as if trying to extract every molecule of oxygen from the bitter air. Within a fraction of a second, his body forced the air back out of his lungs. The warm exhaust crystalized before it left his mouth and lingered in front of his face, even as he gasped another stinging breath.

He cocked his right foot, then kicked it forward. It landed with a crunch. Another deep breath. The routine of exchanging one inadequate breath for another had increased in frequency since he started the five-hour trek toward the summit of Lobuche East.

Blake pulled his left foot free, bent his knee, and slammed the metal spikes of the crampon into the jagged ice two feet above his right. He transferred weight to his left leg and pressed down, testing its stability. His foot shot downward as the brittle ice cracked and fell away. With his right foot firmly planted, and with aid from the ice axe he clutched in his right hand, he kept his composure, never putting tension on the fixed rope to which tethered him.

Faulty footing had become expected in these last few hundred feet of the climb. Because of the cycles of melting and refreezing, small cavities, called "ice cups," riddled the side of the mountain. The frail ridges along the craggy surface proved less than reliable on more than one occasion, particularly in the last half-dozen steps. He set his left crampon again and pushed and pulled his six-foot-three frame a few feet closer toward his goal.

At over 19,800 feet above sea level, the effective oxygen in the air had dropped from 20.9 percent to a mere 9.9 percent. Every foot of progress up the forty-five-degree slope of the ice wall was labored. Beautifully painful.

As Blake dislodged his axe to reach up and bury it again, the icy surface appeared ablaze in a blinding orange glow. The sun emerged over the tall peaks in the distance and cast a blanket of light over the entire face of the mountain. Blake turned his head toward the sun, soaking in its warmth. Water droplets formed on the thin layer of ice encrusting Blake's unkempt beard, revealing hints of its natural red color through the silver frost.

For a second, a mere fraction of what would ultimately be a two-week journey, Blake lost himself in the moment. The dull aching in his legs melted just as the ice would. He gazed at the gleaming disk cradled deep in the gap between Everest and Nuptse. The sun's rays burned through the wispy clouds and rippled off the highest peak on the planet.

Whether there was something to be said about the Buddhists' and Hindus' beliefs in the sanctity of this place, or only a product of mild hypoxia, Blake might have found what he had come for. Had he needed to come within the shadow of the top of the world to find a moment of peace? To quiet his mind and forget, if only for an instant, the torment of regret? Of grief? He could have lingered. He was sure he could live out his days in that spot.

"We're so close, it's right there," hollered Greyson Whitby, "Woo, I'm king of the world!"

Greyson's shouts snapped Blake's mind back to reality, as if a bucket of ice water had awakened him from sleeping.

Fool.

"Sure, you are, Greyson. Just keep moving." Blake looked up at the hindquarters of the pudgy man tethered to the fixed line above him.

He felt guilty about his dismissive tone, but his patience had been wearing thin with Greyson Whitby since they met at Everest Base Camp two nights prior. And he wasn't the only one. Whitby, a British airline executive based out of Hong Kong, had no business hiking Hyde Park, let alone the snowy peaks of the Himalayas. Blake wasn't climbing Everest, or even Ama Dablam. Unlike Whitby, Blake knew his limitations and that attempting such a feat without enough knowledge or experience could put the other climbers in extreme danger.

But Whitby had paid his way, just like everyone else, and because trekking to Lobuche East required no technical climbing skills, there was nothing to say he couldn't join.

In Blake's estimation, the endeavor required physical fortitude and a set of brass balls — neither of which Whitby seemed to possess. Blake had to admit though, Whitby was motivated. Because there he stood, first in line and only feet from cresting the 20,075-foot peak. Then again, the credit for that impossible result rested squarely on the shoulders of their guide, Tashi Dawa Sherpa.

Blake twisted and looked down at Tashi effortlessly moving up the steep slope ten or fifteen feet behind him. Beyond Tashi, there were several small groups about a hundred feet apart. Blake could see the last group, miniature figurines of the people he had shared a meal with the night before. He reminded himself of their names so he could congratulate them when they arrived at the top. Nora, Dario, and their guide, Gem, or... Jam.

"You okay, Mister Blake?" Tashi called up.

Blake replied, "Just Blake," for the umpteenth time, but realizing the futility, he smiled and said, "great Tashi. Feelin' good."

Tashi's confidence and comfort level amazed Blake. Taken out of context, Tashi looked as though he was out for a stroll on a Sunday afternoon. His breathing was slow and calm, as was his demeanor. On at least three occasions in the past hour he had unclipped his ascender and climbed past Blake to assist Whitby, who kept complaining that his crampons weren't working.

Blake realized how much he appreciated having Tashi with him. Continually impressed with the Sherpa people he encountered in Namche Bazaar, Tengboche and Dingboche, Tashi was another shining example of generosity, mental strength, and religious devotion.

Lucky.

Blake had always respected the forces of luck. For most of his life, he had been a slave to superstition. Not that he couldn't laugh at himself over the absurdity of the proposition that any of it made a difference, but he had to concede that some things just happened for a reason. It would take more digits than he possessed to count the times luck had intervened on his behalf.

Whether it was sitting on a certain side of the Humvee when the IED detonated or deploying to one outpost rather than the other. Or getting turned around one klick before reaching a mountain pass at which the Taliban had amassed a hundred men to ambush the convoy.

Blake saw Tashi's presence through the same cosmic lens because the man was a last-minute addition to the group. The American mountaineer who had guided Blake to Everest Base Camp fell ill after learning he would act as porter to Lobuche for both Blake and Whitby. It became clear what the man was sick of after having spent a few minutes with Whitby.

Tashi had been part of a nine Sherpa team who fixed the ropes and dug the route to Everest a month earlier, so one of the first to summit this season. A feat that contributed to his cohorts treating him with near exaltation. With June around the corner, marking the end of the favorable weather window that defines the climbing season, most of the major expeditions were underway or already completed.

Having bid his final group farewell a day earlier, Tashi agreed to step in as a replacement. Blake got the sense, from speaking with some more experienced climbers at camp, that it was rare to have someone of Tashi's caliber on a basic trek. Given that fact, Tashi was as gracious and patient a man as Blake had ever met.

"My ascender thing is stuck," Whitby yelled down over Blake. The sound of Whitby's voice drew Blake's attention upward. Blake found that he had closed the gap between them to five feet.

Whitby fiddled with his ascender. The piece of equipment, attached to each climber's harness by nylon webbing, contained an internal mechanism that allowed it to slide only upward when attached to the rope. By moving the ascender upward with each step, the safety measure ensured that the climber could not fall more than a foot or two before being caught by the tether.

It was a simple and effective piece of equipment, yet the workings of it had stumped Greyson Whitby. Not once, but twice. Since there was still another hundred feet to go, Blake was optimistic about the chance for a third time.

"Leave it Mister Grey. I help you," Tashi instructed as he approached.

Sure, take your time, Whitby. None of us *have anywhere to be.*

Blake pulled his ice axe and pushed his ascender upward until he caught it. Leaning back, he let the rope take some strain off his legs. He was feeling the full effects of the elevation and, although stopping again annoyed him, he welcomed a moment of rest. He occupied his mind by reflecting on how much they had accomplished before sunrise.

The day had started at the Lobuche High Camp, now some 2000 feet below them. Blake awoke at 1:00 AM and by 2:00 AM, the group had finished their coffee, gathered their equipment, and set off toward the switchback trail that would lead them to their day's destiny. The moonless night made traversing the rocky terrain more difficult than in even the slightest ambient light, something only the moon and a cloudless sky could provide in the remote Khumbu valley region. But headlamps offered some surety, illuminating each step with an ellipse of amber colored light. Blake realized how much he enjoyed that. He had leaned into the sensation of being alone.

Existing only within the confines of a beam of light. Unable to affect anyone else but himself.

By the time they had reached the slabs and could no longer walk without scrambling up the rocky terrain, the group was already twenty or thirty minutes behind schedule. The frost on the slick, exposed rock had proven a challenge for Whitby, who required literal hand holding by Tashi.

With Blake, Whitby, and Tashi being ahead, they set the pace for the rest of the group comprised four three-person teams: five men, three women, and four porters. All capable climbers. Tashi had the most experience and assumed the lead and, during the first hour, moved between the groups to check on each.

The pre-dawn sky brightened as the group reached the crampon zone. Blake was thankful for that, although the glow on the horizon had illuminated how high they had climbed. And how far there was to fall. Never a huge fan of heights, in the initial daylight-exposed minutes a twinge would inevitably materialize in his lower abdomen when he looked back to check on the group's progress. And then he noticed the sensation had subsided. How quickly humans can acclimate.

The shrill voice of Greyson Whitby jolted Blake's mind back to the present moment. The grating sound a perfect antidote to the attention deficit in his brain.

Blake could feel each ranting word out of Whitby's mouth through the rope that connected the two. During his "man-trum"—a term Blake had coined for Whitby's frustrated outbursts—Whitby tugged and bounced and swore, disregarding the measured instructions of the master mountaineer who remained balanced on the slope beside him.

Then it happened.

Blake wasn't sure what registered first, the sensation of the ground dropping out from under him, or the whipping sound of the end of the rope as it flew above him. In a furious effort of primal instinct, Blake smashed his ice axe into the slope. His feet flew out in an arc and he felt the stretch of his shoulder muscle as his body weight bore down, trying to rip his grip from the handle of the axe.

All at once, Blake felt the pain explode from his left shoulder as the spiked sole of Greyson Whitby's crampon drove in deep by the weight of the falling man. The spikes twisted and peeled away as Whitby's body contorted to continue its descent.

Blake reached up with his left hand, grasping at the man's clothing. His fingers found their way into a nylon loop on Whitby's pack a split second before his falling force jerked Blake's arm to its limit with intent to tear him limb from limb. Blake jammed his crampons into the ice to take the pressure off his right hand which had slipped off the axe's handle and grasped the lanyard he had wrapped around his wrist.

Whitby, now upside down, flailed and clawed at the ice with his bare hands, his axe dangling from his wrist in its own attempt to escape down the mountain.

"Greyson, bury that axe. Do it now. Set the axe and push up on it. I can't hold you much longer." Blake winced and closed his eyes as he tried to muster the strength to hold on. A little longer. Just a little longer.

Blake could feel some pressure dissipate. He opened his eyes to find Tashi pushing up on Whitby's shoulders.

"Hold him a little more," Tashi said without a hint of stress in his voice.

Blake watched as Tashi yanked Whitby's axe upward — Whitby's arm with it — and buried it into the ice.

"Okay. You let go," Tashi said. He grabbed either side of Whitby's waist and bounced with his knees to shore up his feet. Blake let go and Tashi guided Whitby around until he had slid right-side-up and was hanging by the strap of the axe. "Okay. You step now." Tashi kicked at the ice near Whitby's feet to demonstrate.

Whitby—who uncharacteristically had not said a word in the past fifteen seconds—did as he was told. He dug his feet in, grabbed the handle of the axe, and stood motionless.

Blake pulled his axe from the ice, repositioned it lower and stepped down two feet closer to where Whitby and Tashi had ended up. For the first time since Whitby's crampon had impaled him, Blake felt the searing pain creep back into his shoulder and radiate down his left arm.

Tashi yelled down to the next group below and waived his arms in the signal to halt. Blake looked down below and could see each group following suit, passing the message to the group below.

"Stay with him, Mister Blake," Tashi said. Blake nodded. Tashi grabbed the rope and drew up the loose end, coiling it as he did. He issued another exaggerated hand signal to the Sherpas below and snapped open Whitby's ascender, disconnecting it from the rope. "Now you." He pointed to Blake's harness.

Blake removed his own ascender from the rope as Tashi took off up the slope, moving at three times the speed that the group had been managing.

Whitby and Blake watched in silence as Tashi disappeared over the crest. Blake felt the urge to admonish the British businessman for almost killing them, but decided that wouldn't help the situation. Besides, what happened here was not the fault of Greyson Whitby or anyone else in their party. Another team set the fixed ropes weeks before this group had arrived. Dozens of groups making the trek over that time had used these ropes.

Again, hanging down from the submission, the rope rippled. Tashi was pulling up the slack to reset an anchor by knotting the rope. Blake realized the previous hand signal had instructed the trailing Sherpas to pull up slack in the line to allow Tashi to drag it over the precipice. A task Blake imagined would take massive strength, factoring in the weight of rope and the multiple anchors along the route.

Blake pulled up on the rope to help. He wondered what might have caused the anchor to fail. He had heard the climbers refer to the top anchor point as being, "bomb proof," meaning the anchor was set with several redundancies, but Blake thought it was a dumb analogy. In his experience, nothing was bomb proof.

Tashi reappeared and made his way back to Blake and Whitby.

"Okay. Ready. We will go now," Tashi said with a genuine smile.

"Tell me what to do and I'll do it," Whitby said. His voice carried a serious quality that had not been present before.

The group clipped back into the line and ascended. Tashi instructed Whitby and, in what felt like only minutes, Blake watched as Whitby reached the summit. He could see the shaken man stare out into the vast landscape. No hooting, no hollering, no jumping up and down. Maybe Whitby was the one who had found what he was looking for.

Blake reached the summit, followed by Tashi. Blake put his hands together and gave a slight bow. Tashi smiled and did the same. The two walked together toward a small area that other hikers had compacted. Tashi motioned to the end of a frayed rope that still protruded from the anchor. Blake bent down and ran his hand along a jagged ridge of ice, perpendicular to the rope.

"Greyson." Blake drew Whitby's attention to the sharp ridge of ice. Blake said nothing else, but Whitby understood. It wasn't his fault. Not completely.

With the rest of the group a few minutes behind, the three sat and enjoyed the solitude of the mountain. Whitby craned his head from one side to the other, as if trying to take a mental panoramic image. Blake couldn't blame him. He also had never seen anything like it.

Blake rooted around in his pack and pulled out a few energy bars. He offered them to the others, who declined. Blake removed his outer layer and stuffed it in his pack. He stretched his legs out and leaned back on his hands.

"How bad?" Tashi pointed to Blake's shoulder. Blake hadn't noticed that blood had seeped through the yellow polyester of his pullover.

"It's nothing. Of all the sharp things I've been stuck with, crampons don't even make the worst ten." Blake smiled.

"It's amazing what you did Mister Blake." Tashi turned to Whitby, "He save your life."

"Yes, I know, "Whitby chimed in. "I don't know how to repay you. I mean, I will. I will repay you."

"You don't owe me anything, Greyson. Do you want to know how you can repay me? The next time you're setting out on one of these adventures. Don't."

Tashi blurted out a quick laugh before he could contain it.

"Done," Whitby said. "I think I've had my fill."

"You have family?" Tashi turned in toward Blake.

"No family. It's just me," Blake answered. He broke his gaze away from the landscape and fixed it on Tashi. "How about you? Where does your family live?"

"No. Three month on mountain. Then stay with other monk. You see? I take vow. No wife. Yes? Only Buddha."

"Oh. You're Buddhist monk. I wouldn't have..." Blake reconsidered his words so to not offend the man. Blake had not considered that the man who wore a North Face jacket and Patagonia alpine pants was a monk. He hated that he had let his own biases influence his perception. He changed the course of his questioning. "So, you live at the Monastery?"

"Yes. Monastery. In Kharikhola. Nine month. All come to mountain, three month."

"Maybe that's the secret Tashi. Simplicity. Solitude. I mean, you seem like a pretty put-together guy. Look at me, my life's kind of a mess."

"Put together?"

"Yeah. Like you're at peace with yourself. You know, happiness."

"Ah. No secret, Mister Blake. Easy. Buddha teach, only open... this," he poked at Blake's forehead, "and this," and again at his chest, "then find true happiness. You see? Yes? Then, life not a mess."

Blake laughed. "I should write that down Tashi. Thanks."

The sound of jubilation broke through the meditative mood as the next group of climbers reached the summit.

Blake stood up. A wave of pins and needles surged behind his eyes and then slowly dissipated. He reached into his pack, pulled out a small oximeter and clipped it to his finger.

Sixty percent.

He tossed the oximeter to Whitby, who clipped it onto his own finger.

Blake peered down the slope toward camp and looked back at Whitby, then down over the edge once more. He let out a sigh, forced a smile and called out to the arriving group, "Congrats Isla! Kris..."

2

The angular rays of the morning sun glinted off the chrome adorning the 1930s Art Deco style arches forming the spire of the Chrysler Building. Levi Farr stood beside the wall of floor to ceiling windows in the modern conference room. *A powerful view,* Farr thought to himself. The perfect place to solidify a monumental deal.

"What's taking them so long?" Dr. Sebastian Roberts groaned.

Levi had almost forgotten his colleague had been sitting in the room. He turned toward Roberts, silhouetting himself against the barbed backdrop of New York City.

"Relax, Seby," Levi said.

Sebastian jutted his neck out toward Levi, as if waiting for the rest of Levi's sentence to arrive. It did not.

"I mean, it's rather rude, don't you think?" Roberts asked.

Levi did not answer the rhetorical question. His mind churned through the mental notes he had prepared. The strategy for the game of hard-ball negotiation to come. He felt good. Confident. A product of his ever-present arrogance. An arrogance demonstrated by the fact he had not engaged his corporate attorneys in the matter.

Levi took in the scene facing him. Dr. Sebastian Roberts, head of the Scientific Division, sat alone at the enormous boardroom table. His back erect against the tall leather chair. His hands folded on the table in front of him as if a protege of Miss Porter herself.

"Seriously, man. Relax. You cannot show any fear, Seby. Trust me, we have the upper hand. You need to look like it."

Dr. Sebastian Roberts and Levi Farr could not be more opposite. A man with squinty-eyes and thick wire-framed glasses, Roberts may have been the least imposing character Levi had ever met. The same had not been said about Levi Farr. At six foot four, 240 pounds, the former Army Ranger's square jaw and booming voice stood out in the boardroom as much as on the battlefield. Levi had brought Roberts to the thirtieth floor of the E 42nd high-rise for one reason. Because no one understood the technology better. No one understood the value more. Now, Farr hoped that his decision to include Roberts would be the right one.

The frosted glass doors swung open with a cacophony of voices. An opening parade of a three-ring circus. The first glimpse at the cast of characters.

"Mr. Farr." Arthur Oran extended his hand. Levi shook it firmly. "My colleagues, Robert Tombs, Anthony Burgess, Linda Belgrade, and Marcus Fleury.

"Nice to meet you all. This is my chief scientist, Dr. Sebastian Roberts."

Roberts reached over the table to shake Oran's hand and resumed his seated pose.

Farr looked past Oran toward three men who had entered the room behind the group.

"Our attorneys, Mr. Farr. They'll be sitting in." Oran motioned to a chair at the corner of the long table. "Please, have a seat."

"Thank you." Farr took the chair positioned at the head of the table. He could sense Oran's urge to protest, which did not materialize. The group each chose a seat and settled in.

"Mr. Farr, I have to hand it to you," Oran started. "I could say that we're making history here today by our mere presence. Never in history, as far as I'm aware, have the heads of the five biggest pharmaceutical companies in the world sat at the same table. And on the same side, no less. Frankly, I'm enjoying the irony."

"I wouldn't go that far." A smirk crept over Burgess's pursed lips.

Levi would have to endure small talk and flattery before the group would dig into the meat of the matter. But Oran was right, and Levi allowed himself to soak it all in for a few moments. His pride swelled as he considered how he had built his company, Techyon, from a small firm that provided corporate and diplomatic security, into what many would consider a giant. From employing a few dozen knuckle-dragging spec-ops buddies to cultivating a stable of some of the world's preeminent experts.

"Who would like to start?" Oran asked.

Levi decided it was time to take control of the room.

"Gentleman, as you know, Techyon is a global leader in the military contracting world. Israel, the United States, and our allies have relied on our firm for everything from specialized tactical teams, cyber-security, weapon systems engineering, and almost everything in between. But our mission, our commitment, is the science. The science that can change the world."

The group allowed Levi to continue with no attempt to interrupt.

"Do you know why I named my company Techyon?" Levi continued without a pause. "It's an homage. A statement of our commitment. As many of you know, my father, rest his soul, was a physicist. He devoted his life to proving the existence of a single particle. The tachyon. He believed that the smallest scientific discovery could have a ripple effect on our understanding of our world."

Levi scanned the room to gauge whether he was losing the attention of the group. He wondered if the prepared speech was coming across as contrived. He cut it short. "Let me cut to the chase."

Levi Farr was a lot of things, but delusional was not one of them. He understood little of the science that Roberts and his people produced. That he had no real qualifications to be in the position in which he found himself. Despite all of it, he had been single-handedly responsible for the meteoric growth of the company. Through hard-learned lessons and unshakable confidence, he beat the odds.

In private circles, he would say he had but two skills. Violence and the ability to lie to anyone, anywhere. Here, he had no use for either.

"Have you reviewed the proposal?" Levi asked.

"Yes." Belgrade jumped in. "At great length, Mr. Farr. I believe I can speak for the group when I say that you have impressed us. Stunned us, in fact."

For the first time since the day began, a smile graced the face of Sebastian Roberts.

"So, you see why we believe it's worth the money," Levi said. "One hundred billion dollars is not only reasonable, but a bargain."

"Mr. Farr, we know what this sum of money can do for you and for the future of your company," Tombs said.

"But?" Levi braced himself for the answer.

"Don't get us wrong. Your asking price is fair. More than fair. The implications of something like this are incredible. It's just..."

Levi waited. Tombs shot a look at Oran.

"Mr. Farr, can we speak with you alone for a moment?" All eyes focused on the quiet scientist sitting toward the far end of the table.

Levi nodded at Roberts.

"Oh. Yes. I'll be right outside should you have any questions. I've brought some additional data that I would love to show you." Roberts gathered his things and exited through the double doors. He poked his head back over the threshold as the door swung closed. "Let me know."

"Mr. Farr." Oran's tone now more direct. "We have a counteroffer for you."

"Shoot." Levi leaned back in his chair. Just as he expected.

"We know as much about you as one can know about a person, Mr. Farr. We've done our homework. We know where you've come from and, if I may be so bold, where you want to go. We believe you understand the importance of discretion. Would you say we are accurate in this assessment, Mr. Farr?"

"Without a doubt." Levi assured them.

"Good, because this conversation does not leave this room. We are prepared to offer you substantially more than your asking price."

"Okay?" Levi almost sang the word. His eyes narrowed as his brain tried to readjust to a twist it had not rehearsed for.

"We are offering five hundred billion dollars." Oran paused. "To kill the program." He punctuated the statement by mimicking Levi's posture, leaning back into his chair and crossing his arms.

"Wait. You want to kill it?"

"Yes, Mr. Farr," Fluery interjected for the first time, "erase all trace that the program ever existed."

"But why?" Levi wasn't sure it mattered. Five hundred billion. With the injection of that much capital, he could expand his reach to where he could dominate most of the markets in which Techyon competed.

"Our actuaries have spent the last week running every scenario," Fluery explained, "and very few of them work out in our favor. The companies represented in this room, Mr. Farr, generate a yearly revenue that exceeds a trillion dollars, as I'm sure you are aware. What you are offering would significantly jeopardize this. We cannot absorb it. So, we need you to kill it."

One of the nameless attorneys pulled a stack of paperwork from a black leather bag and slid the packet across the table to Levi.

"You agree to destroy all evidence, all documentation, every sample, every product, and anything else that can recreate these results now or in the future. We agree to hand you a check for five hundred billion dollars. As easy as that."

"How would that work?" Levi began calculating, considering the logistics of such a proposition. "That much money cannot just appear out of thin air. I'd go to prison, for Christ's sake."

Oran chuckled. It infuriated Levi. It showed Oran had the upper hand. Not Levi. It was never Levi.

"We have that covered, Mr. Farr." Oran's confidence was on full display. "We have recently developed an experimental drug, an Alzheimer's treatment. Nothing novel, but it has potential. The application for clinical trials has not been filed at this point. We will tout this drug to the media as a miracle discovery and the first ever joint venture, spearheaded by the people in this room, to purchase the so-called 'groundbreaking technology' from none other than..."

"Techyon," Levi said.

"Techyon." Oran repeated. "Techyon gets the money and a little publicity on top of it. We'll take a loss and issue a statement about how hopeful we were about the potential of the treatment and what a shame it was that it didn't offer the miracle cure we had hoped for. Or something along those lines. The bottom line is that we will handle the minutiae, you handle your end of the deal. Can you do that?"

During Oran's diatribe, Levi had already decided. He had flipped a switch in his brain that toggled between doubt and complete resolve, as if the brittle switch had buckled under the immense weight of five hundred billion-dollar bills.

"Yes. You have a deal." Levi opened the packet of paperwork.

"Good. But let us be clear," Oran added, "this means all evidence. Including the kind that has a pulse. I know I don't need to spell it out to you of all people, but are we clear on this point? Can you live with that? Having more blood on your hands?"

Levi understood there was no choice to make. This wasn't a request or a negotiation. These people had the resources to take him out. And anyone else that stood in their way. And knowing what he did now, there was no path backward. He was in it. Deep.

Oran leaned in and peered into Levi's eyes. "Can you?"

"I can barely remember a time when my hands were clean." Farr said. The callousness of the former soldier and mercenary bubbled from whatever shallow place it laid buried. His eyes deadened. "Consider it done."

"Good." Oran stood up from the table. His four counterparts followed suit. Oran motioned to the three attorneys, who remained silent. "They'll help you finalize everything. Good meeting you, Mr. Farr."

The five walked through the doors and barreled through the small reception area.

Sebastian Roberts jumped in his seat at the abrupt entry of the herd. He raised his hand meekly as he stood. "Mr. Oran, I..." Oran passed by without a glance, followed by each of the other industry titans, and disappeared down the hallway.

"Nice to meet you," Roberts called out. He sat back down in his chair and clutched the portfolio, the most significant portfolio that existed, and waited.

3

Blake squeezed himself out of the rear door of the Suzuki hatchback and walked to the back of the car. The driver—who stood five-foot-two but wore a neon green traffic vest that would have been big on Blake—had already started unloading his bags. The miniature car had been shrink-wrapped with Nike branding. Yellowed and peeling, the graphic obscured much of the rust and crinkled metal that riddled the old box of bolts. He wondered how much they had paid the guy to display the advertisement.

Blake handed him one thousand rupees, the price he had negotiated at the start of the trip, plus an extra two hundred rupees for his effort. Stretching his back, he wished he had thrown in a few hundred extra to ride in the front seat.

The driver got back in the car and moved forward in the line of taxis clogging up the drive that led to the principal building of the Tibhuvan International Airport. The building could have been mistaken for an office in a Delaware industrial park had it not been for the concrete control tower jutting out above it. It was a stop, but not the last, in his journey to nowhere.

Blake headed to the main doors, dodging two motorbikes that were weaving through the vehicular traffic.

Inside, Blake worked his way through the throngs to the ticket counter, the security checkpoint, and then the bag check. A worker directed him to throw his bags on a towering pile of multicolored duffels and backpacks. Blake ran through a mental checklist of the items in his bags and decided there was nothing in them that had any significant value to him. Monetary value, yes. But nothing that he couldn't replace. He tossed the bags on the pile and continued toward the gate.

Blake checked his watch. Ahead of schedule.

He spotted an information desk with a few travelers lined up in front of it. He waited his turn and asked the attendant if Wi-Fi was available. The woman provided the password.

Blake punched the password into his phone and connected. He found a seat and plopped down, his legs still sore from the final few days of hiking. The blisters that had formed during the first day had since ripped open and reopened in a daily torturous cycle. He thought about taking off his shoes but decided against it. It had annoyed him in the past when others did so in airports and planes.

He looked around, noting the modern aesthetic. He had noticed the same thing when he first arrived in Nepal. In fact, he found the same to be true in the entire city of Kathmandu. Surprising anachronisms embedded within ancient architecture, customs, and traditions.

The iPhone he had turned off and stowed away since the last time he passed through the walls of the airport buzzed in his hand. He swiped at the device to unlock it and launched the email application. He scrolled through dozens of messages, deleting each one as he went.

Junk. More junk. More junk.

Finding nothing of importance, he checked the voicemail log. Six messages from Griff. He had thought about Griff often during the long stretches of silence that accompanied the trek into the remote regions of the country. Griff, Khat, Fezz and, of course, Anja.

Although he had only known Griff a short time — a fraction of the time he'd known Fezz and Khat — they had formed a bond. Partly because they had shared an interest in exploiting computer systems and partly because of what they had gone through together. Like the unbreakable bond that he, Fezz, and Khat had formed in battle, Griff had been there for him through hell and back. Well, through hell anyway.

Blake touched the screen to play the latest of the voice messages. He pressed the phone to his ear.

"Hey buddy, it's me. Again. Just—"

The audio cut out and the phone rattled. Blake looked at the screen. Incoming call.

Griff.

"Hey buddy, it's me," Griff started.

"You just said that," Blake interrupted.

"Huh?" Griff paused. "It's me. Your long-lost friend. Ya know, digital mastermind, playboy extraordinaire."

Blake had only spoken with Griff a few times over the previous eight months. Not that he didn't want to talk to him, or Fezz, or Khat. It was that he found it easier to compartmentalize the past if the reminder wasn't always present. But it was nice to hear Griff's voice, which, he noticed, had become more strident since they had first met.

"What's up, Griff?"

"Where the hell are you, Mick? I've been calling you for days."

Hearing his nickname stirred Blake. It had been a while since anyone called him that. "I've been traveling a bit. Clearing my head. That sorta thing."

"And you don't call me back," Griff rumbled. "Is it 'cause I'm Black? It's 'cause I'm Black, isn't it, you racist ginger ass?"

An errant smile overtook Blake's face. He came close to bursting out with a full-on laugh. Since he had been traveling, he had met no one with whom he could share the crass, twisted humor common between him and his former teammates. And Griff had been spending too much time with Fezz and Khat.

"You know I'm an equal opportunity hater, Griff. I don't like you very much."

"You love me. Seriously Mick, where ya at?"

"Kathmandu."

"Ah, Kathmandu. That's really, really where I'm going to," Griff sang.

Blake didn't respond. He knew the song, but encouraging Griff was not in his plans.

"Bob Seger? Come on," Griff said. "But where are you, really?"

"Sitting at home. Watching the Golden Girls. What do you want Griff?"

"I've got a proposition for you. Hear me out."

Blake spoke over him. "Here we go. I'm not interested in the proposition, Griff."

"Hold up, brother. Listen. I've gotta go out to Vegas. They're sending me out to poke around the DEF CON conference. The DEF CON conference, Mick. At the Venetian. I know how much you love smart turds with lots of teenage angst and too much time on their hands and I thought..."

Blake groaned.

"No. Really. There's gonna be some great seminars. A chance to keep a leg up in the game. Maybe put a few kids in their place. Ya know what I mean?"

Once upon a time, Blake would have jumped at the chance. The biggest hacker conference in the country would have had a lot to offer his former self. But not anymore.

"First, saying 'DEF CON conference' is redundant. And I appreciate the offer, Griff, seriously I do. But I'm gonna sit this one out. Anyway, I'm sure the CIA wouldn't want me involved." Blake surprised himself for uttering the acronym. He couldn't remember ever saying those three letters out loud. Especially on a cell phone. Normally, he would refer to his former employer as the Agency or not at all.

"Come on, Mick, you wouldn't be there in any official capacity. Just a vacation. You've been hanging around, doing God knows what.

You probably are watching the Golden Girls. And this is a chance to get out. It'll mostly be mingling and whatnot. And drinking. Tons of booze, Mick. Think about it, will ya?"

"Okay, I'll think about it, Griff."

"Great. It's in three days, so don't think for long. Call me later."

"Will do," Blake lied. "Later." He hung up.

Blake dug inside himself but couldn't find any trace of the love he once had for the art of computer hacking, social engineering, or even the entire field of spy craft or special operations. Not after everything that had happened.

He had pulled the trigger when he knew he shouldn't.

He had made mistakes he thought he wouldn't.

He was no longer sure what he was doing, where he was going, or why he was in Nepal.

He looked down at the ticket resting on his knee. KTM to DOH. DOH to CPT. Cape Town International Airport. He picked up the ticket and began flicking it against his arm with a rhythmic beat. His body was motionless. As was often the case, the more still Blake's body, the more chaotic his mind.

He sprung up, put his phone in his pocket, and headed off toward the ticket counters.

Time to go home.

4

"Is this it?" The Uber driver called back to Blake.

"This is fine." Blake called up the app and entered a gratuity. The app asked him to enter a rating for the driver. He touched the icon for the maximum rating. Five stars.

Blake jumped out and dragged his bags from the back seat. The car drove off, leaving Blake standing on the side of the affluent Alexandria street. Parked cars pointing in both directions lined the road.

He had entered an address that was about a half block away from his own. Old habits, he guessed. He lugged his bags along the row of immaculately kept townhouses, a world away from the open expanses of the Himalayas. Even the air smelled different. Polluted. He had never noticed it before. But he was still glad to be there.

As he approached his home, he could see the Dodge Challenger he left parked on the street, in front of his door, had accumulated a thick coat of pollen and dust. Several parking tickets decorated the windshield under the driver's side wiper blade.

Blake dropped his bags and ran his finger over the hood of the car, leaving a thin, shiny streak. He walked into the street, toward the driver's side, and saw the bright yellow boot affixed to the front wheel. He had expected that would happen before he left, but decided it would be better than leaving the car in a lot or trying to find someone to move the car twice a week while he was gone. What he didn't see, at least not right away, was the deep gouge that ran along the entire side of the car. He ran his hand along the serrated groove.

Bastards.

Blake let out a defeated chuckle. Finding out that someone had keyed his Challenger was a fitting end to the longest day in history. A day that had started in Kathmandu over fifty-two hours earlier. Through several layovers and cancelled flights, Blake had inched his way closer to Dulles. During the last leg of the flight, he had half-expected an emergency landing in the Atlantic to drag out the trip that much longer.

Blake humped his bags up the stairs and rested them on the stoop. He punched his code into the lock and the familiar robotic response greeted him. He swung the door open. The warm, stagnant air met him at the threshold.

He walked in and dropped his bags, glimpsing himself in the mirror. He leaned in and swiped his fingers over his cheeks and through his beard. His hair had grown long, not just over the last few weeks, but in the eight months since he had last had a haircut. He looked more like an animal than a man. And he had lost weight while he was away. He could see it in his face. At least he hadn't lost muscle tone — the harsh mountainous region had made sure of that. In fact, he thought he looked more muscular now than when he left. More defined. Although he conceded that it may have just been the style of the tight Under Armour compression shirt that made it appear his shoulder, arms, and chest muscles were about to rip through the fabric.

Normally, Blake would have taken the next several minutes to clear the three-story townhouse, checking every room for any signs that something had been moved or that someone had been there while he wasn't. Not that he didn't consider doing it, it's just that he ultimately decided he would much rather inspect the couch cushions with his rear-end. Besides, while it was once a simple task for Blake to determine if anything was out of place—thanks to an obsessive compulsion that everything be in its designated spot—his routine had become vague over the previous months. And having been gone for so long, he wouldn't have been able to tell anyway. Especially if someone had the intention of covering their tracks.

Instead, Blake picked up the remote control, stretched his legs along the couch, flicked on the TV and, within seconds, succumbed to sleep.

5

D r. Benjamin Becher pulled his knees up to take the pressure off his back. He had been lying on the table for some time but wasn't sure how long. Enough time to predict the interval at which the fluorescent lights would flicker. Accompanied by their tinny tick. As pedestrian as they were, Becher ranked these buzzing and ticking gas-filled tubes as the most important feature in the high-tech facility. Without them, the windowless room would have been shrouded in complete darkness, save a few blinking LEDs embedded in the control panels of various pieces of medical equipment.

Becher wasn't a medical doctor. Not a physician, technically. He was a preeminent geneticist, an expert in human physiology. And as a patient, he had become intimately familiar with most equipment in the room.

"That should do it, Ben." The first thing Dr. Ursel had said in the last half-hour. Ursel grasped the tube and twisted the connector, which unlocked the tube against the catheter protruding from Becher's chest.

Ancel Ursel was the corporate physician. He wasn't leading a research project or developing any new medical technology. He was on hand to care for the upper echelon of the company's cadre of executives and scientists. Becher could have done it himself, but he appreciated Ursel's help in administering and monitoring the treatments. Access to the best. One of the many perks of working for Techyon.

Dr. Benjamin Becher fit square in that category of the best. The best of the best, in fact. As one of the first to sign on to the newly minted Techyon Scientific Division, Becher had the most seniority of anyone, including his boss, Sebastian Roberts. Becher could have risen to the top. He didn't hold a Nobel prize like Roberts did, but he had no interest in bureaucracy. Only in science.

In the beginning, there were only a few. A small group of visionaries. They had given him an extreme amount of latitude to conduct his work, with the funding to match. And that much had not changed at least. The head of several highly secretive projects, Becher felt he had only scratched the surface of what was possible.

"Let's look at the number." Ursel scrolled through a series of graphs displayed on a laptop connected to a machine attached to Becher by a bundle of leads and electrodes.

"Let's," Becher said. He already knew what they would show.

Ursel had a funny way about him. An awkward approach to conversation. Out of touch with non-medical topics. But Becher rather enjoyed the man, and he was happy Ursel had also been one of the people to move from Tel Aviv to the new United States facility a few months prior.

"Let me guess," Becher said. "I'm dying."

Ursel sighed. "You know I don't sugarcoat Ben and I've told you before. The treatments are helping, but I just don't know how long it will matter. I'm confident it will buy you some time, but it's programmed into your DNA. There's only so much you can expect. It's brilliant work, what you've done. It's a huge advancement in stem cell therapy, but for you... right now... the answer is yes. I'm sorry, Ben, but you're almost out of time."

"That's not acceptable." Becher barked. "That's exactly what I need. Time." He didn't mean to direct his outburst at Ursel. It wasn't Ursel's fault. Becher meant to direct his outburst at the rest of the universe. Whatever grand force strung the whole thing together.

"Ben," Ursel said. His inflection transformed the single word into an entire phrase that bore the message, "Take it down a notch."

Becher was aware of the limitations of the treatment he had developed. He knew that his own stem cells, harvested from his own bone marrow, were genetically programmed to persist the condition that was slowly causing his heart muscle to atrophy. But he had the solution. A solution he couldn't explain to Ancel Ursel.

"Whatever we can do to buy some time, I'll do it, alright?" Becher said. "Doesn't matter if it's made worse in the long term. That will be moot when I get what I need. I am so close. I know you don't understand yet, but you will. You'll see. It will be a miracle is what it will be. Hell, it already is."

Becher caught himself and pulled back before he had said too much. Though he was sure that Ursel took his words as the ramblings of a desperate person. Even after everything Ursel had seen come out of the Techyon labs, he had seen nothing like this.

"There are years of discoveries to be had. Advancements we haven't dreamed up yet. And I'm going to be there for them. I'm going to live so I can make sure that those things happen. I promise you." Beads of sweat formed on Becher's forehead as he spoke.

"I hope you do, Ben," Ursel said, his bedside manner on full blast, "and I'll do whatever I can to help you, you know that. The important thing is that you stay calm. Avoid stress. Stay hydrated. And get some sleep if you can." Ursel stood up from the stool and turned to leave. "I'll see you back in a week."

Becher hopped off the table and fastened the buttons of his shirt over the plastic port embedded in his thoracic cavity. He began looping his necktie into the usual Windsor knot.

With both hands, he grabbed either side of an EKG monitor mounted on a tall chrome stand next to the table. With a grunt, he pulled, tipping the contraption. It crashed to the ground and broke into several pieces. He kicked the carcass of the machine until another large piece broke off and flew across the room.

Then Dr. Benjamin Becher straightened his tie, grabbed his jacket, and went back to work.

6

Bang, bang, ring. Bang, bang, bang, ring.

The initial knock woke him, but the rhythm of the knocking and doorbell ringing garnered no alarm or concern. Despite being half asleep, he trusted that anyone who posed a danger wouldn't be knocking.

Blake lurched into a seated position and opened one eye. The light streamed through the slits in the closed blinds. The living room was eerily still, except for the TV mounted above the mantle of the white-bricked fireplace, which played an old re-run of *The Facts of Life*.

Ugh. Worse than the *Golden Girls*.

Blake picked up the remote and flicked off the TV.

Bang, bang, ring.

He didn't know how long he had napped, but figured it wasn't long. At least it was still daylight. He checked his watch.

6:04 AM.

Blake's groggy brain took a moment to accept he had slept straight through the afternoon and night.

"Hang on." Blake's voice cracked.

He pulled himself up and walked toward the front foyer.

Reaching under the thin table, positioned against the wall under a mirror, he slid the Glock 9mm from the holster he had screwed into the underside of the table. He tucked it into his waistband at the small of his back. Better safe than sorry.

Bang, bang.

"Hang on," Blake said, this time with blatant authority.

He peered through the peephole and smiled at the image relayed through the tiny convex lens. The giant head of his friend and former teammate filled the entire frame. Blake unlocked the door and opened it.

"Jesus, Mick. What? Were you sleeping? It's six o'clock." Blake could feel Fezz looking him over as he pushed his way inside. "Rough night?"

"I don't remember," Blake quipped.

Fezz looked down at Blake's feet.

"Did you sleep in your shoes?"

Blake just stared at him, not wanting to award him a response.

"Come here." Fezz wrapped his arm around Blake and slapped him on the back twice. Any harder and he could have knocked the wind out of him. Blake did the same. "Got any coffee in this joint?" Fezz asked as he walked down the hallway toward the kitchen.

Blake followed. He could use some himself.

"Shit, Mick. How long has it been? Six months?"

"Eight," Blake said. He switched on the Keurig and pulled out the plastic reservoir to fill it.

"Eight months. Damn. You look... good," Fezz said, with an obvious lack of authenticity. "I like what you've done with the place."

Fezz motioned to the pans and other kitchen items laid out on a towel next to the sink, as if set out to dry but never put away.

"I've been busy," Blake said.

Fezz took a seat on a stool at the island in the center of the kitchen. He rested his arms on the granite countertop.

"Apparently you have, brother, because Griff has been calling you for days. He's headed to the airport to catch his flight out to Viva Las

Vegas. Wasn't sure if you had changed your mind about going with him. I told him I'd stop in."

"I'm not going to Vegas, Fezz." Blake replaced the filled reservoir, clamped down the handle on the coffee pod, and started brewing. "Nothing good can come of it."

"If by 'nothing good' you mean winning big on the craps table and spending the night with a couple of Tropicana showgirls, sign me up, too." Fezz laughed.

"That's the last thing I need." His serious tone did not match the levity that Fezz had been attempting to inject into their exchange.

Fezz was trying to cheer him up, to make light of the situation. It was how they had always done it. Most times they were relentless in breaking each other's stones. Often crossing the line to insult. But there was no one that Blake trusted more than this man. They would often call each other brother. And they meant it.

"I thought I was in a good place, Fezz." Blake spoke slowly, measuring each word. The emotion behind the abrupt statement was palpable if the expression on Fezz's face was any judge. "When it was all done. After we had finished our business. After we made our decisions, right or wrong, and we delivered vengeance. It felt like the end of the chapter. The beginning of a new one. But it wasn't, Fezz. It really wasn't."

Blake paused. Fezz didn't speak, allowing Blake the opportunity to gather his thoughts and get them off his chest.

"It's just what we do, right?" Blake continued. "Bury the doubt, the pain, the anger. It's the only way we could operate. Hell, we all would have been dead a long time ago if we didn't have that ability. I guess I figured this last time would have been the same. But it was different. It was personal."

The coffee machine spat the last drops into the mug. Blake grabbed it and passed it across the island to Fezz, who held it like a toy teacup in his enormous hand. Blake started a second cup for himself as he spoke.

"While I was traveling, I realized it had never been personal before. The lives we took. Even the collateral damage. It was for a cause. The greater good. It was never about me, or you, or Khat, or any single person. It was about the mission. And I was good with that." Blake ran his hands over his face and rubbed his temples. "I don't know. I'm rambling."

"Mick," Fezz interjected, "do you remember in Syria, I recruited that woman who had gotten tied in with Al-Nusra. Fatima was her name. She had the nine-year-old daughter. You and I built a swing for the kid out behind the safe house. Remember how she'd swing on that thing for hours?"

"I remember," Blake said.

"I set up Fatima with a tracker so she could lead us to the Al-Nusra training camp. Except I knew she had already been made. I knew they were taking her to her death, but I let her go anyway. Because we needed to know where they would take her."

"Yeah, that was messed up." Blake admitted.

"It was extremely messed up. And so was I. For a long time. I had to tell this little girl her mom was dead. A woman that did nothing but help us. Knowing that I could have prevented it. I was most pissed off at myself for letting it get to me. Letting it get personal. But do you remember what you said to me?"

Blake shook his head.

"You said, 'It's always personal. Otherwise, you wouldn't be here.' And you were right. It's our care for what happens to the people that allows us to bring down such brutality on others. We were always invested. Having to shoulder the consequences is our cross to bear."

"I sound like a wise man." Blake smiled.

"You had your moments," Fezz jabbed. "The thing is, moving forward isn't the same as moving on. It's okay to move forward with your life. Maybe you never get back in the game, I'm not saying you should, but you're the best at what you do, Mick. You shouldn't have to hide from it."

Fezz glanced at the stairway just off the kitchen. His movement drew Blake's attention to it. Blake hadn't ventured down those stairs and into the custom-built vault in months. He hadn't even considered it. The room full of computers and state-of-the-art equipment had sat dormant. Patiently waiting for a surge of electricity to once again pulse through its veins.

"Anyway," Fezz said. He gulped the last bit of coffee in his mug and stood up from the counter. "Enough of this serious, heart-felt crap. I've gotta hook up with Khat. We've gotta make a quick trip that never happened to a place that doesn't exist." Fezz smiled.

"Good luck with that." Blake extended his hand. Fezz shook it with a firm squeeze. "It's good seeing you."

Fezz walked to the door and opened it. Blake watched from the kitchen.

"Vegas, man. Vegas." Fezz nodded. And with that, he left.

Blake sipped his coffee and stared into space. Puttering about the kitchen, he put away the pans and tidied up the counter as his mind churned away. He finished his coffee, washed the two mugs, and placed them in the cabinet, turning the handles so they pointed outward. He looked around at the room, settling his focus on the entrance to the basement stairs. Hardwood steps to the past.

Blake walked over and descended the stairs to the vault's door. He walked at a normal pace, as anyone would, but he felt as though he had teleported there. Taking a deep breath, he punched in the numbers and heard the large cylinders slide inside the thick, rein-forced door. He pushed it open and walked into the darkness.

Blake ran his hand along the wall and touched the switches of the electrical panel. He switched them on in rapid succession, bringing the room to life.

Fans whirled, disks spun. A familiar symphony.

The screens on the desk in the middle of the room came to life. Blake walked to the desk and sat in the chair. The screen greeted him with the flashing cursor of a terminal prompt. The little square of flickering pixels represented an entry point to an infinite number of possibilities.

The rabbit hole.

Blake picked up his phone, dialed the number, and held it to his ear.

"Fine, Griff. I'm in."

7

The digital compass dial spun as Blake rotated his phone. He had arrived late the night before and was just getting his bearings in the expansive Venetian hotel complex. While checking in, he had glanced at a floor plan mounted on a wall near the front desk. From where he stood, his destination was due southeast.

"Room for cream?" The barista stood poised to pull the lever and dispense the final ounce of coffee into the paper cup.

The Starbucks kiosk was on the first floor of the Palazzo, a few feet from the elevators to Blake's suite on the forty-ninth floor.

"Yes, thank you," Blake said. He took his coffee black and slapped a lid on it to help him keep from spilling as he walked. The distance to the auditorium—in the enormous conference center that was once part of the historic Sands hotel—was a quarter of a mile away, but the walk there would not require leaving the building. He would have to hustle to make it in time.

Blake touched his phone to the electronic pad to pay for his coffee, then set off toward his destination. He realized he could not make a bee line. Forced to walk south, he hugged the east wall until he spotted a sign overhead which pointed out the direction to the conference center.

The sign, like everything else in the place, mimicked old world Italian architecture. Frescos covered the ceilings and faux stone pillars lined the corridors. Blake had spent some time in Venice and Rome years prior, and this was no substitute. But he gave them credit because he had almost forgotten he was in the middle of a desert.

He looked at his watch and picked up the pace to a mild jog, letting the signs guide him in. He reached the security checkpoint, emptied his pockets, and passed through the metal detector. The machine beeped and blinked. He rechecked his pockets, pulled out a quarter he had missed, and tossed it into the plastic bowl. A security guard motioned for him to back up and pass through the detector again. This time, the machine did not complain.

Blake gathered his belongings and followed the crowds to the main expo area. He meandered through hordes of people gathered around booths adorned with giant screens, art exhibits, and video arcade games. Several DJs blasted techno tunes, the next one picking up as soon as the previous was out of earshot. The size of the operation was stunning. Over thirty-thousand people would attend, but the whole thing seemed impossibly large. He wondered why he hadn't attended the annual event sooner.

Blake made his way toward the auditorium where he had agreed to meet Griff. The vinyl sign, pulled taut between two folding stands, read "Resist the Reset: Breaking Through Wallet Isolation," and displayed a picture of the speaker, Adam Holt. Griff had chosen the speaker because he remembered that Blake had been interested in the topic. During their research in Bitcoin the previous year, Blake had discovered an article by a graduate student about securing cryptocurrency hardware wallets by separating the user and kernel processes into two CPUs, resetting the user processor between tasks. Blake was curious to find out how Holt had worked around this method of sandboxing.

"Mick," Griff waved as he worked through the crowd toward Blake.

Blake gave Griff a nod. The strange collection of people in attendance grabbed his attention. Many wore button-down shirts, others were in shorts and T-shirts, while others arrived in strange costumes and eccentric makeup. Blake couldn't think of any other place he had been that was so diverse. Age, race, style, status, skill. Every combination was represented. In his jeans, T-shirt, and thick beard, Blake represented the casual red-headed caveman demographic.

"Let's go in, it's about to start," Griff said, as he reached Blake. "You don't want to miss the beginning."

Blake really didn't care. He would have rather been at Spritz, the little poolside joint he'd seen on the website, having a breakfast burrito and maybe a Bloody Mary. But he didn't want to let Griff down.

"Nope, don't want to miss it." Blake followed Griff into the room.

The two found seats in an empty row of chairs toward the back. Griff took out his laptop and set it on his thighs. One of the organizers was speaking at the podium.

"—if you have questions at the end. And with that, please welcome Adam Holt."

A lackluster round of applause followed.

"Thank you. It's great to be here today. Can we get this up on the screen?" Holt motioned to someone offstage. The two towering screens behind Holt at both ends of the stage lit up. Both displayed the words Resist the Reset. "Great. Let me start by telling you a little about myself—"

"How was your first night?" Griff whispered.

"I got in at almost 1:00 A.M. I had a bite and went to bed. Not that exciting. What did you do?"

"I played blackjack for a few hours. I started with like forty bucks and at one point I was up six hundred. I lost it all, though. But hey, at least I was only out forty. Also, I was talking to this guy from Texas. He was sitting next to me at the table. Said there's this little dive bar down by Freemont that has great food, live music. Said it's the best place no one knows about. I know you like the hidden gems, figured maybe we'd hop over there tonight. Check it out."

"Sure Griff, whatever you wanna do," Blake was half listening to Griff and half to Adam Holt.

"Great." Griff turned back toward the front of the room.

"—before going to work for Sizzle, where I serve as Chief Technology Officer. It was the—" Holt rattled on.

Griff shifted in his chair toward Blake. He whispered, "Bet you a C-Note you can't hijack those screens."

Blake snickered. "I don't want your money, Griff."

"You don't want my money because you can't do it?"

"Please," Blake dismissed. "I'm in no mood."

"I bet I could do it." Griff poked.

"Uh. You're such a child. You know damn well I can," Blake said, a little louder than he intended. He dropped his voice. "The projectors are on the Wi-Fi and I'm assuming so is your laptop. It's not like there's a high level of security on these things, there'd be no reason for it."

"No reason 'til now." Griff laughed. He held the laptop out toward Blake.

"Give me it." Blake snatched the computer from Griff's hands.

Griff was trying to get Blake to engage. A simple task for someone of his ability. But a challenge had been issued, and Blake couldn't resist.

"What's taking so long, Mister Wizard." Griff goaded within seconds of Blake's fingers touching the keys.

Blake hammered away at the keyboard and slid fingers around the track pad. Griff tried to look on, but Blake turned the screen away. After about ninety seconds, Blake declared victory.

"Done."

Griff reached to take the computer, but Blake pulled it back toward himself. "Hold on, one more thing."

After another minute, Blake grinned and tossed the laptop back onto Griff's lap. It landed with a thud.

"Careful with this thing," Griff protested.

Griff looked at the screen. Blake looked at Griff's face, waiting for the reaction. A reaction which came as a burst of suppressed laughter. If Griff had had a mouth full of water, he would have spit it over the three rows in front of them.

Blake reached over, opened the screen preferences, and clicked the icon that looked like a projector. The two giant screens flickered, and the prepared slide was replaced with one that contained only the words, "I made up most of this on my way here."

A raucous laughter erupted from the crowd. Holt stopped. His eyebrows tilted, showing his perplexity. The clamoring settled down and he continued. "As I was saying, the entire purpose was to prevent the kind of vulnerabilities found in the Ledger and Trezor wallets, but—"

"My turn," Griff whispered, almost giggling. Griff toggled the output back to the laptop screen; he deleted the text, typed his own, and selected the projector.

"I live in my Mom's basement."

The crowd erupted again. Even louder than the first time.

Blake let out a hearty laugh. Griff laughed louder, causing Blake to laugh even more. Blake laughed so hard he had tears in his eyes. It had been a long time. And it felt good.

The crowd began looking around, trying to spot the culprit. The laughter morphed into a chatter that prompted Holt to pause, again.

"What am I missing?" Holt said. His headset microphone feeding-back slightly.

Griff could have switched it back, but Blake was glad he didn't. He got a kick out of seeing how long it would take Holt to figure out what was going on. A woman in the front row stood up. Blake couldn't hear her, but he could guess what she was saying as she pointed to screen.

Holt turned to look. He took the message in stride. "Brilliant. For the record, my mother is a wonderful woman. With a very comfort-able basement. Now, if you wouldn't mind."

Blake yelled out, "We don't mind." All eyes turned toward the back of the auditorium. Griff's eyes widened. Griff had not expected Blake to speak up. Blake sat back, unfazed by the attention. He nodded toward Griff, who fumbled to switch back the feed.

Holt craned his neck until the screens displayed the correct information. He continued. "So, as I was saying. Vulnerabilities—"

Griff leaned over to Blake. "Wanna see what else is going on?"

"I thought you'd never ask." Blake had already determined within the first two minutes that there was nothing he would hear that he didn't already know. He stood and walked toward the end of the row. Griff followed. The pair slid into the aisle and sauntered to the double exit doors.

"What did I tell ya, you're a child." Blake smiled and wiped some remaining moisture from under his eyelid.

"I'm a child? What would possess you to do such a juvenile thing?" Griff faked his astonishment.

Blake slammed the door's latch bar and pushed it open with his hip as he shoved Griff into the door frame.

Griff pushed through the door to the cacophony of the main floor. Blake was already ten feet ahead of him. Griff smiled.

"Ladies and gentlemen," Griff said to a crowd that wasn't listening, "he's back!"

8

Haeli Becher strutted through the lobby of the Waldorf
Astoria with a purpose. Her eyes locked on the elevators
ahead, she was keenly aware of everyone and everything
around her.

The place was fancier than she had envisioned. Sleek and
modern. No expense had been spared to demonstrate the preten-
tiousness sought after by the discerning clientele.

A couple stood at the front desk. The man wore an expensive-
looking suit, but with no tie and the top button of his shirt open. The
woman, wearing a simple black dress that sat off her shoulders, was
as sleek and elegant as the decor.

An older man with a stoic expression and salt-and-pepper hair
passed by from the opposite direction. She heard his gait slow. She
could feel his eyes on her.

Haeli was no stranger to attracting men. Blessed with what many
considered conventional beauty, her soft, pleasing features, bright
smile, silky black hair, and flawless skin had drawn compliments
daily. She had learned to use it to her advantage. But on this day, she
needed just the opposite. And it wasn't going very well.

The clicking of her heels on the polished marble was as accurate as a metronome. The sound of a woman who knows where she's going, she hoped.

She shifted her eyes from side to side. A flicker, really, but enough time to thoroughly scan her surroundings.

Were they all looking at her? Was she out of place? Maybe she should have given more care to what she wore. She had thought the white sleeveless blouse and black pants would have sufficed. Nondescript enough to discourage anyone from remembering her.

She reached the elevators, pressed the upward arrow, and glanced over her shoulder at the desk. A porter was loading the couple's baggage onto a cart. The man and woman working behind the desk were wrapped up in the check-in process. She decided that she was being paranoid. Hundreds, if not thousands, of people passed through every day.

The elevator opened and Haeli stepped in. She pulled a yellow square of paper from her bra and double checked the number. 1211. She slid the paper over her chest until it lodged between her breast and the fabric of the undergarment. Then pushed the button for the twelfth floor.

The elevator moved fast. An LCD display embedded in the wall kept track of the progress. 8, 9, 10. The elevator slowed, settling on the eleventh floor. The doors opened.

Two men dressed in black suits occupied the area between the elevator and the elaborate parlor. The men canted their bodies, opening a pathway between them. They stared at her as if demanding she step out. Haeli backed up against the stainless-steel box in which she was trapped. She let her hands fall just behind her thighs and she balled her fists.

One man spoke. "That's okay, we're going down."

Haeli let out the breath that she realized she'd been holding in. Her fingers relaxed as the doors closed and the elevator lurched upward.

Relax.

The doors opened to the twelfth floor. The sitting area and

48

hallway were empty. She felt relief, but the tension in her shoulders would have disagreed.

She followed the order of the numbers affixed to each door until she reached the one that read 1211, and knocked lightly.

The door opened a crack. She could not see anyone peeking out at her.

"Haeli?" he whispered.

Haeli raised her sight line and saw the man's face peering out from what seemed like several feet above her. At five foot four, she was used to looking up at people, but not that much. She guessed the guy had to be at least six foot eight.

"Dr. Wentz?" Haeli responded.

Karl Wentz opened the door and hurried Haeli inside.

"Were you followed?"

"I don't think so." Haeli noticed that the tall man was sweating. His face was gaunt and his movements were sporadic. Maybe she was right to have been paranoid. Something had put the fear of God in this man.

Two chairs faced a small table in front of large panes of glass that looked out onto the Las Vegas strip. Wentz pulled one chair out. Even this simple motion was awkward.

"Sit down," Wentz said. "I'll try to make this quick, but I want you to listen to what I have to say. It's important I tell you everything I can and then you'll never see me again."

Haeli sat. Wentz pulled out the other chair but didn't sit in it. He paced in a tight circle like a dog chasing its tail in slow motion.

"You don't know me, but I feel like I know you in a way. I worked with your father. Not for long, I mean, they hired me just as your father transferred from Israel. It was an excellent opportunity. I mean, it was supposed to be an excellent opportunity. But I saw something I shouldn't have. I didn't mean to. Believe me, I wish I hadn't."

Haeli tried to let him speak but was already growing tired of trying to decode the nervous rambling.

"Is my father okay?" Haeli interrupted.

Wentz stopped and let out an audible sigh. He adjusted the matching red plush chair and sat facing Haeli. If she had been standing, the pair would have been eye-to-eye.

"I don't know, Haeli. I had to run and came here to warn you. I couldn't live with myself if I didn't. If I didn't tell someone. I couldn't warn him, I couldn't go anywhere near that place. So, I'm telling you." Wentz's speech dropped to a disconcerting level. "Haeli, you and your father are in danger. Extreme danger."

Haeli's mouth opened as if she was going to speak, but no sound came out.

"I came here to give you this." Wentz produced a small blue thumb drive and held it toward Haeli. Haeli reached out and Wentz grabbed her hand and pushed the device into her palm. With his other hand, he closed her fingers around it and squeezed. "It's everything that I could access. It's proof that what I'm telling you is true. That they are planning to wipe the Eclipse program..."

"Wait. You're losing me," Haeli interrupted. "I don't know what that is. What is the Eclipse program and what does it have to do with me?"

"You don't know? Eclipse has everything to do with you. It's—"

The left side of Karl Wentz's head exploded. The skin peeled back like a grotesque piñata. His head hadn't moved, and his stare remained fixed on Haeli as if he were going to finish his sentence. The blood and brain matter that painted half the room said different.

A high pitch rang in her ears even though she had never heard the shot. The subtle clink of the glass and the whistle of the round passing into Wentz's temple and then into the far wall was all she had heard.

Haeli's mind railed against the scene in front of her. In a daze, she acknowledged the sensation of the warm droplets hitting her face by rubbing her hand along her cheek, smearing the blood down her face and onto her hand.

Only a second had elapsed before the entire picture became clear in her mind. The small, clean hole and shallow crater that hadn't previously been present in the thick pane of glass. The nervous man with half a head that sat before her. It all crashed down on her in a single moment of clarity.

Get down.

Haeli dove for the floor as another round smashed through the window and whistled overhead. She dragged herself by her elbows toward an interior door. Another round cracked through the glass. She reached up and pulled down on the handle, popping the door ajar as she dropped back to the ground. A fourth projectile left its mark on the pane and struck the wall behind her with a thud. The translucent pockmarks formed a pattern from right to left, dropping lower each time a new one appeared. It was a matter of time before one bullet blindly found its mark.

Haeli pulled the door open by the bottom corner and found another door behind it. She laid as low as she could and smashed her fist against the bottom of the second door, pleading that someone be in the adjoining room. Anyone.

She called out frantically, "Is anyone there. Help me, please."

The door cracked open. Haeli looked up to see a pair of brown eyes staring back at her from the dimly lit room.

Although the woman's eyes were the only thing visible behind the complete coverage of the burka, Haeli could see the obvious fear in them. And she didn't blame her. Covered in blood and yelling like a lunatic, Haeli couldn't have guessed why the woman didn't slam the door on her, or even refuse to open it in the first place. The woman stepped back and allowed Haeli to low crawl into her room.

Haeli scanned the room, noticing the drawn drapes, and she hopped to her feet. She closed both adjoining doors and took a breath. She needed to plan her next move.

Haeli opened her hand and checked the memory stick she had been grasping with all her might. While covered in blood, it didn't appear damaged. She tucked it into her bra.

The Muslim woman had retreated to the corner of the room, near the window. She remained silent.

"Don't touch the curtains and get away from the window," Haeli ordered. She grabbed a glass off the dresser and held it in front of the peephole. If someone were on the other side, they'd send a round through. Satisfied it was clear, she put her eye to the peephole that looked through to the hallway.

A plan. That is what she needed.

And fast.

THE HULKING MAN in the black suit held the H&K semi-automatic pistol high, inches from his face, and pressed his back against the wall to the left of the door marked 1211. He motioned to his associate, who had assumed a similar posture on the right side of the door. The man on the right swung around and kicked the door directly below the handle, shattering the door frame and violently swinging the door open.

Both men filed in, the muzzles of their pistols leading the way. They cleared the room. Each step leaving a gory imprint in the carpet.

"Where is she?" the big man said.

His partner waved his gun toward the adjoining room. Taking the initiative, he quietly opened the outer door and pressed his ear to the inner one.

"Move." The big man's foot came crashing on the door without further warning. His partner skirted to the side in time to not become the target.

The door exploded inward, and both men rushed in with a singular purpose. To kill Haeli Becher.

But Becher was not who they found. They knew Haeli Becher well. They knew her face. And the woman sitting on the bed, wrapped in a bed sheet, trying to cover her hair with a pillowcase was most definitely not Haeli Becher.

"Talk to me," the radio squeaked in both man's ears.

The big man answered. "She's not here."

"What do you mean she's not there? She couldn't have gone far. The rest of the team is on the perimeter, we'll nab her if she tries to leave. Anderson, you track her down. Trinity, you find the thumb drive."

The radio went silent for a moment but cut back in. "And no witnesses."

As if choreographed, both men turned toward the cowering young woman and solemnly shook their heads.

HAELI LEANED into the street and waved at the cab driver. The car blew by without slowing.

Come on. Come on.

She waved down another, which to her relief, pulled over a few feet past her.

Haeli rushed to the car, opened the rear door, and hopped in.

"Just start driving," Haeli said.

"Of course." The young middle eastern man was amiable enough and didn't seem perturbed by Haeli's short temperament. He eased out into traffic and headed south on Las Vegas Boulevard. "Where are you heading?"

The question didn't even register in Haeli's mind. She yanked the burka up under her buttocks, pulled the entire garment over her head and then used the heavy fabric to wipe her face and hands. The driver's gaze met hers in the rear-view mirror.

"What are you doing?" he yelped. "I can see you."

Haeli gathered her hair and pulled it tight toward the back. She pulled an elastic from her wrist and twisted it around the ponytail.

"No worries," she replied, "I just converted."

9

———

"Let me get these out of the way for ya." The man's voice was friendly and upbeat. A contrast to the brooding style he had seemed to cultivate. Tattoos covered his arms and crept up the side of his neck. His bald head was polished and gauged spacers filled the inch-wide holes in his earlobes. This man was familiar to Blake. Not that they had met before, but in the sense that most of Blake's friends possessed a similar quality. An outward appearance that would make the average person cross the street to avoid meeting them on the sidewalk. A rough, hardened exterior that housed a heart of gold. As servers go, Blake found the man beyond attentive and decided he would leave a sizable tip.

"What else can I get for you guys? Another round?"

"I'll take another Pappy," Blake said.

"Hook me up with another mule." Griff added. Each word more exaggerated than the last.

"You got it." The server carted away the balanced stack of plates and empty glasses.

"You know how I can tell when you're drunk?" Blake asked.

"Because I'm slurring?" Griff answered, slurring.

"Because you have a personality." Blake laughed.

"Screw you. At least I'm not nursing my drinks. I'm drinking 'em like a man."

"Yeah, nothing says manhood like a few sprigs of mint." Blake mocked. "This, my friend, is an eighty-dollar glass of perfection. You savor it. Got it?"

"And that's why you're buying," Griff said.

Blake hadn't said so yet, but he was, in fact, buying.

Blake had been sold on the place within the first five minutes of arriving. Primarily because the dominant feature of the bar was a wall of some two hundred bottles of whiskey. Scotch, bourbon, rye. Various ages and locales. Each fastened upside down and fitted with a dispensing stopper that allowed the bartender to draw a perfect pour with the touch of a lever. Blake had planned to sample a few varieties that he hadn't tried before, but as soon as he discovered that they stocked Pappy Van Winkle 20-year-old Kentucky Straight Bourbon, he scrapped the entire plan. Pappy was his favorite, and it was rare that he found it on the menu.

"I have to say, this was an excellent find, Griff. Your gambling buddy came through. Great food. Better drinks. The atmosphere, very interesting."

Stickers, chotchkies, and eclectic art covered every inch of the aging interior. The wooden floors were raw and every chair in the dining room was different, as if each had been purchased from a different garage sale in a different country.

"I like it," Griff agreed. "I'm glad you came out, Mick. Out west, I mean. Not that it's helping me get any work done. I have to submit some kind of report after this, so I've gotta buckle down a bit. Tomorrow." Griff tipped back the copper mug and jiggled it to free any last drops of liquid that might be clinging to its sides. "Tomorrow I'm all business."

Blake wondered what Griff's mumbling had sounded like in his own head. Probably perfectly intelligible.

"I can take care of business, Mick. You know that." Griff fully committed to his new tangent, as if a different conversation had engrossed him. "I've been in the shit too. You know that. I've been shot down. Right? You know I can handle myself."

"Yeah, I know that, Griff." As amusing as Griff's non sequiturs were, Blake wasn't placating him with validation. He meant it.

"'Cause I don't know if Fezz and Mick know that. No, you're Mick. Fezz and Khat, I mean. It's always like, 'you stay in the van and do that voodoo that you do.' Ya know? You did both, Mick. I've heard all the stories."

"Listen, Griff. For what it's worth, and I know you won't remember this in the morning, but Fezz and Khat know what an asset you are. They've told me outright. And I'd be glad to have you by my side when the shit hits the fan."

"Ahhhh, ha, ha. This guy." Griff stood up from the table and pointed at Blake. "This guy." The few people who turned their attention to the disruption immediately lost interest and returned to their own conversations. All but one young woman sitting at the bar. The petite blonde had grabbed Griff's attention.

"Hi there," Griff called across the bar.

"Sit down." Blake considered that it may not have been a good idea to order another round.

"What," Griff said. "Did you see that? That woman's into me."

"I'm sure she is." Now Blake was placating him.

The server dropped off the Moscow Mule and two-fingers of bourbon, neat. "All good for now?"

"All good," Blake replied.

"Hold up. I wanna buy that girl a drink. Whatever she's having." Griff pointed out the woman.

"No problem." The waiter moved on to the table behind Blake to check on the couple that had been sitting there for the past hour.

Whenever in a public place, Blake made it a habit to observe. To casually keep track of people's movements. Their body language. A habit that was so engrained, he was not conscious that he was doing it. But he had gathered that the couple behind him was going through a rough patch. He had overheard most of the conversation.

Argument, really. He agreed with the woman. She had some valid points.

"Why don't you find a..." Griff stopped himself. Blake knew what he was going to say. He was going to spew some crap about playing the field or getting back out on the market, or some other sage wisdom about why he needed female companionship. But at eight Moscow Mules deep, Blake was impressed that Griff retained enough of his faculties to know it wouldn't have gone over well. Griff changed the subject back to his own priorities. "I'm going to hook up with that girl tonight."

Blake shook his head.

"What? You don't think I will?"

"Not to burst your bubble, buddy, but did you notice that she's with a dude? He's been chatting her up for the last half hour. You snooze, you lose." Blake sipped his bourbon.

"Well, he's not there now, is he?" Griff said. "Looks like I've got a shot."

Griff was right. The muscular guy in the tight T-shirt who had been stuck to the woman for the past half hour had disappeared. Blake was surprised he hadn't noticed the man exit.

The waiter delivered Griff's gesture — a pink concoction garnished with a paper umbrella. Blake watched as the server pointed Griff out to the young woman. The woman nodded and took a sip of the drink. Griff remained engrossed in his own cocktail, but Blake noticed that she had stood up and was moving toward them.

"You sly dog," Blake said. "Look alive, brother. Incoming."

Before Griff made any indication that he had heard Blake, the woman was standing at the edge of the table.

"Thank you for the drink, that was sweet," she said. "I'm Sandy."

Griff hopped up, kicking his chair back in the jerky maneuver.

"I'm Griff, nice to meet you."

Blake stood and introduced himself. Sandy extended her tiny hand with her palm down as if she were the Queen of England. Blake wondered if she expected him to kiss it. He reached out and shook it.

"Mind if I join you guys?"

"Not at all." Griff pulled out one of two empty chairs and tucked it in behind the woman as she sat.

"So, do you live here, or just visiting?" Sandy shifted her body toward Griff.

"Just visiting," Griff said. "Business trip."

"Oh, what do you guys do?" she asked.

Griff shot Blake a look. They would often make up stories about what they did for a living. Anything but the truth. Often, they'd have fun with it, seeing who could come up with the most outlandish career. But Blake thought it'd be more fun to go the other way.

"We sell insurance. Griff here is quite the salesman. Actually, you're looking at Anchorage's top producer, two years running."

Griff's eyes widened and fixed on Blake. His jaw clenched so hard it was visible through his cheeks. He knew exactly what Griff wanted to say. Insurance? Couldn't have been firefighters, or deep-sea divers, or MMA fighters? Blake smiled back at him.

"Oh. That must be, uh, interesting." Sandy fiddled with the tiny umbrella.

"Nah. It's just temporary," Griff said. "The money's good, I couldn't pass it up. Plus, I mean, I couldn't have been a Navy pilot forever. I mean, life's not all about thrill and danger." Griff leaned in closer and softened his voice. "Or maybe it is."

Blake chuckled under his breath at Griff's attempt at being smooth. But, as ridiculous as it sounded, that part was true. The Navy had afforded him the ability to get his master's degree in computer science, and his extraordinary skill had not gone unnoticed. The Agency recruited Griff before he even finished the program. As much as Griff loved flying, he couldn't pass up the opportunity for his master's degree.

"How about you? You live in Vegas?" Griff asked.

"Yeah, moved here last year. I'm a dancer. Kind of in between gigs at the moment."

"That's too bad," Griff said. "I'd love to see you dance."

Blake noticed Sandy's chair had crept closer to Griff, who was one hundred percent on the mark. She was into him.

"Well, I'm going to settle up and head back to the hotel. I'll leave you kids to it." Blake scanned the room to find the server. He didn't see him, but he found someone else. The muscular man that had accompanied their new friend was now standing by the bar, surveying the room. He appeared to spot what he was looking for. From the direction of his angry stare, his target of interest was sitting next to Blake. The man charged across the dining room.

Blake stood. "Heads up," he said to Griff while keeping a laser focus on the approaching man.

Griff stood just as the man approached.

"What the hell?" The man looked back and forth, unsure who to direct his anger toward. "Get away from my girl."

"Calm down, friend." Blake's voice was devoid of stress. "We're having a friendly conversation. Nothing to get bent out of shape about. Let's take a step back."

"Screw you, asshole." The man's temper flared. "Let's go, Sandy."

"I'm not yours." Sandy reached for Griff's hand. "I just met this guy." She remained seated at the table with her back turned to the aggressive suitor. "Leave me alone."

"You heard the lady," Blake said. "Why don't you grab yourself a cab and we'll all move on. Whatta ya say?"

"Who asked you?" The man moved in closer, not stopping until he and Blake were nose-to-nose. Blake remained inanimate. "How about I kick your ass?" Spittle landed on Blake's face.

Griff lurched forward as if about to lunge at the indignant prick. The table grated against floor. Blake held out his hand, never breaking the lock of the man's glare. Griff backed off.

"I don't want to fight you, friend," Blake said. It wasn't just something one says in these situations. It was the truth. Blake harbored no fear or apprehension. He had made a promise to himself that he would avoid violence. It was a core tenet of his new self. But it was a harder proposition than he expected. Every muscle ached to lash out. To put an end to this man. Blake turned his eyes down and took a step back. A clear message of deference.

"That's right, you don't." The man inflated his chest with victory.

He turned toward Sandy, who had remained fixed in her position, head bowed toward the table. "I'll catch you outside," he sneered.

The man backed away slowly. Either in fear or relief, Sandy's entire body vibrated. Griff placed his hand on her forearm as the man turned to leave.

Blake looked at Griff, his lips pursed, and his chest risen. He had won. By his own reinvented standards, he had done the right thing. But it didn't feel right. There was an imbalance lingering inside of him. And he couldn't help himself.

"I like your shirt," Blake said.

"What?" The man's head turned first, his body following gradually.

Every person in the establishment focused on the exchange taking place. The continuous lack of normal chatter and clanking of forks and knives meant the room was still tuned in.

"Your shirt." Blake repeated. "It's nice. I was wondering if it came in adult sizes."

"You mother—" The man charged. His fist cocked back like it weighed a ton and was being dragged behind him. He swung wide and hard on a trajectory with Blake's face.

Blake moved subtly. An inch or two. Enough to ensure the blow missed him. The man's momentum carried him past Blake and toward the ground, but he regained his balance.

Blake spun to face him. Sandy leapt from her chair and scurried around Griff. She pressed up against his back as if using him as a shield.

Then came another right hook. With his left hand, Blake slapped at the side of the man's forearm, diverting the punch. In a fit of rage, the man swung again, this time with his left. Again, Blake diverted the blow.

The silence of the room had morphed into sporadic outbursts of grunts, groans, and cheers. It appeared to the crowd a choreographed routine as Blake parried and dipped, exerting little energy. That was the point. The enraged man provided all the energy Blake needed to use against him.

The man picked up the empty wooden chair. He raised it up over his head. The chair, heavy and sturdy, would not have been out of place at a farmer's table or country home. Blake held steady as the chair reached its crest and descended toward his head.

With both hands, Blake pushed the chair to the right, sending it swinging in an elongated arc. The other man lost his grip with his right hand but hung on tight with his left. The momentum caused the chair to deviate from its full path, just missing the man's leg and ending up behind him. Blake slid around the man's side as the clunky piece of furniture slowed to a stop. Blake snatched the chair free and slammed it into the back of the other man's knees. The force knocked him backward, causing his legs to kick out like a toddler in a highchair.

The man gripped the arms of the chair to push himself up to a standing position. Blake crashed his foot into the rear leg of the chair, causing it to spin almost ninety degrees, facing the table. The thrust had again knocked the man back into the chair in a comical twist. To anyone who hadn't seen the events leading up to that moment, it would have appeared as though the man had tucked himself for dinner.

The random noises generated by the patrons' reactions had turned to pure laughter. Blake fed off the energy. He stepped on the rear cross-brace of the chair, pinning the man against the table. The man pushed against the edge of the table, furiously trying to escape from the embarrassing prison. Sweat glistened on his face and his desperate movements showed that his own fury had rendered his fine motor skills less than useful.

As if to appease his loyal audience, Blake timed his movement with the man's heaving motions and abruptly removed his foot. The man tipped back and crashed to the ground, knocking his head against the ragged wooden floor.

Blake casually picked up his glass of bourbon and took a sip. He glanced over at Griff and gave him the faintest shrug. Griff shook his head, but the beaming smile on his face gave away his approval.

The man staggered to his feet and stumbled toward Blake, who placed the glass back onto the table.

The man balled his fists and raised them to just below his chin. Then, his body snapped around a hundred and eighty degrees as Griff tapped him on the shoulder. Blake only wished he could have seen the man's face as Griff's fist barreled in and connected with the underside of his jaw. The man collapsed as if the punch had ripped his entire spine out through his neck.

Blake picked up his glass and finished the last sip. He took out his money clip, peeled off several hundred-dollar bills, and dropped them on the table.

Griff took Sandy by the hand. "Let's get you home."

She nodded.

The three walked to the exit in silence, leaving the sleeping man where he laid. No one else moved or spoke, including the staff.

Griff opened the door and Sandy walked outside. Blake held the door as Griff followed. The air outside was heavy and warm, a jolting contrast to the conditioned air of the bar. As the door creaked closed behind Blake, they could hear the eruption of chatter from within.

Blake couldn't help but smile.

10

"**G**ood morning, sunshine. You're alive." Blake looked at his watch. 12:52 PM.

"I'm gonna be a little late." Griff groaned.

Blake held the phone to his right ear while he plugged the other ear with his finger. The bustle of the conference center overwhelmed the crackling transmission.

"You sound like a tank ran over you." The statement had a sympathetic subtext. Blake had been there before. A few too many times.

"I might as well have," Griff scoffed. "Sorry to leave you hanging."

Blake had called and knocked on Griff's door for several minutes before heading to the conference center on his own. Griff's lack of response did not surprise Blake. He never expected Griff to make it back by morning.

"Nah, brother. It's all good. I've been checking out a few of the speakers. Some worthwhile stuff, actually. I'm guessing you had a hell of a night, where'd you end up?"

"Uh. I have no freakin' idea. Right now, I'm standing next to an inflatable pool in some crappy-ass trailer park. Sandy's inside making breakfast."

"I think you can just skip to lunch," Blake said. "You'll have to fill me in on the rest later, I can barely hear you in here. You good getting back?"

"Yeah, I'm good. I'll Uber back soon. I told her I was flying back to Alaska today and had to be at the airport in two hours. Gives us enough time for one more goodbye."

"Ah. Roger that. I'll see you when you get back," Blake said.

"Later." Griff disconnected.

Blake pulled the day's itinerary from the pocket of his jeans. He picked out a seminar called Owning Docker: Attacking and Auditing Containerized Infrastructure. Now comfortable with the layout of the venue, Blake weaved through the booths and exhibits, arriving at his destination with plenty of time to spare.

He chose a seat in the back, settled in, and waited for the event to start. As he waited, his mind wandered. Deep in thought, he entertained any random notion that popped up. He observed the attendees as they entered the room and interacted with one another. He tried to separate them into two general categories, those who were interested in security and technological advancement, and those who were more interested in causing harm, mayhem, or most despicably, hoping to prey on the vulnerable for personal gain. In his world, these two opposite groups were classified as Black Hat and White Hat hackers, a reference to the good guy/bad guy dichotomy of old Western movies. Blake liked to think he fell in the White Hat category.

As a bonus round, Blake also tried to pick out who was representing federal and state agencies. All the attendees knew that most, if not all, of the federal agencies attended the event. Griff was there for that purpose, even if he had applied his own interpretation of his directive to infiltrate, but he wasn't the only one sent on a fishing expedition. His agency would have sent dozens of operatives, all working independently or in small groups. Not to mention the others. FBI, DHS, NSA, DIA, a myriad of private government contracting companies. That did not seem to dissuade anyone from showing up. In fact, it had the opposite effect.

Small-time criminal organizations loved the attention of law enforcement, especially federal law enforcement. Small chapters of biker gangs and the fringes of revolutionary organizations fancied themselves as dangerous and powerful. In their minds, any attention by law enforcement would serve as proof of their self-aggrandizing roles in the underbelly of society. But anyone of consequence preferred to keep a lower profile.

Don't worry about the threat you see, worry about the one you don't.

Blake had no way to know for sure, but he thought he could identify the agents and operatives. The ones he had noticed seemed obvious. He wondered if he stood out in the same way.

The lights dimmed to half their original brightness, and a volunteer began unhooking the rear doors, allowing them to swing closed. A guy in his mid-twenties wearing a vintage Pacman t-shirt and carrying a backpack slipped through the doors before they closed. He ducked into a seat in Blake's row and pulled a laptop from his pack. In the old days, Blake and his teammates would assign nicknames based on some unique feature to people they didn't know. When communicating on coms, it allowed them to refer to people without ambiguity.

Pacman.

As the last door closed, the roar of the crowd outside the room transformed into a muted buzz.

"Thanks for coming. A bit of housekeeping before we bring out Kip. Please turn your cell phones off." The moderator started with the usual spiel.

The sound of the crowds flooded the room for a moment before receding again. Blake turned back to see the latest arrival. A petite woman wearing tight black jeans and deep purple top. The dark-colored clothing, combined with her black hair and dark features, gave her a mysterious aura. Blake tried to place her in one of his categories. She looked youthful but wasn't a kid. She was beautiful but didn't look as though she spent a lot of time or energy addressing her appearance. She was jittery, but in the same way he might be. Scanning the room. Hyper-aware of her surroundings.

There was a visible tension in her body. He found the woman a curious case.

Pegasus.

It was the first nickname that popped into his head. He went with it.

The woman found an aisle seat about halfway down. She looked over her shoulder, locking eyes with Blake. He winced at being caught staring and looked away. After a few moments, he couldn't help but shift his focus back in her direction.

As attractive as she may have been, Blake wasn't interested in her. Not sexually. That was the last thing he needed. But he found her interesting.

Definitely not a Fed.

Blake had tuned out the speaker. The woman captivated him as her head swiveled back and forth. She'd look over her shoulder at the rear doors, scan the crowd, squirm in her seat, and start the pattern over again. The more Blake watched, the more he realized that the woman appeared to be hiding from something. She didn't seem interested in the seminar's content. Was there someone she was trying to avoid? An ex-boyfriend or something? He reconsidered. The bottom line was that she looked scared. The question was, what was there to fear while surrounded by strangers at a public event? Should he be concerned, too? Should they all? What did she know that no-one else was aware of?

What's your story, Pegasus?

Again, came the rise and fall of the exterior chatter. This time, louder. More distracting. The speaker did not skip a beat, but Blake paid no attention. He looked back to find that two more men had entered the room. Unlike the woman, these men were not a mystery. But their presence was peculiar. Dressed in black cargo-style tactical pants and synthetic black T-shirts, they stood on either side of the door. It wasn't only their pants, their high-and-tight haircuts, or their rigid posture that made Blake so sure. It was their belts. The style of nylon belt screamed military. Were these men federal agents? It was possible.

Thing One and Thing Two.

Both men's eyes darted back and forth as if looking for someone or something. Blake ran through the options. Bomb threat? If that were the case, there would be dogs. There would be an attempt to evacuate the room. Maybe a wanted person? There were several people on the FBI's most wanted list who would fit in just fine at a hacker's conference. But why take the risk of appearing in such a public place. A place teeming with undercover agents?

Blake peeked back at the woman and saw that she had slumped down in her seat and placed her hand along the left side of her face. Were these men looking for her?

He had been familiar with most of the high-level hackers who had not yet been apprehended. But he didn't recognize her face. Then again, he had been out of the game for quite a while. He felt the hair on his neck stand up. The situation grew more intriguing by the second.

Blake turned back toward the doors, trying his best to be inconspicuous. He saw one of the two men lean toward the other. The man spoke too soft for Blake to hear the faintest bit of conversation, but he didn't have to. His motion, pointing toward the area where the young woman sat, said volumes. The scowl on his face said even more. They both moved down the aisle.

The woman peeked over her shoulder just in time to glimpse at the men before they had closed the last forty feet. She leapt up and sprinted toward the front of the room. The meeting space, created by sectioning off a larger ballroom with floor-to-ceiling collapsing partitions, had two exits at the front of the room. These doors, positioned at either side of the portable stage, were marked with glowing red exit signs. It wasn't a stretch to guess that she headed for the nearest one. It also went without saying that the two men would do the same. They picked up their pace. The woman put another twenty feet between her and her pursuers before they kicked it up to a full sprint.

Maybe his judgment was not what it used to be, but Blake's gut told him that something wasn't right. Thing One and Thing Two seemed desperate. Their method was unorganized. If this woman were the target of a federal agency, more agents would have been placed in the room. The two men would have been more inconspicuous, or at least attempted to be. They would have waited until the woman was pinned in from all angles. And then there was Pegasus. She portrayed vulnerability. A genuine fear. He could see it in her eyes.

Blake had watched the entire scene unfold, beat by beat. Every other soul in the vicinity had been oblivious to the performance until the climactic action sequence demanded their attention. It meant, sadly, that he understood the characters in this story better than anyone else at that moment.

In the fleeting seconds that followed the start of the pursuit, a tug of war ensued inside Blake's brain. He had never been one to stand by and watch. He was a man of action who fought for the vulnerable, stood up for what was right. Even if it meant sticking his nose where it didn't belong. But that version of Blake was supposed to have been dead and buried. So why couldn't he shake the instinct to follow? He didn't have time to find the answer. If a few more seconds elapsed, the question would have been moot.

Screw it.

Blake sprung up from his seat, threw his leg over the back of his chair and climbed into the empty row behind him to avoid having to wait for Pacman to let him out. Thing One and Thing Two passed through the front exit door as Blake headed toward the front of the room.

The speaker had paused his presentation and made a comment about the disruption. Blake heard him but wouldn't have been able to repeat his statement. The rest of the participants prattled at one another.

Blake exploded through the exit door and into a long service corridor that ran parallel to the back of the ballroom. It was empty, except for a few buffet serving tables, stacks of chairs, and other equipment that lined one wall. The concrete floor, walls, ceiling, and even the overhead electrical conduit were painted the same shade of gray. Blake looked in either direction. There were fluorescent lights hanging from the ceiling at regular intervals toward the vanishing point, illuminating the openings to several more perpendicular corridors.

Which way would I go if I were her?

There was no difference. Either choice would have followed the same logic as flipping a coin.

Blake listened. He could hear the faint clamoring of what sounded like a kitchen or equipment room. Metallic clanking, the low hum of an air conditioner. He guessed the sound came from the right, but far away. Then he heard the voice of a man. Not the words, but the low cadence at which they were spoken. It came from the left and it was much closer. Blake moved toward it.

He hadn't yet rounded the corner to the first offshoot when he heard the addition of a woman's voice echoing through the concrete maze.

Pegasus.

Blake darted around the corner into an identical scene as the one he left behind. More equipment, more corridors. Only this time it wasn't empty. Two hundred feet ahead stood the woman, flanked on either side by the two military men. Something must have stopped her there in the middle of the hallway. Why not keep running? Blake was missing something.

He could see that each man held a wooden stick. An old-fashioned billy club. And he knew why. Security had been tight. Everyone entering the facility had to pass through metal detectors. These guys were not Feds. Then what? Mercenaries? And what could they want with this young woman?

The men hadn't seen him yet. At least, they didn't react as if they had. Blake closed the distance, hoping to get the jump on them, but when he saw one man raise his stick, he knew he wouldn't make it in time to prevent the woman from being injured.

"Hey, shitbird," Blake said. He hadn't yelled, but his voice carried, amplified by the narrow walls.

Both men startled. They hadn't known he was there.

Blake ambled along, continuing to close the gap. He hoped to distract them from their original task long enough so he could intervene.

"Yeah, that's right. I'm talking to you. I'm gonna have to insist you leave the lady alone," Blake added.

Thing One's eyes darted between Blake and Pegasus. Thing Two's remained fixed on Blake.

Blake met Thing Two's gaze as he neared. A faint smile then crept up on the man's face.

"You won't be smiling for long," Blake said.

"No!" Pegasus cried out.

It all came together in a flash. The scream, the smile. It all registered as the wooden club crashed down on the back of his head.

They're behind me.

At first there was no pain. Only confusion. At one moment Blake was standing. The next, his face pressed against the cool concrete floor. The muffled voices of the men echoed off the walls and again in his head. He could see only blurred shadows, haloed by green light. For a moment, Blake's disorganized mind contemplated whether he was dead. The searing pain radiating from the back of his head, traveling down his spine and through his jaw, dispelled any such notion. He tried to get up but only lifted himself a few inches before his arms gave out. He dropped to the ground in a human puddle.

Hours passed. Or only milliseconds. Or no time at all. He couldn't tell. The sounds of the real-world returned as if someone had turned up the treble on a graphic equalizer. The sound of brutality. The horrible sound of the wooden club striking flesh and bone. Blake could only imagine the grisly state of Pegasus' once delicate face. She was unquestionably dead. And he would be too if he didn't pull it together.

Blake pushed himself onto his hands and tucked his knees under him. He shook his head and tried to focus on the attackers. The images were clearer. He could discern the shapes of the men, but none of it made sense to his rattled brain. Four shadowy apparitions flittered around. Three were much larger than the other.

Pegasus.

Reasoning returned. He could see the diminutive frame of Pegasus, surrounded by three men. A fourth man laid on the ground in a heap.

She's alive?

Blake tried to push himself to his feet, but his knees crumpled beneath him. He could only watch as one man lunged forward, swinging the stick with furious intensity. Blake's face contorted as the stick careened toward the woman. He fought the urge to close his eyes.

What happened next defied explanation. Was he dreaming? Was he still out cold? Blake felt as though he was becoming more lucid, but now he wasn't so sure.

The woman dodged the blow, grabbed her attacker's wrist with both hands and yanked down. She kicked off and launched her feet into the air, using the man's arm as a pivot point. As her legs crashed down on either side of the man's head, she bent her knee and locked her foot around the back of her other leg. Upside down and with a vice-grip on the man's neck, the woman twisted her body, sending the man off balance and crashing to the ground. The woman maintained her hold while she landed on her feet. The man's head twisted violently. Blake expected it to pop off his neck. One thing he was sure of, that man would never get back up.

In one fluid motion, the woman dove toward another would-be assailant with her arms outstretched as if diving into a pool. She slid across the floor, driving her arms between the man's legs, forcing them apart. Before he could swing the club down on her back, she erupted upward, propelling the crown of her head into the man's groin. As he doubled over, she flipped onto her back and delivered a powerful kick. It landed square on the man's nose. She pushed against the man's calves, sending herself skidding out from under him as the gush of blood splashed onto the floor.

Blake's mind may have been chaotic. But it hadn't created the chaos he saw before him. This was real. Unbelievable. But real.

Blake staggered to his feet, his own tenacity forcing him to get back in the fight.

Pegasus wrenched the club from the man's hand and smashed it down on the back of his neck. She turned toward the last remaining attacker. With a flourish, she spun the stick in her hand and took up a fighting stance.

Blake stumbled to the first fallen man and picked up the wooden club that rested on the floor by his lifeless legs. It was heavier than it looked.

The last of the attackers bounced back and forth in a tentative dance. Before he could muster his attack, Pegasus leapt into the air with the stick cocked high above her head. She swung in a downward stroke. The man had been ready for it, easily countering to avoid the blow. What he hadn't been ready for, if his guttural screams were any indication, was the woman's right foot. The stick had provided the perfect distraction for her to land a flying kick on the side of the man's kneecap. His leg snapped at the joint, leaving it grotesquely deformed. She kicked again, further buckling his leg sideways at a ninety-degree angle. The attacker fell on his side.

Blake stood ready. He clutched the club in his right hand. He looked around at the carnage and, after a moment of cognizance, opened his hand and let gravity send the stick clattering across the floor.

"Let's go." Pegasus walked toward him. "We have to get out of here. Can you walk?"

Intense pain enveloped Blake's entire head. It throbbed behind his eyes. He reached to feel the egg-sized lump and the slickness of the blood. He looked at his hand to confirm.

"We'll get that cleaned up, come on," she said.

She took Blake by the elbow and the pair stepped further through the maze. They started slow, gradually picking up the pace. His sense of time had returned, along with control of his nervous system.

They slowed as they reached the last intersection. Seeing no way out ahead, they turned left into another corridor.

As soon as they made the turn, they saw it. A sign in the distance. A sign so commonly used that it often went unnoticed. Emergency

Unleashed

Door. Alarm will sound. With no communication, the pair made a bee line for the door.

The red lever stretching across the door released the latch as advertised. The door swung open and daylight flooded the drab gray tunnel. The only noise was that of the city streets. No siren. No alarm.

"I knew those signs were bullshit," Blake said. He hadn't expected a response, and he didn't get one.

They descended the metal staircase and ran across the loading dock, disregarding any looks they may have garnered from the employees unloading trucks or smoking cigarettes.

They made it to the end of the driveway and rounded the corner onto the sidewalk just before a semi-tractor trailer made the turn from the street. They slowed to keep pace with the normal pedestrian traffic dotting the area. They headed south, toward E Flamingo Road, with no destination.

Pegasus exhaled loudly. "I'm Haeli."

"Blake." He removed his hand from the back of his head intending to offer it to her but bailed on the idea when he remembered the bloody mess. "What just happened?"

"Let's get off the street," Haeli said. "I'll tell you whatever you want to know."

11

A crimson film coated the ceramic basin. Blake flicked his hand through the stream of water, sending the splashes swirling around the edges. With each motion, the deep red color of the pooling water diluted further into increasingly lighter shades of pink until it ran clear.

Blake cupped his hands and splashed a handful of water on his face. He pulled a few paper towels from the metal dispenser and patted his skin and hair, gingerly pressing the moistened towel onto the large lump on his scalp. He checked the paper towel to find only a few specks of smeared blood.

Blake shut off the water and looked in the mirror, tipping his head to glimpse the affected area. As far as he could tell, his hair covered any obvious injury. Satisfied that the bleeding had stopped, and any conspicuous evidence cleaned up, he tossed the paper towel in the bin and unbolted the door. He emerged with caution.

The place was quiet. Dimly lit, except for the light streaming through the windows that faced the street. A long bar ran along one side of the narrow storefront establishment. Nothing appeared to have changed since he'd first arrived and ducked into the bathroom. Three patrons still sat gawking at several screens mounted behind and above the bar, each displaying a live feed of a different horse racing track.

A four-foot-tall wall ran through the center of the room, parallel to the bar which delineated the eight-table dining area. The section was empty except for the one formidable young woman, who sat at the table positioned furthest toward the back wall.

Blake considered walking straight out of the front doors and not looking back. It wasn't a question of whether it would have been the right course of action. The smart course of action. He was resolute that nothing good could come of spending another second in her presence. But he wanted some answers. He didn't need them, but he wanted them.

Blake pulled up a chair.

"Bleeding stop?" Haeli asked.

"Yeah, bled like hell for a bit there though." Blake reflexively reached up and patted the wound.

"Head wounds will do that. Stop touching it." Haeli extended her fingertips and pushed a glass of amber liquid toward him. "Here, I ordered you a whiskey."

Blake started to ask what kind, but he decided it didn't matter. He picked up the glass and took a large swig. Haeli did the same.

"Are you old enough to drink?" Blake asked. Not that he was going to stop her.

Haeli grinned. "I get asked that a lot. A few minutes ago, the bartender asked me the same thing. But, if you must know, I'm thirty-four years old. So, yeah, I'm old enough to have a drink."

Blake didn't hide his surprise. He had pegged her for early twenties at the most. Just one more assumption that he had been completely wrong about. What was it about her that made her so hard to read? "Sorry, you look... I mean, you have a youthful look."

"No worries. I should be the one apologizing. For nearly getting you killed. You were trying to help me, and I want you to know I really appreciate it."

"I don't think I provided very much in the way of help. But you're welcome." Blake paused. "But answer me this. Who were those guys?

I mean, what did they want? And where did you learn to do that? I've never seen anything like it." He could have gone on. "Who the hell are you, really?"

Haeli shifted her eyes toward the table. Blake fought the urge to break the elongated pause, sensing that an answer to at least one of his questions was forthcoming.

"It's my father," Haeli said. "He's in trouble."

"Okay." Blake's inflection meant to encourage Haeli to continue.

"My father is a scientist," Haeli explained. "He works for this private corporation. It's a long story, but we sort of had a falling out and I haven't seen or spoken to him in a while. Anyway, a few days ago, I got a call from a man who said he needed to talk to me in person. He said it was important and that it had to do with my father. That he was in trouble. Of course, I tried contacting my father, but he didn't respond."

"Did you meet with the guy?" Blake asked.

"Yes. Yes, I met him. That's why I'm in Vegas. He wanted to meet here. The guy was a nervous wreck. He told me to make sure nobody followed me, to be careful and all this stuff. When I met up with him, he told me he used to work with my father."

"Where does your father work?" Blake interjected.

"It's an Israeli company. We used to live there, Israel, but he moved to the US when they opened the satellite office here. Anyway, the guy said my father was in danger and he gave me a thumb drive. He said there was information on it I needed to know."

"What was on it?"

"That's the thing." Haeli laid her hands on the table. "When I got back to my hotel, I used the business center and tried to look at it. I plugged it in and could see it had one file on it. A .zip file. I tried opening it, but it asked me for a password."

"The guy didn't mention a password?" It was what she had already implied, but Blake found it hard to believe.

"He must have forgotten. And he told me I'd never see him again, like he was in hiding. So, long story short, when I realized that this DEF CON thing was happening right down the street, I thought there had to be someone there that could help me open the thing."

"If you're worried he's in trouble, why not just go to the police? Give them the thumb drive and let them run with it. They have forensics people who could crack that file." Blake had a feeling he'd receive push back on the suggestion. That there was an excuse brewing behind her piercing eyes.

"I don't know," Haeli countered. "The guy may be a total whack job. It could be a file full of porn for all I know. I just want to see what it is before it turns into a big production for no reason."

Blake got the excuse he expected. He agreed with the logic to a point. He would have convinced himself of something similar if he were in her shoes.

"So, what about Thing One and Thing Two?" Blake didn't need to see Haeli's confused expression to realize he needed to clarify the question. "The guys in the service hallway. Who were they?"

"Oh. When I got to the conference, I noticed a couple of guys tailing me. I remembered what my father's friend had said about being followed, so I tried to duck into one of the shows and blend in. They found me anyway."

"So, you ran into the service hallway where two other guys were waiting. They catch you and try to kill you, or hurt you at least. They split my head wide open, and somehow, you pull some ninja sh—"

Haeli cut him off before he could finish the escalating indictment. "I know. Crazy, right? Growing up, I studied martial arts. For years. I competed in tournaments and that sort of thing. If they cornered me, I just reacted. Honestly, I surprised myself that I had it in me."

Blake tried to hide his skepticism. There was some truth in what she was telling him, he was sure. But by his estimation, what he had witnessed went well beyond martial arts classes. It was the skill of someone not only well trained but also highly experienced. He replayed the event in his mind — the parts that weren't fuzzy — and one detail stood out. She could have kept running further into the network of hallways, but she chose not to. She stopped to face the men. They didn't chase her. She had lured them there. Out of the public eye.

Blake played along. "So, what do you think they were after, the thumb drive?"

"That's the only thing I can think of. Maybe there is something important in that file. Maybe, whatever it is, someone doesn't want it getting out. Do you think you can help open it?"

"That's not really my thing." Blake figured he could play the lying game just as well as she could. "I wish I could help, but I'm a dope with computers. I just came out to visit a friend who was attending the conference."

"Oh. Do you think she could help?"

"He," Blake corrected, "and no, he was called away for work this morning."

"That's okay." Haeli's shoulders sagged as if her lungs had sprung a leak. "You've done enough already. Again, I'm so sorry for all of this."

Haeli's bottom lip shifted upward in a subtle pout. The look meant to be pathetic, yet adorable. It was both, but it wasn't working on Blake. It reminded him of Anja, how she would give a similar look when she wanted something he resisted. The only difference was, from Anja, it always worked.

"It's no problem, I'm just glad you're okay." It was the courteous thing to say. It was also the truth. Blake may not have believed her story. But it relieved him she had come through the attack unharmed. He recalled his certainty that she was dead. That they had mashed her face while he laid on the ground a few feet away, helpless and useless. He imagined what effect that would have had on his own psyche.

"I guess I should get back to the hotel then," Haeli said. She scooted her chair back. It made a high-pitched squeal as it rubbed against the floor.

Blake was sure no one from the conference center had followed them. But what about her hotel? If they had been following her, wouldn't they know where she was staying? "Did you check in under your own name?" Blake hoped he didn't already know the answer.

"Yeah. I didn't think—"

After everything he had seen, why did he still feel protective of this woman? A part of his nature that he couldn't override.

"Okay." Blake interrupted. "You can't go back there. Where do you live? We'll get you to the airport and you can get out of here."

Now Haeli spoke with a conviction he hadn't yet heard. An intensity broke through her sweet veneer. Tears welled in her eyes. "The thumb drive is in my room and I'm not leaving without it. Do you understand? I will not give up on my father. When we walk out of this place, you will go your way and I'll go mine, okay? I'll figure this out on my own."

Whether the outburst was a tactic, a kind of reverse psychology, Haeli's stress had peeked through her collected exterior. Blake hadn't been completely wrong about the vulnerability he'd sensed in the seminar hall. Had he?

"Haeli, listen to me." Blake hardly believed he was saying it. "I will go with you to the hotel. Just to make sure there aren't more of them. If all is clear, you get what you need and get out of there. Then I'll go on my way. Deal?"

A wide grin accompanied a surge of bubbly energy as Haeli hopped up from the table and grabbed Blake's hand.

"Deal," she said. "Let's go."

12

"Here you are. Channel 8." The driver slowed to a stop but didn't put the car in park.

"Have a good one." Blake stepped out onto the curb.

Haeli exited on the driver's side. The car pulled off before she could complete the half circle around the back of it. She passed Blake on the sidewalk and moved in as close as she could to the unremarkable brick building.

"Stay close." Haeli flapped her hand.

Blake agreed and positioned next to her. Without another word, Haeli moved south along the building, which gave way to a chain-link fence securing the entrance to the parking lot of the television studio facility. News vans and production vehicles sat idle behind the gates. Blake scanned the lot but did not detect any movement.

He followed Haeli's lead, hugging the bit of cover that they had, while trying to draw as little attention as possible. At the edge of the motel property, they stopped and acted as though they were having a conversation.

"That's it." Haeli nodded toward the three-story stucco motel. "Right there, second floor, second from the end."

A far cry from the grandeur of monolithic resorts of the Vegas strip, you could have found the rundown building at the end of any random highway exit in the country. Rows of guest room doors were visible along the exterior of each floor. Located in the shadow of the towering Wynn hotel, Blake wasn't shocked that he could only count three cars in the narrow parking lot that wrapped around the building.

"Look." Haeli didn't need to clarify what she wanted Blake to look at. He had spotted the man as he entered the second-floor landing.

"I bet he's one of them." Haeli whispered.

Blake wouldn't have taken that bet. If there was one thing he could spot, it was the guys that Haeli seemed to attract. Wicked men with ill intentions. This one could have been a carbon copy of the men they had encountered at the convention center, except for his clothing. Instead of the telltale tactical look, the man wore a black suit, a black tie, and sunglasses. If the goal were to blend in, he was doing a horrible job.

The man walked to the end of the landing, past the second door from the end, turned around and retraced his steps until he rounded the corner into a passageway leading further into the building.

"One hundred percent," Blake said. "And I'd venture to say there are more where he came from. We've gotta get you out of here."

"I told you," Haeli balked, "I'm not leaving without that thumb drive."

"Haeli, I guarantee you they've already been in your room. Which means they already have the thumb drive. But they're still here, right? Because there is unfinished business. You are the unfinished business."

The start of a syllable formed on Haeli's lips. Blake continued before she could convert it to an audible word.

"I know you don't want to hear it, but you have to be reasonable here. I'm telling you, that guy up there is not messing around. Do you know why he's wearing a suit in one-hundred-degree weather? Same reason as the Secret Service. It's easier to conceal and access a firearm. Not to mention radio communications. There are no metal detectors here. No jiu jitsu matches. You can't judo-chop a .45 caliber bullet—"

Blake halted. He recognized that he had worked himself up to where his next words would be more insulting than helpful. But more than that, it was the look on her face. A subtle crooked smile conveying that she already knew everything he was saying. And she was comfortable with it.

As much as Blake tried to buck his own nature, he continued to be empathetic to her plight. He reminded himself that he knew less than nothing about her. He told himself he didn't care what happened to her. More than anything, he wished that were true.

"I agree that they would have already searched the room," Haeli said. "But I don't think they found it. I hid it well. I'm guessing they would just assume I have it on me. And they'd have a point. This would have been a lot easier if I had taken it with me."

The man in the suit appeared again, completed his circuit, and disappeared around the corner once more. A floor below, another less imposing figure had appeared. A short, stocky woman pushed a cart along the concrete walkway. Although at ground level, an iron railing separated the walkway from the parking lot. The labored sound of the cart's wheels echoed through the empty street.

"I'll go." Blake blurted out the suggestion before thinking it through. By saying the words out loud, he had committed himself to whatever came next. "They're not looking for me. If I go alone, I stand a better chance of getting in that room without being spotted. Just tell me where you hid it and I'll go."

"Thank you, but I can't let you do that," Haeli said.

"Don't be—"

"No," Haeli interrupted. "You don't understand. I go with you or I go alone. I'm not letting that drive out of my sight."

Blake would have been offended if the mistrust hadn't been mutual. He resigned himself from trying to talk her out of it. He even accepted the possibility that Haeli could be on the wrong side of this thing. The only decision was whether he would let her go alone. And that was no decision at all.

"Fine. We'll go together," Blake said. "But we do it my way, agreed?"

Haeli's face lit up. She nodded.

"We wait until our friend pops out again. When he... if he keeps the same pattern, we wait until he retreats around the corner, then cut across the lot to the back of the building and find a way inside."

"Got it." Haeli hopped over the wall and sprinted toward the back of the building.

Unbelievable.

Blake jumped over the wall and ran after her. He reached the corner of the building a few seconds behind her.

"What do you mean, got it?" Blake said. "What part of 'wait' was unclear?"

Haeli reached out and patted Blake on the shoulder. "No time like the present."

Blake tried to suppress the smile, but it crept up on him. Her beaming grin had infected him.

The pair walked past a bank of electrical boxes and a set of metal doors with no handles. They rounded the corner into a walkway that led to the interior of the building. Blake now had a better picture of the motel's layout. What looked like one extensive building from the side was multiple sections that surrounded a central courtyard. A series of walkways connected each section and allowed for exterior access to each room throughout.

They passed several guest rooms and reached the first intersection. Blake peeked around the corner but pulled back to avoid being seen by the sturdy woman pushing the cart. He motioned for Haeli to be still as he heard the squeal of wheels approaching. The noise stopped, replaced by that of a door opening.

Blake peeked around the corner again to see the woman pulling the cart into a room. Its metal door was unlike the brown panel doors indicative of the guest rooms. The door swung open again. The woman emerged without the cart. She walked to the end of the passageway and took a left toward the front of the building. He kept his eyes on the empty walkway a minute.

"I have an idea." Blake motioned toward the end of the corridor. "Follow me."

Blake rounded the corner and hurried to the stairwell that was located just past the utility room and marked with a protruding sign. He could feel Haeli behind him as he started up the stairs. Blake reached the second-floor landing and pulled Haeli against the wall. He listened.

The sound of footsteps scuffing along the concrete filled the landing. The steps grew louder, but the rhythm remained lethargic. Unlike the maid who had been scurrying back and forth, this was the sound of pacing.

Blake pushed his back against the wall. Facing the open doorway, the severe angle made it so he had only a sliver of a view into the walkway. Twenty feet to the right of the door, he could see the opening to the outside where the man in the suit had been appearing and disappearing from view.

The footsteps crescendoed and a flash of black fabric passed from left to right. Blake waited before repositioning himself to see the man's back as he disappeared around the corner toward Haeli's room.

"Now," Blake whispered.

Haeli followed as Blake moved through the doorway and headed left. He opened the metal door and shuffled Haeli inside. The hinges pulled the door shut. Blake stopped it from slamming and eased the door through its last inch of travel until it latched.

Blake looked around, relieved that the gamble had paid off.

"How did you know this was here?" Haeli rustled through the sheets, towels, and toiletry items neatly stacked on a row of metal shelving units.

"I watched the maid stow away a cart in a room just below this one. Unless they have a service elevator, which is not likely, I figure they'd store separate carts on each floor."

Blake pulled one of several gray and white smocks from a row of hooks on the wall opposite to the shelves. He twisted the gold plastic name tag toward him so he could read it.

J. Rodriguez.

He put on the smock and cleared stacks of towels from the bottom shelf of the cart.

"Let me guess," Haeli said. "That's my ride."

"Hop on. I'll try to cover you."

"Give me these." Haeli took the stack of towels from Blake and placed them at the edge of the bottom shelf. She grabbed several more stacks of towels from the shelves and placed them along each edge, leaving an open area in the middle. The distance between the bottom and top shelf was more than enough, but the cavity she had constructed didn't look as though it could even hold a small child.

"Good idea, but the cart's too small for that. There's no way you'll fit in there."

"Watch me." Haeli accepted the challenge.

Haeli removed two stacks of towels on the end and handed them to Blake. She slid into the opening, pulled her knees up and pressed her chin into her chest. To Blake's amazement, Haeli had contorted herself to a size he couldn't have imagined. He thought he could have been watching a magic trick.

"Put those stacks back on the end and stack a bunch more on top of me," she said.

Blake did so, then stepped back to survey the result. In a million years, he wouldn't have guessed there was someone under the stacked rows of terrycloth if he hadn't seen it with his own eyes.

Blake rolled the cart to the door. The wheels were misaligned and rusted. It would not be the smoothest of rides. He lifted one stack of towels from the area where her head was situated.

"You okay?" he asked.

"I'm fine. Don't dilly dally."

"I need your key," Blake said.

The heap of towels undulated. Two thin fingers protruded from the opening. Between them, a white plastic key card.

Blake placed the last stack back on top of Haeli's head. He opened the door and wheeled the cart into the walkway. He turned left and headed toward the sunlight. Within seconds, the man in the suit appeared around the corner and started walking toward him.

"Good afternoon, sir," Blake said.

The man walked by without the common courtesy of a response. *Would it kill you to say hello?*

Blake looked over his shoulder. Beyond the man that had just passed by stood another. Another black suit. He wondered how many there were.

Blake picked up his pace, turning the corner and wheeling toward the second door from the end. He inserted the key card, opened the door, and pulled the cart inside. Out of the corner of his eye, he saw the man in the suit approaching. Blake left the cart in the doorway, propping it open. He moved to the single queen-sized bed and stripped the bedding while monitoring the doorway.

On cue, the man in the suit passed by. Blake noticed him glancing inside. He continued with his fake work, waiting for the next pass. A few seconds later, it came. Again, the man turned to look.

Blake dropped the comforter back onto the bed, hurried over to the cart, and started removing stacks of towels. Haeli extended her legs and slid herself off the cart.

"Hurry," Blake said. "Our friend is curious. I'm sure he'll pop in here again any minute. And I saw another. They're probably swarming this place."

Haeli shoved the bedside chest of drawers to the side. The motion caused the lamp to tip, but she righted it before it fell. She knelt and pulled at the base molding along the bottom of the wall behind the table. The molding tore away from the drywall, pulling a strip of paint with it. Behind it was a foot-long jagged slot that had been punched through the sheetrock.

"Did you glue that back on there?" Blake asked.

Haeli reached in and felt around. "Told you I hid it well."

Blake picked up the comforter from the bed and shook it out. He prepared to replace it to make it appear as though he had changed the sheets and remade the bed. Haeli pulled the small blue thumb drive from the cavity and put it in her pocket. She reached back inside.

"What are you doing now?" Blake's gaze shifted between her and the open door.

"I left one other thing."

The handle of the pistol protruded from the opening first. Haeli twisted and tilted the gun until it was in the right orientation to fit through the opening. She shoved the firearm in her waistband at the small of her back and reached back in the hole.

"Christ." Blake wasn't sure he wanted to know what other surprises she had stashed away. "What is this, Mary Poppins' purse? We're out of time."

Haeli's hand emerged, grasping a smooth black cylinder. Blake recognized the SureFire suppressor. He owned several of them. She had some explaining to do for sure, but this was not the time.

"Get in the cart," Blake said.

"One second." Haeli picked up the molding and pushed it back into place.

Blake heard the footsteps a split second before the silhouette of the man appeared in the doorway. It was enough time for Blake to outstretch his arms, pulling the comforter taut between them and shielding the man's view of Haeli, who remained crouched at his feet. He shook the bedding as if he were preparing to fold it in half.

"Sorry to bother you," the man in the suit said. "I'm out of shampoo. Can I grab another from you?"

The thinly veiled attempt to get a better look inside the room irritated Blake. They were almost home free. He had half a mind to grab the pistol out of Haeli's waistband and make this guy wish he had minded his own business.

In his peripheral vision, Blake could see that Haeli had dropped to the floor and pulled her knees up to her chest. He got the message.

"Sure, no problem." Blake dropped the comforter on Haeli, so it fell in a messy heap. He glanced at the pile of fabric. She had pulled the rabbit out of the hat a second time.

Blake opened two of the plastic tackle boxes sitting on top of the cart before he found the one that contained the miniature bottles of shampoo. He pulled out three and handed them to the man.

"Thanks, Mister..." His stare fixed on Blake's name tag. "Rodriguez. Appreciate it." He lingered for an extra awkward moment and then walked away.

Blake stuck his head out and watched as their adversary turned the corner. He spun around to let Haeli know the coast was clear but found her standing six inches from him.

"We've gotta go. Get in the cart."

Haeli smiled. Her eyes narrowed. Without a word, she leapt on top of the cart and launched herself toward the edge of the second-floor balcony. In a feat of extreme athleticism, Haeli caught the top of the railing with both hands. Her feet swung outward, then dangled below her. She let go and caught the edge of the concrete walkway before dropping to the ground in one fluid movement.

From the moment she left her feet, Blake knew that she was in the wind. She had gotten what she needed. He'd never see her again. He thought he'd be relieved, but he wasn't. Maybe it was curiosity. The need to know how the story ended. But it was more than that. To say that he'd met no one quite like her would have been the understatement of his lifetime.

Blake pushed the cart out of the doorway and walked to the edge of the railing. He looked down at the parking lot. There she stood. Staring up at him with wide eyes and a huge grin on her face.

"What are you waiting for?" She said. "Come on."

Blake laughed at her ridiculous posture. Arms extended like she was going to catch him. Blake looked around. He decided Haeli was right.

Take the window while you can.

He threw one leg over the side and lowered himself until he hung by his hands from the deck of the walkway. He dropped, bending his knees to soften the impact as he landed on the asphalt. Then they ran.

They put at least a half mile between them and the motel before stopping to catch their breath. Back in the heart of the strip, the crowds of pedestrians brought a sense of safety.

"You were great back there," Haeli said through rapid breaths.

"You too." Blake pulled his hair back out of his face and fought through the tightness in his chest. "You are full of surprises. If I'm being honest, that was the most fun I've had in a while. I haven't felt this much like myself in a long time."

Haeli dropped her head. "If *I'm* being honest, I should tell you I haven't been." She paused. "Honest, that is. Not entirely. There's a lot more to the story that you should know."

"I know." Blake walked past her. Haeli kept pace. "I figured you'd tell me when you were ready."

"I know you don't trust me, Blake, but I trust you, whether you believe that or not. You didn't have to help me, but you did. After what happened at the conference, any other person would have run away and not looked back, but you didn't. From what I've seen, we have a lot more in common than you think. That's why I want you to know the truth. Can we start over?"

Blake slowed. "How about we start with your actual name?"

"Haeli is my real name, honest to God. Haeli Becher."

"Blake Brier." He held out his hand. "Nice to meet you, Haeli Becher. Tell you what, since you're short a hotel room, why don't you stay in mine for the night. You can fill me in when we get there."

"In your room?"

Blake realized how his proposal had sounded. Judging by her reaction, he wasn't sure if Haeli was offended or delighted. He hadn't been shooting for either.

"Let me restate. What I meant to say was, I'll stay with my friend Griff and you can have my room. By yourself."

"I thought they called your friend away on business."

"I haven't been entirely honest either," Blake rebutted.

"Touché."

"What do you say?" Blake pressed. "Take the room?"

"Yes. Thank you, Blake Brier. You are a gentleman."

Blake grinned. "Don't go pigeonholing me yet, Haeli Becher."

13

Blake rapped his knuckle on the door. When Griff got to the door and looked through the peephole, he threw the door open.

"There you are, brother," Griff said. The shift in his expression gave away his surprise to find Blake accompanied by an attractive young woman. "Oh, hello."

"Hi," Haeli said, with a meek wave.

"Griff, this is Haeli. Haeli, Griff." Blake rushed through the obligatory introduction. "Can we come in?"

"Yeah, come in." Griff stepped out of the way to allow entrance to the suite. Blake motioned for Haeli to enter ahead of him. She did.

Blake stepped in and Griff closed the door. Waiting a moment for Haeli to move from the hallway to the living room area, Griff leaned in as if he were going to reveal a profound secret. "You dirty dog."

Blake shook his head and walked in to join Haeli. He found her pacing, her feet tracing the swirling pattern of the area rug that covered the faux stone tiles between the couch and two chairs.

"Sit down," Blake said. "Relax."

Haeli took half of his advice. She moved to the couch and perched herself on the edge of the cushion.

"Do you want something to drink?" Blake asked.

"Water."

"I'll grab it." Griff bypassed the living area as he moved to the kitchen, separated from the sitting room by a bulky island counter-top. He pulled three bottles of water from the fridge and delivered one each to Blake and Haeli.

"Sit down for a sec, Griff," Blake said. "I spoke with Haeli and we agreed—well, she agreed to fill you in on some developments you've missed."

"What are you into now?! I was only gone for a few hours." Griff sounded apprehensive, but Blake knew better. Intrigued? Of course. Excited? Definitely. But apprehensive, no. It wasn't a tool that existed in either of their sheds.

"Do you want to fill him in, or...?" Blake said.

"Go ahead." Haeli replied.

"Okay. I'll try to make a long story short. Haeli thinks we can help her. She has an encrypted thumb drive that contains information related to her father." Blake turned to Haeli. "What's his name?"

"Ben. Doctor Benjamin Becher," Haeli answered.

Blake continued. "So, a guy who works with Dr. Becher gives Haeli the thumb drive and tells her that her father is in trouble, then takes to the wind, leaving her with an encrypted drive with no pass-word. Haeli tries to get in touch with her father but can't reach him and doesn't know where he is. Sums it up, right?"

Haeli nodded.

"All right," Griff said, "we can work with that. Do you think the person who gave you the drive is telling you the truth? Seems like if he went through the trouble to give it to you but didn't tell you how to access it, he's just playing games, no? Do you have reason to think your father would be in trouble? What kind of doctor is he?"

"He's a scientist," Haeli said.

Blake jumped in again. "And—" he bowed his head and parted his hair to reveal the wound, "—a couple of thugs gave me this when I interrupted their meet-and-greet with Haeli, so I'd say there's prob-ably something to it."

Blake left out the part of the story where Haeli dismantled four armed men and saved his life. He wasn't embarrassed. Or ungrateful. But it was another story. One that he thought would be best left to Haeli if she expounded.

"Now that adds another dimension." Griff's excitement spilled over.

Griff had been itching for some kind of task. A mystery to solve, a damsel in distress, or anything that would somehow make Blake realize that he was born for action, or some other garbage. A ridiculous notion that was no doubt planted by Fezz and Khat. But it didn't work that way. Not in reality. He would rather eat a bullet than crawl back to the CIA.

Plus, Blake hadn't committed to anything, as far as he was concerned. He was returning a favor, nothing more. Even if he had rather enjoyed it.

"I told Haeli that we'd look at the file and see what we could do. I hope you don't mind if I stay with you, Griff. I've offered Haeli my room for the night. If we can get her what she needs, she can take it to the police, and she'll be on her way home. Right?"

Blake looked at Haeli and nodded as he spoke. The habit had been so ingrained that he rarely noticed he was doing it. But the subliminal tactic had proven effective in the past. Nodding yes while asking a question made it subconsciously difficult for the other person to say no. In this instance, Haeli would have agreed regardless. There wasn't any other choice.

"That's right," Haeli said.

"Wait a minute," Griff protested. "We're not going to leave it at that, are we? What if there is something to it?"

"Who are you, Robin Hood? Since when are you in the vigilante business?" Blake asked in jest, but he knew it was unfair. Griff had been sucked into the vigilante business the moment he met Blake. The instant Blake had asked him, Fezz, and Khat to put aside their principals, morals, and their oaths to uphold the laws of the United States. All in the name of exacting revenge.

"Who are you? Because I thought you were Blake Goddamned

Brier," Griff bellowed. If Blake didn't know any better, he would have believed that Griff was pissed.

"Stop." Haeli yelled. Her lips quivered as if she was trying to suppress her rage. That, or she was on the verge of tears. "I do need your help. There's no one else to turn to. I can't go to the police. I have no one I can trust. It's a colossal mess and I think I've created it. My father could be dead already and it's my fault."

Griff shot Blake a look. Blake had nothing to shoot back. Neither said a word.

"I told you I didn't know who those men were or who they worked for. That was a lie. I know who they are. They work for Techyon. And until a few months ago, so did I."

"Techyon, the military contractor?" Griff asked.

"You were an operative." Blake's face gleamed with the glow of enlightenment. "You're a mercenary. A highly trained, deadly, holy crap mercenary. That explains everything. The convention hall, the Glock, the silencer. It was obvious, I mean, I thought you were going to say Mossad. Wait, were you? Mossad?"

"No," Haeli said. "My father started working for Techyon before I was born. My mother died when I was a year old. We lived on the Techyon compound in Tel Aviv throughout my childhood, as far back as I can remember. My father was bound to his work. If he wasn't sleeping, he was working. Always saying he was on the verge of a new discovery, always an excuse why we couldn't spend time together. There weren't any other kids around, so I made friends with some people who worked there. They taught me shooting, hand-to-hand combat, all kinds of fun stuff. I didn't know any different, it was all a game to me. When I got old enough, I went to work for them. It was a natural fit."

"Then how did you end up on opposite sides?" Blake asked.

"Over the years, my missions grew bigger. More important. More secretive. More intense. I travelled the world, moving in and out of the shadows, doing things I can't talk about. One day, I was surveilling this guy—let's just leave it at that—and he was with his family. They seemed so content and it dawned on me I've never had a life. Not a real life. Not like everyone else. I never went to school with other kids. I never had friends and family or had to struggle to pay student loans or work my way up from some menial job. I missed all of it."

"What'd you do, quit?" Griff asked.

"Yes. I went to my father and told him I was going to quit. He tried to warn me. He said that it wasn't possible. Like they owned me or something. That just made it worse. We had a big blow-out over it, and I left. I just up and walked away. My father must have left a hundred messages, pleading for me to come back. I deleted them. Every single one, so I'd forget. Why did I do that? I should have just listened to him. I should have taken his calls."

"And you think they're using your father as leverage to force you back?"

"I don't know, I guess so. After I left, I came to the United States, moved around, saw some things I always wanted to see. I was lying low, but I wasn't in hiding. I kept my same phone, used my real name. No one ever showed up on my doorstep. Until one day, I got the call from Karl Wentz."

"Who's Karl Wentz?" Blake's attention had focused with the intensity of a laser beam after learning Haeli had worked for Techyon. He was familiar with the company, with the company's owner Levi Farr in particular, but he let Haeli say what she needed to say.

"Wentz was the man who gave me this thumb drive." She produced the small plastic device from her V-neck shirt. "He's the reason I know I'm in deep. Before he could give me the password, they took him out. Sniper. Textbook Techyon, I'm sure of it. And I was next. Trust me on that. I escaped, but they must have tracked me down to the conference center."

"You know too much. Is that it?" Blake verbalized his mental scratchpad. "They give you some time to reconsider and when you don't, you're deemed a liability and you're eliminated. It still wouldn't explain what all of this has to do with your father."

"It shouldn't have anything to do with him," Haeli responded. "There isn't anyone at that place more loyal than him. I've worked with plenty of people who have retired or moved on to other gigs. It never seemed to be a problem. There's something else going on here. Dr. Wentz mentioned something about a program. He called it Eclipse. But I've never heard of it."

"We have to look at that drive." Griff was almost giddy over the prospect of getting a glimpse at anything that might detangle the sordid web Haeli had spun in front of his eyes.

Blake ignored him. "Where's your father now, then? Tel Aviv?"

"In his messages, he said that he was transferring to the United States. A new facility dedicated to the Scientific Division of the company. He didn't say where. I wouldn't expect him to have said. His work is secretive. The location of a clandestine laboratory is not something you leave on someone's voicemail."

"Why are you telling us this?" It had just dawned on Griff that they were complete strangers.

"Because I know who you are," Haeli said. "Both of you."

"Okay," Griff said. "What's my last name?"

"I don't mean I know you personally. I mean, I know what you do. Special Forces? CIA? DIA? Am I close?"

"I work for the State Department, if that's considered close," Griff said.

"Uh huh. That's what I thought." Haeli settled back into the couch cushions.

Blake looked at Griff and shook his head. Griff's eyes widened and his hands twisted in a lazy 'What did I say?' gesture.

"First thing's first. Let me see your phone," Blake held out his hand.

She turned it over. "Switched it off after we left the conference center. Figured they had used it to track me."

Blake checked that it was off and handed it back.

"You need to get rid of this, we'll pick you up a burner."

The statement was practical enough. Flowing effortlessly from his lips, considering the betrayal it had inflicted on his intentions. To the casual observer, it would appear he was getting involved.

Griff had sprung up from his chair, then returned with his laptop in hand. "May I?

Haeli handed Griff the memory stick. He slid a tab to expose the metal USB jack and inserted the stick.

"Let's have a look." Griff ticked away at the keyboard. "This is good. Better than good."

"What is it?" Blake moved to a spot over Griff's shoulder.

"Standard Zip 2.0 encryption," Griff said.

Instead of having to deal with the more secure AES Encryption, which would have required the use of classified technology, they had a simple task of breaking the Standard Zip 2.0 encryption, which required a common password recovery tool.

"Do you have what we need?" Blake asked.

"No. And it would take days on this laptop anyway," Griff said. "But I know where we can get what we need."

"Where?" Haeli chimed in.

"The expo hall. One vendor, I think they're called Sumatra or something like that. I stopped by their booth. They showed a pre-configured forensic computer system. It was one of these twenty-five-thousand-dollar jobs. A good amount of processing power, multiple graphics cards, water-cooled, hot-swappable RAID, you know, the usual. The vendor was showing the speed of the system with Passware."

"Passware? What is that?" Haeli got up from the couch and crowded in next to Blake so she could see what they were looking at on the screen.

Blake was glad to see Haeli trying to stay in the loop, but the raw hexadecimal representation of the encrypted file couldn't have meant much to her.

"It's a software product for breaking passwords," Blake said. "Mostly using dictionary attacks, brute force, that sort of thing. It's commercially available, so not useful for the stuff we normally deal with. But in this case, it'll work fine."

Haeli threw her arms around Blake. "Thank you, thank you, thank you."

The soft floral fragrance of her hair made his pulse quicken. His arms yearned to wrap around her. But he was strong willed. In the battle between his mind and body, there was no contest.

Blake reached up, gently grasped her wrists and separated her arms until she dropped them to her side on her own. "It's no problem."

"Now." Griff shut the laptop's screen and pulled the thumb drive from the USB port, oblivious to the awkward interaction that had just occurred. "We just have to steal us some screen time."

14

Blake pulled the handle of the fourth and last set of doors leading to the exposition area.

"Locked," he said.

It surprised no one.

There were other options. An infinite number of them. But this option was the quickest and easiest. The proverbial bird in the hand. If only they could get in.

"You didn't think it was going to be that easy, did you?" Haeli's demeanor was more upbeat than expected, considering they had been at it for over forty-five minutes.

The cleaning crews, maintenance staff, and security guards swarmed in unpredictable patterns. It had taken patience, timing, and a lot of luck to avoid being spotted. The daytime, with its herds of people, brought a sense of anonymity. It was something Blake only considered in retrospect after having experienced the opposite effect. Now, he was one of a few rats in a several million square foot maze.

"It's a matter of time before someone comes by," Griff said.

Blake had already considered that contingency. A kiosk located to the right of the row of doors would provide enough concealment for all three of them if a security team forced them to duck behind it.

Haeli was already rummaging through the packets of registration paperwork, class schedules, and product brochures laid out on the kiosk counter.

Aside from the security personnel, Blake worried that cameras were mounted within the mirrored glass drones that protruded like boils from the paneled ceiling. That no one had accosted them yet meant that no one was monitoring the video feeds. With the place closed, management didn't see a need for live monitoring. Blake was glad they weren't trying to pull off something like this in the hotel or casino.

"These should do the trick." Haeli held up two large paper clips that matched those binding the packets of paperwork together. "They're not ideal, but unless either of you have a set of lock picking tools, we're going to have to go with it."

Haeli appeared confident, and after what Blake had seen, he wasn't about to question her ability to make it work. Blake figured Griff felt the same way as he also said nothing.

Haeli straightened each clip and then re-bent them, using the corner of the counter as a fulcrum. She narrated as she did so, as if she were giving a master class on the art of breaking and entering. "If I double this one up and bend it into an L, I should be able to use it as a tension wrench. Then I just have to put a couple of kinks in this one so I can use it as a rake."

Blake was well familiar with the tools and methods associated with picking locks. Doing so with a couple of paper clips, not so much.

"All right, MacGyver," Blake said. "If you pull this off, drinks are on me."

"Nice." Griff included himself. "Two nights in a row."

"Not for you," Blake said, his tone dramatic. "You're cut off."

Haeli slid the short end of the L-shaped paper clip into the lower portion of the key slot with her left hand. She inserted the other clip above it and moved it in and out. With each movement of her right hand, her left delicately pressed down on the long section of the makeshift tension tool. The rhythmic movements would have been imperceptible if it weren't for the slight flex in the two spindly pieces of chrome coated metal.

The L-shaped paper clip traveled. Haeli pushed it until it completed its arc. She slapped down on the door handle and pulled the door open.

"I hope we're talking top shelf." Haeli gloated as she went through the door.

Griff and Blake stepped in behind her. Blake checked that the push bar on the inside actuated the latch before allowing the door to close.

"I know where it is," Griff said. "You two stay here, I may need you to buy me some time if anyone comes poking around."

Blake nodded.

Griff skittered off between the booths until he was no longer visible through the signs and screens and tall, colorful backdrops.

"Do you think it's too late?" Haeli asked.

"For your father?" Blake shook his head "I don't. No one ever won a battle by thinking they already lost it."

Haeli shook her head slightly. Her gaze darted around his face and then came to rest after meeting his. Blake felt as though she could see through him. "Who are you, really? And don't tell me you work for the State Department."

"Let's just say in a past life I've had some experiences not unlike your own." Blake measured his words for a few beats. "I know how hard it is to come to terms with the real cost. And how hard it is to put it behind you."

Haeli looked at the ground. "I thought when I walked away, I'd never look back. That I would walk out to the world and be a regular person. I was kidding myself. It's too late for me. And if something happens to my father..."

Blake waited for her to continue. The thousand-yard stare—past his shoes, past the floor, past the center of the earth—meant her monologue had continued inside her own head.

"Look, I know what you think you want," Blake said, "and I hope you find it. But don't for one second think it won't be a constant struggle. I've seen what you can do, who you are. It's in your blood. And no matter the wake of destruction you have left in your path, no matter what regrets you have, it'll pull at you until you take your last breath. It's a choice you must reaffirm every single day."

Haeli looked up at him, giving him another once-over. "Are we talking about me, or you?"

Both of their heads snapped around at the metallic sound of the handles on the right-most set of double doors jiggling. Then the second from the right. Then the third.

"If that door opens," Blake said, "act like we're having an argument."

The fourth set jiggled and then the door creaked open.

Haeli disregarded the plan. She reached up and wrapped her hands around Blake's head; her thumbs framed his ears and her fingers stretched around the side and back of his neck. She pulled him toward her and pressed her lips against his.

Blake committed to the ruse. There wasn't enough time to debate.

It was forceful at first, but Blake could feel Haeli's fingers softening, releasing him from his obligation. The warmth of her lips, the sweet taste of her tongue drew him in. His hand found its way to her lower back without him realizing it, and now it was him who drew her closer.

It was a staged kiss. A concocted distraction. So why did it feel like passion? Like comfort? Blake could have remained in the moment for as long as it existed, because that's what it was. A moment. And when it was over, it would never happen again.

"Hey, I'm talking to you," the man yelled. It was the first time the voice registered in his ears.

Haeli slowly dropped from her toes to flat feet, pulling at Blake's bottom lip with her teeth. She smiled and gazed into his eyes, ignoring the security guard that stood only two feet away.

"I'm sorry," Blake said. "Are we not supposed to be in here?"

"No, you're not supposed to be in here. This area is closed. Off limits."

The man was unarmed, Blake thought, but he wasn't sure. The guard was older, salted strands intermingled with his otherwise peppered head of hair. He wore a jacket with the Venetian logo over the breast pocket and carried a handheld radio. He hadn't asked about Griff, so Blake figured he hadn't seen them on the cameras.

"Oh my God, Roger. You said no one would see us in here." Haeli's voice came off shrill and laced with a midwestern accent.

"Baby, give me a break, huh." Blake turned to the security guard. "I met this lovely lady in your casino and, you know, we were just looking for a quiet place to talk."

"I'm going to give you ten seconds to get out of here. Go get yourself a room like everybody else."

"Sure thing." Blake did his best to be non-confrontational.

The security guard opened the door and held it. "Let's go, people. Move it."

Blake and Haeli exited past the guard to the hallway. Another man, about the same age and dressed in the same uniform, approached.

The original security guard said, "Paul, will you escort these love birds back to the casino entrance? And did you lock these?"

"Bobby locked up over here," the other man answered.

The original man keyed his radio, "Bobby, meet me in the office."

BLAKE PULLED out a stool and Haeli sat facing the bar. Blake spun his stool around. The high leather back rubbed against the bar rail. It was the closest place they noticed where they could sit without gambling. It also had a decent view of the passageway to the conference center. Blake wondered if Griff knew they had been shooed away.

"A deal's a deal," Blake said. "What are you having?"

"Johnny Blue. 'Cause they don't have Pappy."

Blake was going to say something funny about how she was the perfect woman or about what a coincidence it was that they had the same taste. But then he realized it was too much of a coincidence. Griff must have put her up to it.

"Now we wait." Blake kept his gaze on where he hoped Griff would emerge.

The bartender made it over to them and took Haeli's order.

"Johnny Blue, neat please." She put her hand on Blake's forearm.

"Same." Blake did not avert his attention.

Haeli let her hand linger for a few more seconds than needed. His skin burned under her fingers.

"There he is." Blake slid off the stool.

Griff emerged, stopped, and surveyed the room. Blake walked toward him, but Griff signaled that he saw him, and Blake returned to his stool as Griff made his way over.

"I got it," Griff said.

"Thank you." Haeli jumped off her stool and hugged Griff. Blake wondered if he had misinterpreted Haeli's intentions when she hugged him in Griff's room. Had it been a friendly gesture? But then there was the kiss. There was no misinterpreting the kiss.

Unless he had misinterpreted it.

"You're the man," Blake said. "I take back everything I said earlier. What are you having?"

"I'm all set," Griff said. "I need to run upstairs and take care of wiping that surveillance video before anybody gets curious. I'll meet you up there in a few and we'll look at what's in this file." Griff handed the thumb drive to Haeli. "You hang onto it 'til then."

Haeli took it and secreted it in her bra.

Griff turned and took a few steps, then turned back. "Quick thinking in there. Must've been awful."

"You saw that, huh?" Blake grimaced. He knew Griff would get a lot of mileage out of it. Griff's wink solidified it.

The bartender placed the two glasses down in front of Blake and Haeli.

"Bye Griff," Haeli sung.

Griff smiled and vanished into the crowd.

Haeli picked up her glass and placed her hand over her chest. "Whatever is on this drive, I'm glad you'll be there to see it with me."

Blake didn't know what to say in response. He picked up the glass and stated the truth. "Me, too."

15

D r. Becher depressed the button on the end of the Eppendorf pipette, releasing the prescribed amount of liquid into the tube. He ejected the plastic tip with a satis-fying click. Becher swirled the mixture and held it to the light. The chemicals would denature the DNA, separating it into individual strands for sequencing.

"Tell me some good news," Becher said.

He didn't expect the Deoxyribonucleic acid to respond. Not just yet. But it would eventually speak to him. It would reveal whether the experiment had been a success.

Transforming the DNA into digital data to be analyzed had been a tedious process. Not because it was difficult—it was a mostly auto-mated process that had become pedestrian in the decades since they invented it—but because it took time. Lots of time. And his patience was growing thin.

He had used a thermocycler to automate the Polymerase Chain Reaction process needed to amplify the DNA. By applying heat, the Taq Polymerase enzyme synthesized two new strands of DNA using the original two as templates. Two exact copies. Over the entire cycle, the process was repeated thirty or forty times, doubling the DNA each time, until it made billions of copies.

Becher himself had been working on a similar amplification solution in the early 1980s. He had been close to pioneering a patented technique of his own when Dr. Kary Mullis released his paper, eventually snatching the Nobel Prize in 1993.

But the amplification was a means to an end. Generating enough DNA for the high-tech sequencing machine to detect each nucleotide as a corresponding chemical caused the machine to fluoresce. The result would be a sequence comprising four letters, A, C, T, G. The order in which these letters appeared would give him his answer.

Typically, lab technicians conducted this kind of menial work. But Becher insisted on doing it himself. It was the only way he could be sure that the results were pure.

"Knock, knock," Sebastian Roberts said as he poked his head through the doorway.

Becher recognized the voice without having to turn around.

"Come in, Seby." Becher kept his focus on his work. "To what do I owe this visit?"

"Wanted to come and check out the new place. See if you needed anything. I went to your quarters. I don't know why, I should've assumed you'd be working in the lab."

As bosses go, Roberts was ideal. He wouldn't dream of telling Becher how to conduct his work, and he had never denied Becher's requests for funding. But if Roberts was there, Becher knew there was an ulterior motive.

"You flew all the way out here to see if I needed anything?" Becher said.

"No, not just that. Levi asked me to speak with you in person."

Becher placed the last tube in the tray and turned to face Roberts, who now had Becher's attention.

"What is this about, Seby? Levi could have called me himself."

"It's about Haeli." The forced smile fell from Roberts' face as if it had been taped on over the sullen expression.

"Have you heard from her? Is she all right?"

"It's not good Ben. She's alive, but she's gone rogue."

"Rogue? What is that supposed to mean?" If the lab work had worn down his patience, Sebastian Roberts was using every remaining granule.

"All I know is what Levi told me. He received information from his men that Haeli has gone rogue. I mean, she's lost it. Killing innocent people. Committing crimes. What did he say?" He made several clicking sounds with his tongue. "Something about her going off the reservation."

"That's ridiculous." Becher could hardly believe what he was hearing. Was Roberts serious? Was this a sick joke? "Seby, you know Haeli. Does that sound like her?"

"No, it doesn't. But I'm assured that it comes from a trusted source. You know what she is capable of, Ben. And she ran away. Doesn't it make sense that she could have just snapped?"

"No. That makes no sense at all. I need to find her. Talk to her. You'll see that your information is sorely mistaken."

Roberts slapped his hand onto the counter that separated the two men. "You don't get it. Levi has deemed Haeli a danger to the public. You know what that means. They will neutralize her. Levi's already ordered it."

"No. No. No." Becher's voice stepped up a few decibels with each repetition of the word. His face reddened. "Where is he? I want to talk to him."

"He's still in Israel, but he's flying to Nevada in the morning. He'll be here early. Ben, I don't think you'll change his mind. He sent me here to get your help. He's expecting your cooperation on this. What am I supposed to tell him?"

"You tell him to wait." Becher barked. "Not to do anything until I speak with him. I need him to understand. All of you to understand. I need her, Seby. She's my only hope."

"I'll tell him. But I don't think it'll go over very well."

"Do it." Becher said, unable to mask his irritation in the least bit. "Now leave. I need to get back to work."

Becher turned his back to Roberts. After a few moments, he

heard Roberts sigh. In defeat, Becher hoped. He waited for the sound of shuffling feet to fade before checking over his shoulder to confirm Roberts had left. He walked to the desk in the corner of the lab and picked up his cell phone.

"Danger to the public. Ridiculous!"

He opened his text messages and scrolled to the thread labelled Haeli. He typed, *Haeli, watch your back, they* —

Becher paused a moment before holding his finger down on the backspace key. The cursor jumped backward, swallowing each word until there were none.

16

Blake inserted the key card Griff had given him. A green LED illuminated, accompanied by the click of the disengaging latch. He and Haeli entered and moved down the hallway to the living room.

"Griff?" Blake called out.

The door to the bedroom was open. There was no movement within.

"Be right there," the muffled voice responded.

The sound of a toilet flushing came from beyond the bedroom. A few moments later, Griff appeared in the bedroom doorway, drying his hands with a washcloth.

"So, we ready to do this or what?" Griff flashed a toothy grin.

"I'm ready." Haeli sat on the edge of the couch cushion.

"How did it go with the surveillance?" Blake asked.

"Piece of cake," Griff said. "Ya know, we could do some damage if you ever wanted to go all Ocean's Eleven on this place."

"Yeah, I don't think so," Blake said. "But for the record, you'd make a pretty good Basher Tarr."

"Basher?" Griff grimaced. "I'm Danny."

"Please. He's the big picture guy. There can be only one Danny. That's clearly me."

"Guys, focus." Haeli raised her hand in the air with the blue thumb drive pinched between her thumb and forefinger.

Griff picked up his laptop from the kitchen island and sat next to Haeli. Blake chose a spot behind the couch for a better view of the screen. Haeli passed the drive to Griff, who inserted it into one of the USB ports.

The file finder window popped up, revealing the contents of the drive. The original zip file named "1.zip" was still present and now accompanied by a folder of the same name. Griff double clicked to display the contents of the folder.

The window presented four icons representing the extracted files. Three PDF documents and one with an unknown type and a raw file extension, each named with a random series of numbers.

Griff clicked on the first file. It automatically opened the PDF viewer software and displayed the document.

"Blueprints." Griff stated the obvious.

"Of what?" Haeli asked.

Griff scrolled through the file and did not respond.

"Looks like some kind of industrial facility," Blake said. "Wait. Stop there."

Griff took his hand off the track pad.

Blake leaned over Griff's shoulder and pointed at the screen. "These, right here. Laboratories. I think we're looking at Techyon's facility. Does this look familiar, Haeli?"

"No," she said. "I don't recognize the layout at all. If this is Techyon's facility, it would have to be the new one. It's definitely not Tel Aviv."

"Open the next one," Blake said.

Griff did so. This time the document comprised one page. A satellite image of lower Nevada. The metropolitan sprawl of Las Vegas was visible. About a hundred and twenty miles northwest of Las Vegas— judging by the scale printed on the lower left corner of the Google

Maps image—was a red circle. A line that would result from dragging a finger around the touch screen of a phone or tablet.

"What's that supposed to mean?" Haeli asked. "There's nothing there."

Haeli was right. The circle indicated some importance of the location, but it was drawn on what appeared to be an empty section of the Nevada desert. A homogenous brown patch between two darker colored strips, their crinkly textures indicative of mountain ridges.

Griff zoomed in. The resolution of the image was high, but there was still no sign of any man-made structures. "Maybe this was the planned site."

"Then the thing hasn't been built yet," Blake said. "Look at the date."

The time stamp printed on the bottom of the image was from a week prior.

"I assure you they have built the new facility," Haeli said. "It was almost completed before I left. And my father told me in his message he transferred months ago."

"We're assuming this map relates to the blueprints," Griff said. "Maybe it's not. Maybe it's marking something else."

"Possible," Haeli said. "But it'd be a huge coincidence that Wentz asked to meet me here, in Las Vegas, the only major city within hundreds of miles of this desert valley. If he had fled from Techyon, as he claimed, wouldn't it make sense?"

"There are other possibilities," Blake said. "They could camouflage the structure to appear to be the desert floor. Or it could be underground. It wouldn't be the only underground facility in Nevada. Hell, I could name off a half dozen belonging to the U.S. government."

"Let's not get hung up on conjecture, there are a couple more files here," Griff said. "There's bound to be more clues." He clicked the X to close the map and double clicked the next file. A window prompted Griff to choose which application to use to view the .raw file. Griff chose the plain text editor. "Raw is right." Deep wrinkles sprawled out from the corner of his eyes toward his temples. "It's a data file, just a bunch of random letters. Encoded."

"Those aren't random letters," Haeli said. "It's genetic data. Trust me. Just don't ask me what it means."

Griff scrolled through what seemed to be thousands of pages full of letters. Even though the letters represented data and not human-readable text, Blake's brain picked out words on each page. Act, Cat, Tag, Tact.

"I don't know what we're supposed to do with that," Blake said. "Check out the next one."

Griff brought up the last document in the folder. There was no ambiguity to the contents of this file. The heading read Project Eclipse Lab Journal and the subtitle Dr. Benjamin Becher.

Griff read out loud. "Week 1. Fertilization was successful. The host is in exemplary health."

"How long is this journal?" Haeli asked.

"Long." Griff flicked his finger on the track pad. Pages scrolled by. Week 50, Week 100, Week 300. "We're only a fraction of the way into this thing. There has to be twenty- or thirty-years' worth of entries in here." Week 400, Week 500.

"Stop!" Haeli grabbed his wrist. "Go back. A little more."

They all saw it. Week 539. Haeli's name flew off the page. She grabbed the laptop and slid it onto her own lap.

"Haeli continues to progress. Reflex times, fast twitch muscle density and relative strength continue to progress at 0.2 percent week over week. While overall readings are lower than the models predicted, it is still possible for her to meet all goals should she continue to progress at the same rate or higher through puberty. Blood tests suggest signs of elevated hormone levels. It is likely that the onset of puberty is imminent."

Haeli sat still, hunched over the laptop, mouth agape. Blake wished he had the words. He was at a loss, but he couldn't imagine how this affected Haeli. A simple passage with such horrible weight. He wished she would stop reading there.

Blake had always tried to be cognizant of the events that defined him. To weed out the insignificance of everyday life and break the sum of himself down into individual parts. He believed it a worthwhile pursuit to identify those instances that deflected him from his original trajectory. Whether it was something as heavy as taking someone's life or overhearing a piece of advice that resonated, Blake thought he had been successful in mentally cataloguing such instances.

Until one event, a nuclear detonation that made all other experiences mere firecrackers erased all others. Blake discovered that the real deal didn't need to be contemplated or cataloged, and it couldn't be missed or forgotten. He became it, and it him. This was Haeli's nuclear moment. She would never be the same.

Haeli scrolled, coming to rest on a random page. She read aloud again.

"Week 786. Test results confirmed the ailment to be the common cold. With every sign that Haeli fully recovered and is operating at full capacity, I administered the yearly proficiency test. The two-week delay should not be significant enough to offset next year's scheduled testing. The full report was forwarded to Mr. Farr and Dr. Roberts at the start of the week. Yearly progress has technically increased but has significantly slowed to a rate of 0.045 percent. I stand by my previous assessment, as always, that there is no other conclusion to be drawn other than complete confidence that the genetic manipulation has demonstrably increased Haeli's aptitude, speed, and strength. It is my opinion that Haeli should transition to real-world training and evaluation when deemed appropriate."

"Haeli," Blake said. He wanted to plead with her to stop. To close the laptop and never open it again, but it would have been an unfair demand. She needed to know. Besides, she didn't appear interested in any attempts at persuasion. She lifted her hand and continued scrolling.

She continued. "Anecdotally, proof of the experiment's effectiveness was apparent in the so-called combat tournament. Haeli faced several of Mr. Farr's most experienced and highly trained men and, in my assessment, held her own. Because of the weight and muscle mass differential, I can conservatively estimate that, pound for pound, Haeli's effectiveness exceeded that of her opponents. Let me digress. At the risk of sounding overly sentimental for posterity's sake, I was proud of her. Also note: Dr. Ursel reported that Haeli regained consciousness during overnight phlebotomy and EEG analysis. They increased the dosage of methohexital 120mg with positive results."

"Wow," Griff said. Blake couldn't blame him for his sudden loss of vocabulary. And he was glad someone broke the ice.

"Is this real?" She sounded stuck between laughing and crying. "What the hell am I reading? What am I, an experiment? This thing makes it sound like I'm a mutant, one of the X-Men. Like I'm not even human."

"You're human, Haeli." Blake placed his hand on her shoulder. "Think about it, though. What you did in the conference center, you decimated those guys. Did you ever wonder how you could do that?" Blake winced at his own statement. He had meant well, but the words had come out more condescending than consoling.

"Wait, what did you do at the conference?" Griff said. "Why is this the first time I'm hearing about this?"

Haeli ignored the question. "If this is true, it would explain a lot. Why these people took any interest in me. Why they devoted hours everyday training me, teaching me. It was their job. And I...*I was a fucking experiment.*"

There it was. The anger Blake was expecting. The sense of betrayal. The tip of the iceberg.

"It's incredible," Griff said with tone-deaf excitement. "They were building a super soldier. It's downright diabolical. Who the hell are these people?"

"You're not helping, Griff." Blake's face flushed.

"I've gotta google it." Griff tapped at his phone.

Griff's lack of empathy for the girl astonished Blake. He had to consider his own reaction, too. Was he being too coddling? And why was he so concerned about protecting her feelings? She was a killing machine. If her list contained his name, she'd erase him from existence without care or concern.

"I thought I knew who I worked for, but now…" Haeli rested her hands on the top corners of the laptop screen. She tilted the screen toward the keyboard about an inch, and the glow lifted from her face. Then, losing her internal battle, tilted the screen open again. Its light reflected in her dark eyes.

"Here's Wikipedia." Griff skimmed. "It says 'Techyon is a military contractor, science and technology company found by Levi Farr.' Let's see, 'Farr was born in San Francisco.' Oh, check this out, 'Farr's father, an American physicist at Stanford, and his mother, a biologist from Israel, died in a boating accident when Farr was seventeen years old. Farr put aside his plans to pursue a Doctorate at Stanford to join the military. He served eight years in the special forces before starting his own company, which he named Techyon as an homage to his father, who had been working on detecting the existence of the hypothetical Tachyon particle.'"

Haeli rolled her eyes and grunted. "I've heard that story a thousand times."

Griff continued skimming and paraphrasing the article. "'Farr invested a sizable sum, left to him by his parents and enlisted the help of former team members to get the company off the ground.' Oh, listen to this, it reads 'Charismatic and sharp, Farr later secured several investors who allowed him to hire the top scientific minds available. In ten years, Farr transformed Techyon from a small diplomatic security, support missions and cyber security firm into a tech giant. In its current form, Techyon has its divisions advancing in the fields of smart weapons, biological weapons, genetics, and cyber warfare. The company holds hundreds of contracts with the United States Department of Defense and Israel Ministry of Defense and has a net worth of approximately one-hundred billion dollars.' Who wrote this wiki, Levi Farr? Charismatic and sharp?"

"I would agree," Blake said. "Let's just say it's undeservedly flattering."

Haeli closed the laptop, slid it onto the couch, and shifted her body toward Blake and Griff. Her face was pale and her eyes bloodshot. "I don't want to talk about Levi Farr anymore. I want to find my father and rid myself of all of them."

"We'll find him," Griff said.

Blake didn't like how much the statement sounded like a promise. He did not make promises he didn't know if he could keep.

"Haeli," Blake said. "Why don't you get a few hours of sleep. It's late. We'll make a couple of calls in the morning and see what we can do. Okay?" He stepped around the couch and offered his hand. "I'll walk you down to the room."

Haeli reached up and allowed Blake to pull her to her feet. She walked toward the door.

"I'll be right back," Blake said.

"Uh huh." Griff didn't appear convinced.

Blake entered the hotel hallway and found Haeli waiting for him. They strolled the five hundred feet to Blake's room and stopped in front of the door.

"I know it's a lot," Blake said, "but you'll be able to think more clearly after some sleep." Blake handed her the key card. "You may have to swipe this a few times to get it to go. It's temperamental."

"Got it." Haeli said.

Blake paused. "Goodnight, then."

Haeli's shoulder twitched and before Blake realized it, her hand was in his.

"You don't have to go," Haeli said. "I mean, it's your room. You can stay. I wouldn't mind the company."

"Yes, I do. Have to go. Goodnight." Blake turned and walked away and fought his urge to glance back at her. It wasn't until he reached Griff's door that he heard the door to his room open and close. He glanced back at the empty hallway.

What have you gotten yourself into?

17

Levi dropped his bag on the brown leather sofa and inhaled the sweet fragrance of wood and varnish. Stained mahogany covered every inch of the eight-hundred-square-foot office. The bookshelves, ornate wall and ceiling paneling, and over-varnished floors would have been more typical in an Ivy League library than this modern facility.

The mammoth desk weighed a literal ton and had to be built in place by old-world artisans. What money could accomplish never ceased to amaze Levi. Not just the quality of the work, but the willingness of the men to place themselves in such a compromising position for triple the amount they would gain from typical projects. No one would ever be able to torture them into revealing the location of the facility.

Few people would ever see the office, making the cost more absurd. But to Levi, it was a punctuation mark. A testament to his success.

Levi wrapped his hands around the paws of the two lions carved into the mahogany wall panels behind the desk. He pulled the heavy doors, sliding them apart to reveal the living quarters beyond.

The four-thousand-square-foot luxury flat made the stodgy office seem an anachronism. Modern art hung on the stark, glossy walls. Brightly colored furniture spotted the floor for a minimalist effect.

Levi touched the screen embedded in the wall just past the entrance. He called up a preset code to shift the color of the lighting and start a rendition of Lionel Hampton's 'It Don't Mean a Thing' which was subsequently piped into every room.

Levi had spared no expense in automation. Every appliance, big or small, connected to the central brain. In addition to the automation, Levi relied on two staff members to maintain the residence.

With their own connected quarters, Greta and her sister Sofia could easily access the residence to cook, clean, stock and otherwise look after Levi's comfort. The only direction he gave, the only non-negotiable job requirement, was that he never see them. Ever.

Levi opened the Sub Zero refrigerator and found it fully stocked with pre-made meals, snacks, juices, and a variety of India Pale Ale, sourced from New England. It seemed Greta and Sofia excelled in their new roles.

Levi pulled a pint-sized can of beer free of its plastic ring. He checked his watch and returned it to the top shelf of the fridge.

Too early.

He walked to the office, moved his bag beyond the sliding doors, and closed himself inside the shrine of mahogany.

Levi sat in the high-backed leather chair for ten seconds before checking his watch again and springing to his feet. He walked to the glass-topped bar, flipped one of the crystal glasses over, and poured himself a scotch.

A knock came at the door as he took a sip. "Come in. Oh, it's you." He hadn't intended it to come out with such disappointment, but Sebastian Roberts was not who he was expecting.

Roberts stepped in and stood in a submissive posture. "Do you have a second?"

"Depends. Where the hell is Loftus?"

"I don't know," Roberts said. "I wanted to talk to you about Becher."

"That's why I need Loftus. He should have been here four minutes ago to update me on his team's progress."

"I don't mean Haeli, I mean, yes, I do mean Haeli, but also Ben."

"What about Ben? Did you talk to him? Did he give Loftus what he needed?"

"Not exactly," Roberts said.

Loftus appeared in the doorway. He stood at attention.

"Get in here."

One thing Levi missed about the military was the clear hierarchy. The stars or bars or chevrons told everyone what they needed to know about their place in the pecking order. Loftus would have been the equivalent of the Colonel, Levi figured. He had contemplated implementing military style titles at one time but realized it would cause unnecessary harm to morale. Guys who served in the military and achieved rank could have felt as though Levi had demoted them. There couldn't be more chiefs than warriors, and where they came from, they were all chiefs.

"Tell me it's done," Levi said.

"I'm sorry, sir. There was a problem. My team had her pinned down, but she escaped. The good news is Wentz will no longer be an issue."

"I don't give a crap about Wentz." Levi's blood pressure skyrocketed so he felt lightheaded. "Explain to me how your entire team could have her and then let her escape."

"She had help." Loftus paused but, after not receiving a response, took the hint that his answer was insufficient. He elaborated. "She met with Wentz in a hotel room. We tracked her there, covered the room, sent Sullivan up on an adjacent roof to get a clear shot. Rest of the team covered the room, elevators, and lobby. Turned out she had a disguise. Someone helped her by giving it to her."

"A disguise. That's your excuse? She had a disguise?"

"It's worse." Loftus's legs swayed as if they would buckle. "We tracked her down to this conference. A computer hacker thing. She killed two of my men, disabled the other two, and escaped again. And—"

"And?" It took everything Levi had to calm himself. To act the part of someone who did not want to kill the man with his bare hands.

"We think she had more help. Benson was staking out her room. There was a guy. A redheaded guy with a beard that came by to clean the room. He disappeared, leaving his cart, the bed unmade. Benson found someone removed a piece of the molding and we think she sent him in to get something. Probably what Wentz gave her."

"Tell me something," Levi said, his voice soft and measured. "Was Sullivan killed?"

"No sir, it was—"

"Good," Levi said. "You're relieved of your command, effective immediately. Sullivan will head your team. What's left of them. You will depart for Tel Aviv this afternoon and take up your new position."

"Sir? But—"

"That will be all." Levi dismissed him.

"Sir, but what position?"

"Diplomatic security, something that you could once do without screwing up. I suggest you leave now before you're scrubbing toilets or out on your ass. Copy?"

"Copy." Loftus did an about face and scurried out of the room.

"You were right," Roberts said. "Maybe she is dangerous."

Sebastian Roberts had been so quiet, Levi almost forgot he was still in the room. It was becoming a theme.

"I'm going to Las Vegas, Sebastian. This is something I'll have to do myself. There's too much on the line to leave it to these bumbling idiots."

"Levi, I wanted to tell you I talked to Ben, and he was not helpful."

"It doesn't matter," Levi said. "I don't need his help. I'll find her. I'll take care of it."

"But maybe Ben's right," Roberts reasoned. "Maybe it's not a good idea. I mean, Ben says he needs her. That his research isn't complete. We both know Haeli. She was a solid employee, a solid person. Maybe we can salvage her. Ben wanted me to ask you to talk to him before you did anything. I told him it wasn't likely but—"

"Fine." Levi said. "I'll speak with him. I'll hear him out. Okay? I would prefer to avoid this ugliness if I can. You know that."

"Thank you." Roberts stood up to leave. "You know, when I came in here, I thought it was a little early for scotch. Boy, was I wrong!"

Levi gave a contrived chuckle and raised his glass to the feeble attempt at levity. He watched Roberts leave and close the door behind him before picking up the phone and dialing three digits.

"Gas up the chopper and be ready to go in twenty. We're going to Las Vegas."

18

"Cream and sugar." Griff handed one of the two mugs to Haeli. "And black for the gentleman. Served in an exclusive, limited edition Venetian Hotel collector's mug."

Blake accepted the mug in the way an actor would accept an Oscar and took a generous swig. An action he regretted after losing a layer of skin off the roof of his mouth. He rubbed the result with his tongue.

"Thanks, Griff," Blake said. He directed his attention to Haeli. "How'd you sleep?"

Blake was sure he knew the answer. Glowing skin replaced the previous night's mottled look. Her eyes no longer red but clear and focused. Her natural appearance was a sign that, while her mind may not have been rejuvenated, her body was.

"I managed," she said.

"Well," Griff said, "Mick and I went through some of this stuff in more depth. Hope you don't mind."

"No, that's fine." Haeli waved her hand to dismiss any concern. "But can I ask you something? Why do you call him Mick?" She turned to Blake. "Why does he call you Mick?"

Griff laughed. "What else do you call a dirty Irishman?"

Haeli burst into laughter. "Of course. Mick. I should have guessed that."

Blake shook his head. "Please don't encourage him. Someone's going to overhear him one day and kick his ass."

"Sorry," Haeli said over Griff's thunderous laughter. Her own laugh trailed into a sigh and then a grunt as she cleared her throat.

"Griff calls me Mick because our buddies call me Mick. And they call me Mick because, well, what else do you call a handsome, strapping young Irish lad?"

"Okay, Mick. I'll buy that." Haeli put her hand on his knee and squeezed.

"Want to know what we found out?" Griff sat and took a sip of his own coffee.

"You found out I'm the Israeli government's secret weapon?"

"Well, sort of," Blake said. "They intended for you to be a secret weapon for the United States Government. The U.S. funded the Eclipse project in the early 80s, hoping to build the perfect soldier. It seems the Department of Defense expected more dramatic results, as your father had indicated, because they pulled funding about fifteen years later. Techyon saw the benefit and kept you in-house."

"It is really amazing what your father pulled off in the early eighties," Griff said. "The program was well ahead of its time. Some of the genetic technology is just now becoming mainstream."

"And there's something else." Now Blake put his hand on her knee. She shot him a crooked smile. "There were others. A bunch of them. But none of them developed the aptitude and capability that you did. You were, for lack of a better term, the winning formula. It's no wonder they weren't willing to let you leave."

"I don't know. There are a lot of capable guys who work for Techyon. In operations, at least. Former special forces folks. The best of the best, really. I'm no more useful than any of them."

Griff steered the conversation back on track. "But that's not what we really wanted to share with you. We found something useful."

Blake realized his hand was still resting on Haeli's thigh. It didn't feel uncomfortable, but it should have. He pulled back his hand and followed up by scooting his body several inches backward.

"Which is?" Haeli asked.

"We took another look at the satellite image," Griff said.

"And," Blake added, "we pulled up all the archived Google map images from the past few years. It turns out one was cataloged about eleven months ago. Show her."

Blake stared at Griff while pointing at the laptop tucked in a chair between its cushion and plush arm. Griff excavated it and flipped it open.

A satellite image filled the screen. The same desert valley they had viewed the night before. Only this image was different. The valley appeared even more homogeneous than before. Griff zoomed in tight.

"It's blurry," Haeli said.

"It's pixilated. Scrambled," Griff said. "On purpose. You realize what that means? Someone went through some trouble to make sure they obscured this area. Someone with connections."

Blake stepped in. "If Techyon was building a facility here, it would be impossible to hide it from the air while it was under construction. Even if there wasn't a giant hole, there would be vehicles, equipment. We checked with the FAA, they designated this area as restricted airspace a year and a half ago. But they released the restriction a few months back."

"Couldn't that mean it's something the U.S. government was building or is operating?" Haeli asked.

"Not likely," Blake replied. "The federal government owns 84.9 percent of the land in Nevada. This area isn't part of it. In fact, this land is owned by LTF Holdings out of the Bahamas. Which looks to be your typical shell company."

"Okay, so if there is something there not visible from above, we can still drive in." Haeli's back straightened. Her pitch ticked up a notch. The news had encouraged her. "We can grab a Jeep or something and do a little recon."

"We could," Blake said. "Or we could hike in on foot. Either way, I doubt we'd be able to get close."

"What we need is a helicopter," Griff said.

"And someone to fly it," Haeli shot back.

Haeli must have noticed the instant silence because her eyebrows pushed up toward her hairline as she looked at Blake. Blake smiled, lifted his arm, and extended his index finger. Haeli's eyes followed the finger to its target.

"You fly?" she asked.

"Is that hard to believe?" Griff said.

"No, no. I just didn't know. Where do you fly? I mean, what do you fly?"

"Right now? Greater D.C. Rotor Club. On the weekends. But before that I flew for the Navy."

"Wow." Haeli added a singsong inflection to the praise that peaked in the middle.

"Yes, ma'am." Griff stood up and tucked the laptop into the gap of the cushion. He collected the coffee cups from the table and carried them off to the attached kitchen. "I was a career aviator before I left to join the Agency. Could have kept flying, too."

Haeli shifted her right knee, so it bumped against Blake's left. She mouthed the words, "Agency. I knew it."

Blake smiled and shook his head.

She doesn't miss a trick.

"So, we need a helicopter." It seemed reasonable coming from Haeli's mouth.

"Well..." Griff's bravado waned. "It's not that easy."

Blake interrupted, "One of Fezz and Khat's buddies—he left the team before I joined—opened a *sightseeing* business out here. Helicopter tours. Let's give Fezz or Khat a call and see if they can give us an introduction."

"I know who you're talking about," Griff said. "I can't remember what they said his name was."

"Get Fezz on the line," Blake said.

Griff pulled his phone from his pocket and leaned against the kitchen counter.

Haeli crowded in toward Blake. "Listen, there's something you should know. I'm not a huge fan of heights."

"Neither am I," Blake said. "Don't worry, if we can pull off commandeering a helicopter, I'll be going with Griff."

"I didn't say I wouldn't go," Haeli clarified, "I'm just letting you know I have a bit of a thing."

"I'm saying you won't go," Blake countered. "If we can find a way to do this, we'll be flying to a desolate area with no idea what to expect. Let's say we find Techyon. Let's say we're caught. Well, then we would have brought you right to them. Plus, it would be easier to claim ignorance if it's just us. A couple of guys they've never heard of who took a wrong turn while on a sightseeing trip."

"Here," Griff said, "Fezz is on speaker." Griff placed the phone down on the table between them.

The phone rattled the glass tabletop as Fezz's voice distorted the tiny speaker. "Blake, Griff says you're already in some craziness. I knew you'd have a good time in Vegas."

"Yeah," Blake said toward the device. "Very relaxing. We wanted to ask you, does your buddy still have that helicopter tour business out here?"

"Peter Grant," Fezz said. "And yes, I believe business is going well. He's expanded from what I understand. Based out of Henderson Executive Airport. Nice place. You remember about two years ago, Khat and I went to his bachelor party? They lent you out that week. Kiev, I think."

"Yeah, I remember," Blake said. "The Kiev part, that is."

"Well, while we were out there, Peter took us up over the canyon. Great guy."

"What are the chances he'd be willing to lend us a helicopter?" Blake asked.

"Pretty good if it's coming from me. Especially if I let him know the great and powerful Apollo's gonna fly it." Fezz laughed. The resonance caused the phone to rattle itself around a quarter turn.

Blake made a mental note to explain the joke to Haeli later. Apollo had been Griff's pilot callsign in the Navy. According to Griff, fellow pilots bestowed him with the moniker because he had let his hair grow an extra eighth of an inch during flight school, causing an onslaught of ribbing that he was trying to look like Apollo Creed. The color of Griff's skin was the only apparent attribute he had in common with Carl Weathers, which made the name funnier. Griff was proud of it, though. According to Fezz, Griff spent the first six months with the Agency trying to get Fezz and Khat to call him Apollo, all but ensuring they never would unless it was to goof on him.

"I'll call him right now and I'll get back to you," Fezz said.

The phone's display returned to the home screen, signifying that Fezz had disconnected.

"He'll get it," Griff said.

"I know he will," Blake said.

Haeli lifted her hands in front of her with her palms facing out. "I just have to say, you are some good people to know."

19

Levi stood in the ten-by-ten lobby. He meandered around as if it were the Guggenheim where he could absorb all the sights the space offered. He scanned the walls as he moved, with no particular interest in what he was perusing. Several plaques, issued in appreciation by the Special Olympics, a crime stoppers tip-line advertisement, a shadow box holding an original Las Vegas Metropolitan Police uniform from 1973. He tried to come up with a word for it.

Prosaic.

There were two doors. One leading from the outside and one leading further in. He checked the handle of the interior door. Still locked.

He had made four passes around the lobby already. Each trip ended at the thick glass window to a grimy reception office area. The same window through which he had informed the attending officer that he was there to see Lieutenant Jackson. It had been ten minutes since the pudgy officer disappeared through the door at the back of his cramped little terrarium.

Levi knew the layout of the Las Vegas Metro Police Department

Digital Intelligence and Surveillance Unit, or DISU. He had been there before under similar circumstances. And he was always welcome as long as Lieutenant Lenny Jackson was in command.

The building itself had once been the offices of the Parking Authority. Although repurposed and outfitted with a myriad of advanced technology, it didn't appear to have been cleaned since his last visit. Along with his familiarity with the restricted area of the building, he was also familiar with the thirty-second walk to Jackson's office.

How then did the worthless pissant get lost on the way?

Patience was not Levi's strong suit. The same was true about empathy, humility, generosity, or any other redeeming quality. Levi had no delusions. He knew full well he didn't have the qualities that garnered people's affection, trust, or admiration. But he had something better. The ability to fake all of them.

The interior door flew open and the handle crashed against a plastic stopper affixed to the wall. Lenny Jackson, along with the pudgy officer, appeared.

"I'm so sorry, Levi. Didn't know you were waiting," Jackson said. His eyes narrowed and burned a hole through his subordinate's face.

The officer mounted his defense. "I had to go to the bathroom quick."

"Next time," Jackson said, "when someone says they're here for me, you get me immediately. And if you ever see this man again, you just let him in."

The officer nodded and retreated.

"It's not a problem, Lenny," Levi said. "It's good to see you."

"You, too."

The men shared a handshake and walked back through the door, letting it close behind them.

Levi got down to business. "I've got a high-profile issue. I need someone found immediately. For the safety and security of the fine people of Las Vegas, of course. I brought several reference images. Multiple angles, high resolution. Should be easy."

They pushed through the door at the end of the hall to the main floor of the unit. The color temperature of the ambient light was a mixture of the fluorescent fixtures and the dozens of flat panel monitors, mounted in tight rows along almost every wall. Each screen displayed a different feed from cameras mounted throughout the downtown area of the city.

Levi knew that the angles displayed were a mere subsection of what was available. They covered almost every corner of the strip. But that wasn't all. The DISU piped in the internal feeds from every casino and club, police cruisers, taxis, social media posts, and a host of other sources.

Artificial Intelligence had made it possible to monitor the unwieldy number of images streaming through the unit every second. They had shown many of the capabilities to Levi during his last visit, including the Shot Tracker system which could detect and analyze the position, type, and duration of any shots fired within the city. Used in connection with the surveillance systems, Las Vegas Metro Major Crimes had increased solvability of firearms-related crimes eight-fold.

The software Levi was most interested in, the reason he stood in that room at all, was facial recognition. He knew from experience the power of the software. Given reference images, the system could locate, in archives or in real time, any individual. Not only locate, but stitch together a video that included all appearances of the person throughout all sources in chronological order.

A breathtaking yet disturbing video montage. A day-in-the-life production featuring a main character who would be oblivious to their role.

"We'll use this bay." Jackson pulled up a chair to one of the twenty cubicles filling the center of the room. "What do you have?"

Levi pulled a thumb drive from his pocket and tossed it to Jackson. He inserted it, pulled up the contents, and flipped through the images of Haeli.

"These will do," Jackson said. "Not your typical bad guy, though, is she?"

"That's an understatement."

Jackson didn't probe further, relieving Levi. He'd rather forgo making up a story to satisfy his old friend.

Jackson dragged the images to the software window and used the mouse to select parameters.

"Two days," Levi said, before Jackson could ask.

"Two days it is." Jackson clicked the bright green button labelled Start. "And we're off."

Images flashed on the screen. Single video frames culled from matching clips. Some images depicted hundreds of people on street corners and flashed by so fast, Levi couldn't tell if Haeli was in the crowd. But the computer could. The amazing artificial intelligence driven software found a match and plucked her from the obscurity of the masses.

"How's business?" Jackson asked.

And now the small talk.

"It's going well, how about you?" Levi deflected.

"You know, we always have job security around here." Jackson snickered.

"Tell me," Levi said, "can we watch this video while it's working?"

"Sure, we can watch from the beginning. It'll just take a few minutes to churn through the rest. Once it's done compiling, it will automatically add transitions between the clips and output an MP4 video. I'll put it back on your drive if there's enough space."

"That would be great. Do you mind if I..." Levi took hold of the mouse and clicked the play button. High resolution video filled the screen. Levi smiled at the sight of Haeli's face. She briskly walked along the sidewalk to the front entrance of the motel. Levi let it play. The feed switched at the instance Haeli walked through the glass doors and into the lobby of the motel. A lesser quality video picked her up inside as she approached the reception desk.

"Gotta love technology," Levi said.

"You're telling me," Jackson said.

Levi could see that Jackson took pride in the capabilities his unit had amassed. A valuable quality in a commander.

He scrubbed ahead until he saw the lobby of the Waldorf Astoria and again until the gaudy carpets of the conference center filled the frame. He watched as Haeli skittered through the crowd into one of the ballrooms and sprinted for the exit. The video jumped to the exterior loading dock area of what Levi assumed was the same building, right as Haeli burst through the door. But now someone accompanied her. A man. Levi clicked the mouse to pause the video.

"Can you zoom in on this guy?" Levi asked.

Jackson took control of the mouse. The image hadn't zoomed all the way in before it clicked in Levi's brain.

"Blake Brier." Levi was sure of it. But how? It made zero sense. The synapses in Levi's brain fired at overclocked speeds but couldn't make the slightest connection.

"Who's Blake Brier?" Jackson asked.

"A guy I used to know." Levi answered while his brain remained occupied with processing the visual input.

Jackson pointed to the progress indicator. "It's done processing if you want me to copy it over."

"Hang on just a moment." Levi slid the play head to the end. The very last frame of the video displayed an empty hotel hallway. Doors lined either side and the sequential numbers were visible. Levi backed up the video several frames until a door opened and Haeli emerged in reverse. One foot, then the other, then her body, then her face. Rolling the video backward made it appear as though she summoned the door to close against her hand.

"Where is this?" Levi asked.

"That's the Venetian. Palazzo."

Levi looked at the time stamp on the video and then at his watch. "Five minutes ago." Levi leapt up and pulled his phone from his pocket. He poked at the screen and held it to his ear.

"Sullivan," Levi said, "get to the Palazzo. She's there now. I'll text you the room and a couple of screenshots of what she's wearing. Do not let her get away. I'll be right behind you."

Levi hung up without waiting for a response. He snapped a picture of the screen.

"Do me a favor," Levi said.

"Sure." Jackson stood.

"Make a copy of that video, I'll pick it up later. I'm going to finish this."

20

"Are you sure we need this?" Griff huffed as he hoisted the metal case into the rear of the SUV. The ground-penetrating radar unit that Fezz and Khat had arranged came disassembled in several heavy road boxes. The cumbersome nature of the unit was not Griff's problem. Griff would have to fly low — extremely low — to use it. Blake agreed this wasn't ideal, but it would be nice to have if the thermal imaging and visual inspection failed.

"We might as well take it, we needed the thermal anyway," Blake said.

At least they had lost little time. The campus of the University of Nevada, Las Vegas, was just around the corner from where they had started. The equipment was on loan for a week, supposedly for archaeological exploration, although they'd only need it for a few hours.

The young man who provided the equipment appeared from around the side of the SUV, holding a clipboard. The graduate student followed instructions dictated by the department chair to a tee. And he asked no questions.

"Sign this." The kid held out the clipboard.

Blake took it and scribbled on the highlighted line. The student looked at it for a moment. Probably wanted to comment on the fact that the wavy line was not at all legible. He said nothing and retreated to the garage bay with the paperwork.

Blake swung the rear door closed and climbed in the driver's seat. The passenger door opened, and Griff threw himself into the seat.

"All right, I got shotgun then," Griff said.

Blake saw the irony in Griff's choice of words. He may have been riding shotgun, but he didn't have one. Or any weapons at all. Blake had the feeling that was something they should have remedied before they took the trip. But he understood what Griff meant by the comment. It was peculiar that Blake had taken the wheel, seeing as though Griff had rented the car and driven to the university. But his one-track mind had kicked into full gear. He was on a mission.

The twenty-minute drive to Henderson Executive Airport was quiet. Devoid of the usual banter. Blake figured they were both saving it for when they met Peter Grant. From everything they had heard, he was a legendary ball-buster.

Blake should have used the time to reflect on what he was involved in. What he saw as the best-case scenario. And what the contingency plan would be in the worst case. Instead, he watched each passing strip mall and wondered how many massage parlors one town could support.

He spent some time considering where he would be if he wasn't in the outskirts of Vegas. Skiing in the Alps? Maybe. Kayaking in Canada? That was something he had wanted to do. But he couldn't shake the feeling that none of it would have been as fulfilling as what he was doing now.

He met Haeli by chance. And there was no way to unmeet her. There was something about her that resonated in him. It was more than a physical attraction, although that part was undeniable—no matter how hard he tried. They were kindred spirits, as if she was the female version of him. And vice versa. It was dangerous. But as much as he didn't want any part of her life, he didn't want to not be part of it either. The bottom line was that he was a screwed-up individual. Good for no one.

Blake turned onto Jet Stream Way. "This is it."

If they had been expecting the freeways, ramps, and rotaries of a major airport, they wouldn't find it here. The place was an airstrip in the middle of the desert, flanked by several hangars.

Blake pulled into the parking lot. The sandstone-colored buildings, positioned on two sides of the lot, made him feel as if he were pulling into a mall.

There were a few modest signs affixed to the tops of the buildings, but one brand stood out among them, thanks to the oversized billboard. 'Spirit of the West Sightseeing and Tours,' it read. A giant arrow pointed toward a similar sign a few hundred feet north.

"How will we find him?" Griff asked through his shit-eating grin.

Blake didn't respond.

They left the SUV and followed the billboards. The front entrance faced the tarmac, not the hangar doors as Blake would have expected. Those were located around the side.

Blake watched as a Piper Arrow motored down the runway and took flight. If he weren't looking at it, he'd think a lawn mower was taking off.

Blake could identify the model because he had taken a few lessons when he was younger, and the school used the Arrow for training. He enjoyed the lessons but decided not to continue because of a lack of time and budget. Mostly budget. These days, Blake could afford to buy a dozen of the small planes, but he had no interest in flying.

"Mick? Griff?" A voice sounded from behind them.

They looked at each other with the same apprehensive expression before slowly turning around.

"Peter Grant?" Blake said.

"That's me. The Duke of Henderson in the flesh. But you can call me Kook." Grant administered two enthusiastic handshakes.

Grant did not look like what Blake had envisioned. His long blonde hair, tan skin, Birkenstocks, and surfer-esque vocal tone made Blake want to draw him a map to southern California.

"Thanks for helping us out," Griff said.

"Come on, any friend of Fezz and Khat is—" a smile took over Grant's face, "—a sorry son of a bitch." Grant laughed and slapped Griff on the shoulder twice. "Let me show you my beauty."

They walked north, towards the edge of the tarmac, where two small fixed-wing aircraft and three helicopters sat, tethered by straps to hooks embedded in the asphalt.

As they walked, Grant wrapped his hand behind Blake's neck and rested it on his shoulder. "Fezz tells me you're a hell of a pilot."

"That would be Griff," Blake said.

Grant pulled his arm away, drifted toward Griff and put his arm around Griff as if a mirror image. "Fezz tells me you're a hell of a pilot."

"I hold my own," Griff responded.

"Well this, my friend is an EC130. She's the best I've got."

Griff looked the aircraft up and down as if it were a pinup model. "Nice. Very nice. What's the top speed on this puppy?"

"One hundred and fifty on the safe side. Manufacture lists the never exceed speed as one-seventy-eight, but I've never pushed her that hard. Have you flown one before?"

"Sure have." Griff shot Blake a look to convey the opposite of what he told Grant.

"Good. I've got a couple million dollars sunk into this baby. Wouldn't want it to get any booboos. Know what I mean?"

Several million dollars.

The strength of the brotherhood. That this man, who he knew only by name and a few exaggerated war stories, would lend two complete strangers his aircraft, based only on the word of another, blew Blake's mind. Then again, Blake wouldn't hesitate to do the same if the tables were turned.

"So? What do we got goin' boys?" Grant's bleach-blonde hair bounced as he spoke.

"We're looking for a secret compound in the desert," Blake said. "Built by a sociopathic narcissist, so we can rescue the genius father of a genetically modified super-soldier."

"Dang, dude," Grant responded, "you could have just said none of your business." Dead air hung between them for a few moments until Grant laughed.

Blake felt confident Grant was stoned out of his gourd.

"Let's get her fired up." Grant whooped. He leaned in and lowered his voice. "How are you guys for fire power?"

"Light," Blake said.

"Dude. Come with me."

Grant jogged off toward the hangar. After the few beats it took to process the conversation, Griff and Blake went after him.

They walked through a waiting area, then through a small office before emerging into an unfinished space that looked like an automotive garage. Engine parts and tools were strewn over stainless-steel workbenches. An eight-foot-long wing laid between two sawhorses.

Grant approached two pieces of plywood that would have appeared to be leaning against the wall if it weren't for the beefy hinges and padlocked latch. Grant unlocked the padlock and swung the plywood outward.

What lived behind the makeshift doors was more than Blake imagined. Dozens of rifles, shotguns, pistols, knives, even brass knuckles. Blake wouldn't have been surprised if there were grenades and C4 in there as well.

"Now that's a collection," Griff said.

Griff was right. This stash rivalled Blake's own.

"Take whatever you want, man, just bring it back when you're done," Grant said. "Unless there's a body on it, then don't bring it back."

Blake wanted to take one of each, just in case. But he selected only the most useful.

"You really don't mind?" Blake picked up a Colt M4.

"Not at all, dude. Take what you need. That's a good choice right there."

It was an excellent choice. Out of all options, Blake gravitated toward the good old M4 Carbine. The 5.56 mm round was nasty, and it felt comfortable.

"Excellent, as long as you don't mind, we'll take two of these and the two 1911s." Blake pointed to two Kimber 1911 .45 caliber semi-automatic pistols mounted to the inside of the cabinet by rubber-coated metal brackets.

"Done." Grant handed the two pistols to Griff. He leaned the second rifle against the wall and closed the cabinets.

"What time should I expect you back?" Grant asked.

"A few hours," Griff said.

"Cool," Grant said. "Pull your truck around to the tarmac and we'll get you loaded up. I'll throw some ammo on there for ya, too."

"I'm gonna need to have a talk with Fezz." A smile crossed Blake's face. "You are nowhere near as big an asshole as Fezz said you were."

Grant chuckled. "Oh, yes I am."

21

Haeli turned the valve to the left. Enough so the water felt refreshing. A relative chill. She placed her hands on the tile in front of her and leaned, stiff-armed, as the cool water cascaded over her body. Any success of washing the tension from her muscles was negligible. She spun the handle to kill the water.

She walked to the wrought iron towel rack. There were no shower doors or curtains to contend with. The floor raked to ensure water found its way to the drain. She selected one of the plush white towels and applied it to her hair.

She looked at herself in the wall of mirrors spanning floor to ceiling behind the jacuzzi tub. She tightened her stomach, deepening the grid of indentations that delineated her rock-hard abdominal muscles.

It wasn't uncommon for her to catch herself critiquing the girl in the mirror. And most of the time, she was happy with what she saw. The rigorous training and physicality of her job had staved off the inevitable softening and sagging she imagined would have crept up on her by the age of thirty-four. But now she examined her form in a different way. Any genetic modification would have been incredibly minor, as evidenced by the fact that she didn't have a tail or a third arm. But staring at her dripping wet body after learning the truth, she couldn't help but feel like Frankenstein's monster.

She finished drying off and retrieved a sturdy paper bag from the bedroom. She pulled out several items of clothing and laid them across the bed. Two pairs of jeans, two thin-strapped tank tops, several pairs of undergarments and socks, and a form-fitting mini dress, just in case.

She put on a pair of jeans and a tank and returned to the enormous glass for a verdict.

It worked.

For street clothes, Banana Republic wasn't her style. But it had been the closest store she could find in the hotel that wasn't centered on handbags or jewelry, and simple utilitarian clothing was all she needed.

She flicked on the television and tuned to a national news network, then sat on the bed and brushed her hair while she watched.

The talking heads droned on about a Wisconsin Housing Authority corruption scandal. Based on the rampant and pure speculation that appeared to constitute the bulk of the arguments, Haeli surmised that there was nothing of importance going on in the world at the moment. Nothing the press knew about, anyway.

She left the TV on as a background filler until she had finished brushing, then flicked it off.

With the room falling back into silence, Haeli realized how difficult it was going to be for her to sit idle, holed up in this hotel room, while Griff and Blake executed the reconnaissance mission. She knew it was the right play. But it stung to be on the outside. It was a new feeling. For as long as she could remember, she had been the first one called in.

The confines of the suite, spacious as it was, felt tighter and tighter as the seconds ticked by. The need to keep the curtains drawn didn't help matters either. But she'd promised Blake she would not leave the room for any reason. And she intended to keep her promise.

Besides, it wouldn't be long. Presumably, Blake and Griff were already underway.

Fully dressed, except for her shoes and socks, Haeli left the bedroom and wandered around the rest of the suite. She opened the fridge, took out a V8 juice with half an intention of drinking it, then returned it and closed the fridge. She paced around for a couple of minutes before landing on the couch.

The layout of the room, donated to her by Blake, differed from Griff's. While both suites had a master bedroom, two bathrooms, a kitchen, a living room, and multiple large closets, Griff's room only had one door that opened to the hallway. Blake's had a second, in the bedroom. In addition, this room didn't have the short hallway leading to the exterior door. The door opened directly into the living room.

From the couch, the door was in full view. She stared at it. It stared back at her. Beckoning her to break her promise.

Haeli wasn't sure which floor plan she liked better. She decided it didn't matter. With any luck, she'd be moving on shortly. Putting a plan in motion to rescue her father.

My Father.

Haeli eyed the console table to the right of the exterior door. It wasn't the table that sent her mind spinning, but the contents of its drawer. Haeli had placed her cell phone in that drawer after shutting it off the prior evening. The only number her father knew to reach her on.

She moved to the table and opened the drawer. She reached in and picked up the Glock 19 handgun. With the suppressor attached, it had barely fit in there. She placed the pistol on top of the table and withdrew her phone.

Haeli intended to keep certain promises. Only she knew the difference between the promises she'd keep and the promises she wouldn't. This one fell into the latter category.

She pressed the power button and allowed the device to boot up. The home screen appeared, and she pressed the icon for text messages. She waited a moment for data to sync. There was nothing. No messages from her father. No messages from anyone.

She opened the visual voicemail application and confirmed there were no messages pending, then returned to the text messaging app. She touched the thread labelled Dad and typed.

"I'm worried about you. Please get back to me and let me know you're OK. I love you."

Haeli hit send, waited for the telltale tone that the message went through, then held the power button until the screen went dark. She slid the phone in the front pocket of her jeans, and she froze.

The faint sound of three electronic beeps thundered in her ears. Her heart thumped in her chest. She had heard this sound almost every time she tried to key into the room. It was the protest of the temperamental electronic lock rejecting the key card.

Haeli darted to the far side of the door, scooping up the silenced 9mm by the handle with her right hand, her finger on the trigger. She pressed her back against the wall and waited. She didn't have to wait long.

The scratching of the plastic card being inserted into the slot came again. This time there was a single, longer tone. The latch disengaged, and. The door cracked open.

The muzzle of the pistol came through first. Followed by the hand and vascular forearm of the man who wielded it. The pistol swayed back and forth.

The gap between the door and the frame was only about two feet. Enough for the man to get a decent picture of most of the room. She was glad he hadn't pushed the door with any force. It would have pinned her behind it.

More of the arm appeared. Haeli leveled her pistol at his head and waited.

The man's head and shoulders came into view for only a split second before Haeli pulled the trigger. The bullet tore through the man's neck, in one side and out the other. He dropped his gun and clutched at his neck with both hands.

Haeli stepped back, then exploded into the door, knocking him to the floor and slamming the door shut.

The man laid face down. The arterial blood spurted several feet at first, with less and less pressure on every pulse. Haeli felt a fleeting twinge of disappointment that he hadn't even seen her face before he died.

She leapt over the heap of a man and bolted to the bedroom. There were more of them. There always were.

Haeli held the pistol low and cracked the door that led to the hall-way. She heard the thud of the boot slamming against the door and the splintering of the wood. She stuck her head out in the hallway, just in time to see two men rushing in the living room entrance. She seized the moment.

She launched herself into the hallway, half sprinting before her feet touched the ground. It was another half second before she registered a man standing at the end of the hallway, fifty feet in front of her. She shifted her weight as if carving snow with the edge of a snowboard. The carpet burned her bare feet as she slid to a stop. She looked over her shoulder and confirmed her assumption. Another man at the other end. Neither had their guns drawn.

Haeli counted it as a minor victory. There were cameras in the hallway and there would be no way to clean up the aftermath if they took her down there. If discretion still mattered.

There was one option left. She sprinted toward the closer man, eyes as focused as lasers and with an equal amount of intensity.

She closed the gap.

Forty feet.

Thirty feet.

The man planted his feet, bent his knees, and balled his fists. His body language conveyed that he was preparing for the fight. His eyes held the fear of a matador caught by the charging bull.

Twenty feet.

The man hadn't moved. He was gauging his plan of assault from her reckless abandon. It would give him the advantage if he timed it right. But there was a method to her madness. She'd guessed what he'd do. She bet everything on it.

Ten feet.

Haeli veered left and smashed through the stairwell door. She bound up the stairs three at a time.

Deep, emphatic voices and heavy footfalls echoed through the shaft of the stairwell. There were more men, at least two of them. She hoped they were below her.

Haeli reached the first landing and pulled the door. Locked. Easy to get in, not so easy to get out.

The door flew open on the landing below and the man hit the stairs, coming after the fight she had promised him.

A shot rang out, the crack amplified to a deafening explosion by the cinderblock shaft. The pinging of the bullet ricocheting off metal handrails followed.

Haeli hit the next landing. Locked. She continued pumping her legs, controlling her breath, until she reached the last landing. A dead end.

She pulled the door, which swung open freely. The flood of blinding warm light and heat washed over her. It had been a day since she'd seen daylight or been out of the climate-controlled environment of the hotel. She had almost forgotten about the heat wave. The frying pan of a roof was a sufficient reminder.

Haeli bolted across the rooftop. The white gravel laid atop the sticky tar and asphalt scraped and embedded itself in the soles of her feet.

She scanned the roof as she ran. A grid of bulky air-conditioning compressors filled the open expanse. Beyond them, at the corner of the building, was a construction area, cordoned off by orange plastic netting. The bright red truss of a construction crane sprouted from the corner like a mighty redwood. The crane's jib jutting out over the abyss. Looking at it made her queasy.

Haeli dove behind one of the air-conditioning units and landed on the blades of her forearms as the first of the men erupted from the relative darkness of the stairwell. The sting of the scrapes on her elbows surged for a moment. Haeli lifted her bent arm, pistol still clutched in her right hand, and used her left hand to wipe away the remaining pieces of gravel from her right elbow. A trickle of blood streamed to the edge of the knobby bone and a single drop fell to the ground, splashing on the gravel. The glare of the sun off the white gravel set the crimson stone apart like a ruby.

Oh shit.

Haeli glanced down at her feet. Bright red splotches led from her bloody feet around the side of the metal box. A bedazzled trail leading the men directly to her.

She could hear the slow, methodical crunching under foot. While she couldn't risk peeking her head out, she didn't have to. She could envision the scene unfolding on the other side of the scorching hot sheet metal. The men had grouped up and were converging on her position, tentatively and cautiously.

Now or never.

Haeli crouched like a sprinter on the starting blocks and set her sights on a unit one row back and diagonal to her position in the orderly grid. A clear path, but she'd be in the open for several feet. It was worth the risk.

She pushed off, taking three long strides before diving, arms outstretched.

Shots rang out. Too many and too close together to count. The bullets twanged as they pierced the sheet metal and embedded in the guts of the compressor. Steam hissed through the bullet holes.

Haeli sprung up to one knee and launched herself toward another unit, further back. The shots came again. The twangs came again. The hissing started again.

She didn't have time to inspect herself for any damage. She didn't feel the searing pain of a bullet wound, but her adrenaline level was so high that she might not have.

She sprinted again, this time blindly firing three shots in their direction. The men took cover of their own, buying her a few seconds. She hoped.

Haeli reached the last row of units. She slipped over the flimsy construction netting and surveyed the area for an adequate fighting position. There was little cover and only a handful of mediocre options for concealment. She turned her attention to the base of the crane. The truss, made of tubular steel, was mostly open except for a four-foot-wide steel plate that ran up one side. The steel plate, about a half inch thick, was what she needed. Climbing up the thing for even a few feet was not.

Haeli moved to the truss and climbed through the diagonal supports. She looked upward. The vertical lines of the four main tubes converged in the distance. A ladder, welded to the steel plating, ran all the way up toward the horizontal jib and what she assumed was the control room.

She psyched herself up.

It's only a few feet.

The massive crane had been built to carry large or heavy payloads to the top of the roof. Tens of thousands of pounds. Heavier than Haeli's one-hundred-and-twenty-pound frame. Still, she measured every step, as if her weight would tip it over.

The blood dripping from her feet made the thin rungs of the ladder slippery. Her left arm did most of the work, pulling her body upward. She used the last three fingers of her right hand to steady herself while keeping full control of the pistol.

Haeli climbed about fifteen feet until the thick metal sheet shielded her entire body. She wrapped her left arm through the rungs and then passed the pistol to her left hand. She kept the business end of the suppressor pointed down the shaft and pulled her phone from her jeans. She powered it on.

Come on, come on.

When the screen came to life, she brought up the dial pad and punched in Blake's number. Blake hadn't sent his contact to her—hell, she wasn't even supposed to be using the phone—but he had written it down in case she needed it, and she had memorized it.

"Who's this?" Haeli struggled to make out the words over the background noise.

"It's Haeli. I need your help."

"Hello?" Blake said.

Haeli raised her voice. It would have been audible across the roof and would give away her position if they hadn't already seen her climbing. But she had no other choice. "It's Haeli."

"Haeli? Is everything alright? We just took off."

Haeli tipped the phone so that the microphone pointed directly at her mouth. She belted the words as loud as she could. "I need you. Please. Get to the roof. The roof!"

Haeli shoved the phone back in her pocket without bothering to hang it up. She transferred the 9mm to her right hand and held her aim.

The crunching of the footsteps grew closer. She closed one eye and looked down the sights, waiting for a target to appear. And appear it did.

The man ducked under the cross supports. The left side of his body came into view first. He looked up the hollow shaft. Haeli didn't get a glimpse of the gun in his right hand before double tapping the trigger.

One round buried in the top of his shoulder. The other in his left eye. He crumpled to the ground.

Haeli climbed another fifteen feet to put distance between her and the next wave. Like lemmings, they came.

The second man got a couple shots off. Haeli fired three. All three found their mark. She could see the blood running from three distinct holes in the man's cheek as he fell on the other dead man.

The third smartened up. He came around to the open sides of the truss and, instead of climbing in, fired at an angle. Haeli could see the sparks fly off the cross supports before she took aim through the triangular gap and squeezed off three more rounds, putting an end to the threat.

A secondary boost of adrenaline hit Haeli as her brain processed how close the incoming rounds were to striking her in the chest. She figured that, outside of the steel plates, the truss was twenty percent metal and eighty percent air. Surviving any battle was about luck, and she was worried she had used all hers up.

Haeli climbed further. The cover of metal plates was no longer enough. She needed distance. She needed to be a smaller target.

She continued climbing until she reached the horizontal truss. She stopped. The height was dizzying, but the angles were better. When viewed from below, a steeper angle meant more metal would conceal her position. It was the best she could do under the circumstances.

She scanned the corner of the rooftop. No one was visible. The view of the other side with the array of air-conditioning units was still obstructed. She had no way of knowing how many reinforcements had arrived. The entire team, she figured.

She heard the whizz and crack of the supersonic round fly by before she heard the rifle. She caught a quick visual of the two men climbing the ladder far beneath her. The nearest one with his arm wrapped around the rungs and a rifle pressed against his shoulder. She pushed with her legs and threw her body up and onto the horizontal jib. Her dangling right arm squeezed off five rounds. She had pulled the trigger six times, but the last pull answered with only a click.

A metal grate lined the underside of the horizontal truss. More luck. Without it, Haeli would have fallen straight through the wide gaps, hundreds of feet to her death. She'd rather have taken the bullet.

Still lying on her stomach, the grate did little to obscure the view of the ground. It was as if she floated in mid-air. She couldn't let it cloud her mind. She was now unarmed. The men were approaching fast. The only direction she could go was further out. She was being made to walk the plank and there was no option to swim.

The gravity of the circumstances had gotten the best of her. Could she disarm the first man, take his weapon and kill the second before they shot her? Maybe. Could she do it while suspended hundreds of feet in the air? Maybe not. A smile washed over her face. The irony, or rather the beauty of it all, was that she would never need to find out. At least, that's what she heard in the sound of the thumping rotor.

22

Blake parted the side doors of the EC130 as the marque atop the fifty-three story Palazzo tower came into view. He sat on the floor and kicked his legs out onto the step mounted high on the legs of the skid. He brought the holographic sights of the M4 up to eyeline and, using both eyes, ran the red dot along the roofline of the building.

Griff flew in close, staying well above the protruding arm of the tower crane.

Blake counted five men, spread out around the base of the enormous truss. But no sign of Haeli.

Griff got closer still. Blake could see the men were armed. A few with pistols, others with rifles. He clicked the button on the noise cancelling headset so he could communicate with Griff over the incessant whapping of the rotor.

"I don't see her," Blake said.

Blake's earphones crackled. Griff's voice followed. "If those guys are still there, then they're looking for her. She's hunkered down somewhere."

Then Blake saw her.

The delicate, bare arms waving over a head of blowing black hair.

"Griff, on the crane!" Blake yelled in an unintentional attempt at piercing Griff's eardrums.

Blake felt the helicopter jerk. Griff had gotten the message loud and clear. Mostly loud. Griff tilted the craft forward and to the left, pulling back once they hovered directly over Haeli.

Blake keyed up his mic. "Get closer."

Griff eased the altitude lower.

The crack of the rifle was barely audible over the roar of the helicopter, but Blake had already caught the muzzle flash out of the corner of his eye. He raised his rifle, trained the red dot on the man, and fired. He went down. The rest scattered. Blake kept his sights trained on the bank of metal air conditioning units.

The head, hands, and pistol of one man peeked over the top of a unit. Blake picked him off with a single shot. The impact of the bullet with the man's head carried so much energy that the cloud of atomized blood and brain matter was visible, even from Blake's altitude.

Blake waited a moment. Seeing no one else wanting to play whack-a-mole, Blake dropped his rifle to the deck and reached down to grab Haeli's outstretched hands. Haeli stood on her toes but couldn't reach.

Blake clicked his mic on and locked it in place so he could communicate without having to use the button each time.

"A little further Griff, I've almost got her."

The helicopter lurched lower.

Blake wrapped his right hand around Haeli's left wrist. She did the same. He crossed his left hand over and grabbed her right wrist and pulled.

The first few inches were easy, but Blake felt a resistance. Haeli's head dropped. He glimpsed the man that had latched his meaty claw onto Haeli's ankle.

The right arm of the man was a mangled, bloody mess. It hung limp by his side. But his left arm, muscles nearly bursting through his skin, was working fine.

"Higher, Griff," Blake said.

The helicopter jerked. The weight increased. Blake hung on tight.

The one-armed man now dangled by Haeli's ankle, his own feet swinging beneath him. Blake could see him when he swung out.

"He's going to pull you down," Blake yelled.

"No, he won't," Haeli yelled back. "Let go of my right hand and give me your gun. Don't worry, I won't let you go."

It wasn't her words that convinced him. It was her smile. Blake let go, reached into the back of his waistband, and pulled out the Kimber .45. He flipped it around and pressed the handle into Haeli's palm.

Haeli kept her eyes on Blake. Her dark, knowing, smokey eyes pierced through him and his pulse quickened. It wasn't until this moment, with her life in the balance, that he truly came to terms with why that was. It wasn't just that he didn't want her to die. Of course, he didn't. But he didn't want to lose her at all.

Haeli dropped her right hand to her side and fired off three rounds, never breaking her gaze or her mischievous grin. Blake felt the pressure on his grip lighten as the man's body fell and crashed onto the crane jib. Blake was thankful that Griff hadn't veered too far in any direction. A group of tourists had gathered below, their heads turned up toward the hovering helicopter. A body falling from that height was liable to take out a few of them.

Griff lifted the helicopter a few more yards, and Blake grabbed Haeli's left wrist with both hands. Haeli twisted around and fired two more shots before Blake saw the second man popping out through the truss. The man's gun went careening toward the ground, but his body remained slumped over the edge.

"I'd like to get on the helicopter now," Haeli yelled.

Blake cracked a smile as he pulled, using his feet to slide himself further in the helicopter, dragging her with him. She got to a knee and then flopped herself to a seat.

Blake picked up the rifle and scanned the roof through the sights. No one. Either the remaining three had fled or they remained hunkered down.

The roof access door, embedded in the protruding cinder block cube, swung open. A man stepped out on the roof as though he were showing up for a dinner reservation.

Levi Farr.

Farr lifted his empty hands in front of him and glared. Blake could see the recognition on his face. The contempt. All wrapped up in an obnoxious smirk.

Blake dropped the rifle. He raised his hand and gave a lazy, single-finger salute.

Farr closed three fingers of his right hand, leaving only his index finger and thumb extended. He closed one eye and jerked his hand as if firing a gun. The obnoxious smirk grew larger.

You'll get your chance, Levi. You'll get your chance.

Griff yanked the collective, leaned into the cyclic, and the three shot off toward the desert, bellies full of sweet, if not temporary, victory.

23

"Five minutes out," Griff said.

Blake pointed to his headset, extended his thumb, and nodded at Haeli to confirm that she heard the message. The fuselage rocked, causing her knees to knock against his.

She nodded as her oversized earphones remained fixed in space, the same way a firefighter's helmet bobbled around on an excited kid's head.

The fifty-two minutes that had elapsed since the Palazzo tower disappeared in the rear-view was sufficient time for Blake's adrenaline level to even out. By the pace of Haeli's breathing, he guessed it was the same for her.

At an hour each way, thanks to the extra distance required to avoid the restricted airspace of Nellis Bombing Range Test Site to the east, fuel consumption would be pushed toward the top end of a comfortable level. Griff cited this as the reason for rejecting Haeli's tongue-in-cheek request for a slight diversion over the Area 51 Air Force installation. Blake figured not wanting to get shot down was a more convincing reason.

The ride had been comfortable. The clear and calm Nevada skies saw to that. And with the doors closed, the rotor noise had subsided enough that they could carry on a normal conversation, despite having to do so by electronic means.

"The tourists got more excitement than they bargained for," Haeli mused. "Probably thought they were watching a stunt show, marveling at how the resorts spare no expense to provide the highest level of entertainment."

"Too bad we missed the rest of the show," Blake added. "I'm sure the cops are swarming the place. Feds, too." Blake turned to look out the window. "How much you want to bet that the casino prevented an evacuation? Wouldn't want to scare anyone away from the card table."

The sun-bleached faces of the scraggy mountains filled the windows on either side. Blake pushed his forehead against the clear acrylic. Sagebrush and cacti spotted the desert below. He abandoned the aerial view for one of Haeli, which was twice as pleasing and a hundred times more interesting.

Griff keyed in. "I'm happy Grant had enough sense to not have Spirit of the West painted on this bird. If he hadn't been able to remove the logo and tail number decals, the sightseeing business would have gotten more than a little unwanted attention."

"Nah," Blake said. "Any press is good press. That's what I heard. Anyway, I think Haeli was the big attraction. And you got to see it firsthand this time."

Griff twisted his body to look over his shoulder toward Haeli and Blake. "Wouldn't have believed it if I didn't." He turned back to the controls.

"Are you impressed?" Haeli directed a coy grin at Blake.

"Hell yes, I'm impressed," Griff said.

Blake waited for Griff's transmission to complete before keying up his own mic. "Impressed is not the word."

There was a bucket full of words that could describe what Blake was. Impressed was the least of them.

"If I didn't know any better," Haeli said, "I'd say Levi recognized you."

Blake winced.

Not a single trick.

"I told you I was familiar with him," he said with a shrug.

"You said you were familiar with him, not that he was familiar with you," Haeli replied.

"We have a bit of a history. It's a long story."

"Longer than... how much time, Griff?"

"Three minutes."

"Fine, I'll give you the Cliffs Notes," Blake said. "Levi and I worked a mission together years ago. He had already left the Army and gone into business for himself by that point. The guy was capable, but more arrogant than Griff. A lot of the contractors were, but Levi was in a class of his own. Bottom line, he made poor decisions. In particular, a unilateral decision to deviate from the plan because he didn't agree with the rest of us. It cost a few great men their lives."

"That sounds like Levi." Haeli sighed.

"The worst of it was that he ended up saving my life that day. And took a bullet doing it. You know what the bastard said to me when we finally got back to base?"

Haeli shook her head.

"He said I owed him one." Blake made a sound that, in his own muffled ears, was halfway between a cynical laugh and a snarl. "I buried three of my friends and I owe him? I owe him nothing."

"I'm sorry." The compulsory words felt sincere coming from Haeli. She leaned forward, put her forehead on his, and closed her eyes.

Blake closed his eyes as well. Maybe it was the close call, or the inevitable drain that came after an endorphin dump. But he felt tired. Or content. It had been so long since he felt that way, he could have mistaken it for something else.

"This is it," Griff said. "Coming up below us."

Blake slid the doors open and poked his head over the side. Still nothing but the brutal desert landscape.

"Take a pass," Blake said, "then swing back for a second one. Make like we're just passing through until I'm set up."

Blake popped open the case and pulled out the thermal imaging device and a large gun with a camera on the front and a screen on the back. When pointed at a target, the colorful image on the screen would represent the temperatures of the various subjects in the frame. Reds, oranges, and yellows where there was excessive heat, and purples, blues, and blacks for lower temperatures. It was a common tool for firefighters, as it allowed them to find sources of heat invisible to the naked eye, such as a fire burning behind a wall or a faulty electrical connection. Law enforcement employed it too. The lights used in illegal grow houses, for example, would cause a residence to stand out from neighboring homes.

Griff pressed the left foot pedal to kick the tail of the aircraft to the right. He completed the one hundred and eighty degree turn and headed back over the valley.

Blake aimed the thermal imager at the ground. The desert floor glowed in reds and oranges; an expected result due to the hundred-degree ambient temperature in the valley. Accompanied by blue squares littering the desert floor.

Blake tilted the screen toward Haeli. She used her hand as a visor to shield the glare of the sun as she leaned in.

"Air vents," Haeli said.

"Air vents," Blake agreed.

It was what Blake expected if an underground facility lay hidden beneath the sand. The exchange of fresh air and means of egress would be imperative in the event of an emergency, and the climate-controlled air of the interior would escape.

"No doubt there's some structure under there," Blake said. "Can't say for sure it's Techyon."

"You saw Farr. In Las Vegas," Haeli said. "Which, let me add, is a hell of a long way from Tel Aviv."

"I know. But in order to do what I think you want to do, we need to be one-hundred percent positive."

"Can you save the images?" Haeli asked.

Blake examined the rubber buttons on the back of the device. He pushed the one printed with a small picture of a camera. The screen froze for a moment before white titling appeared, super-imposed on the live image. It said 178deg_0000001.jpg.

"Affirmative," Blake answered.

"Good," Haeli said. "We'll compare the layout of these vents to the blueprints we have. If it matches, will you concede?"

Blake would have, but he planned to give Haeli a hard time by mentioning the blueprints themselves were unverified. He didn't get the chance.

"We've got company," Griff said.

Blake felt the centrifugal force of the hard turn. He steadied himself to avoid slipping out of the open door. His stiff arm reflexively swung to prevent Haeli from falling out. He dropped it after realizing that she hadn't budged.

"It's a goddamn Little Bird," Griff said. "Comin' in fast."

The G-force came again.

Blake's stomach fluttered. Not at the force, but at the words. Little Bird.

The United States Army had used versions of the Boeing MH-6 since the early 1980s. It had become an invaluable tool for special operations over the years. Small, light, and fast, the Little Bird was perfect for insertion, extraction, and assault. The attack variant, the AH-6, was often outfitted with a devastating array of weapons, including M134 Miniguns, Hydra 70 Rockets, and four Hellfire or Air-to-Air Stinger missiles.

On several occasions, Blake had witnessed the destructive power of the "Killer Egg," a nickname earned by the bulbous shape of its fuselage.

Blake's team, accompanied by several Navy Seals and Army Rangers, had used two MH-6J and two AH-6J helicopters to assault the compound of a high-level terrorist in Baidoa, Somalia. Little of the stone building remained at the successful conclusion of the mission. Nothing discernable remained of the eight souls who attempted to defend it.

Blake understood their Eurocopter stood little chance and based on Haeli's wide eyes and death grip on his triceps, Haeli also understood.

"I'm not going down without a fight." Haeli grabbed the rifle that rested against the edge of Blake's seat. She dropped the magazine, inserted a full one, and smacked the bottom to make sure it seated properly. She opened the door on the right side of the aircraft and scooted toward the edge, letting her feet rest on the skid step.

A black nylon strap with a carabiner sewn to the end hung from a steel rail above the door. Although meant to attach to a body harness, Haeli spun her arm in a small spiral, wrapping the strap around her right arm several times. She shouldered the rifle and leaned against the strap, using the tension to steady her aim.

Blake leaned over Griff's shoulder and retrieved the second M4 rifle from the empty front seat. Through the front windows he glimpsed the Little Bird bearing down on them. It was headed straight at them, or rather Griff was headed straight at it. Both locked into a catastrophic game of chicken.

Griff didn't have the time or the obligation to explain what he was thinking, but it made no difference. Blake understood the tactic. By turning and running, they would be at a disadvantage. Griff would need to close the gap for evasive maneuvering to be effective.

The good news was the guns and rocket pods that normally bristled from the attack variant of the Little Bird were absent. In their place were exterior bench seats and overhanging anchors, a typical setup for personnel transport and fast rope insertions. Without ordinance or heavy munitions, they at least stood a chance.

Blake took his position at the unoccupied door. He wrapped one of the nylon straps around his own arm and pulled the rifle's charging handle. A live round ejected, bounced off the deck, and careened toward the desert floor.

Better safe than sorry.

"Hold on." Griff was calmer and more collected than while he slept.

The floor dropped out from under them as Griff dipped hard and banked to the left. For a moment, the open air of the left door switched places with the floor. The effect was such that Blake experienced near weightlessness; an illusion dispelled by the angry nylon boa constrictor that bit into his arm.

Blake craned his neck to see Haeli leaning backward, her legs still extending up and over the edge of the door opening. Above her, the underbelly of the Little Bird eclipsed the blue sky like the shutter of a high-speed camera. It's rotor-wash tore through the cabin as it passed.

The floor tilted back to meet the horizon. The tail kicked to the right. Blake got the first closeup look at their adversary as the Little Bird spun around in an equal but opposite maneuver. The gold foil of the Techyon logo against the matte black paint glinted in the sun. Blake felt a flood of relief. Not only because they had been right. They were in the right place. But also because they hadn't stumbled upon another United States military installation.

A thousand scenarios had run through Blake's mind. And his conscience. The most concerning would have pitted him against his own. Using deadly force against U.S. servicemen and women would not have been an option and would have severely undermined their chances of surviving the encounter. It was a moral standard that he was sure Griff shared, and more certain Haeli didn't.

Fortunately, Blake held no such loyalty toward Techyon or the people who would seek to harm Haeli. He had already chosen a side. Blood had been shed. For Blake, the wisdom he acquired in the schoolyard would ring true throughout his entire life.

Once the teams are selected, the only thing left to do is win.

The Little Bird rotated until it faced the broad side of the EC130. Blake could see the pilot's neutral expression. The mirrored surfaces of the man's sunglasses appeared as though sunlight streamed from two huge, empty eye sockets. Both aircrafts hovered, each pilot waiting for the other to make the first move.

"Hold it steady, Griff." Blake lifted his rifle and trained the sights on the pilot. The man's face showed no reaction. Not at first. Then, Blake noticed the edges of his horizontal mouth turn upward as the helicopter began to slowly rotate to the left. Blake kept the rifle levelled until the left side of the helicopter came to view.

Blake pulled the trigger of his rifle at the first glimpse of the man perched on the exterior bench. A reflex provoked by the sight of a tableau he had seen many times, in many variations. The hunched posture, the arms bent upward grasping the tube resting upon his right shoulder, the iconic shape of the rocket-propelled grenade at its end.

The rifle rocked against Blake's shoulder. The vibration of the bolt being slapped backward by the pressure of built-up gases and then slammed forward by the tension of the spring travelled from his orbital bone to his inner ear. The metallic clank overshadowed the report.

A comet of flame, followed by a white smoke trail, streamed high over the tail of the EC130. Blake lost sight of the projectile but assumed it would find a target in the empty expanse of desert.

A second man pulled the launcher from the first man's shoulder and dragged him inside the cabin of the helicopter. The jet-black battle dress uniforms that both men wore obfuscated any leakage. The 5.56 mm round had found its target, but Blake couldn't be sure it was enough to incapacitate the man. The Little Bird rotated to face them again.

"They're reloading." Blake flicked his rifle's selector switch to full automatic. He took aim at the pilot and emptied the magazine. Cloudy marks marred the thick Lexan windshield, and sparks flew from metal posts. The pilot's smug face remained unscathed.

Griff's voice crackled. "We're making a run for it."

"Roger." Haeli dragged the heavy canvas bag from the seat. It hit the deck with a clatter. She reached in and withdrew three loaded magazines and slid the bag toward Blake. She rested the magazines by her right thigh and shifted her body aft.

Griff made a quarter turn toward the north. The nose of the helicopter dipped as the huge engine whined. The ground moved backward like a conveyor belt. Faster and faster. The Little Bird gave chase, keeping within twenty yards.

The EC130 lurched. The nose flew upward. The conveyor belt stopped and reversed direction as the rotors of the Little Bird passed only a few feet beneath their skids.

Griff banked to the south. The engine screamed.

Blake shifted his body again, putting his right knee on the deck and his left foot on the skid step. He pinned his right forearm against the outside skin of the fuselage, as far as the strap would let him, to steady the rifle.

One hundred yards past the tail rotor, the Little Bird was completing its turn and accelerating toward them.

Haeli opened fire first. The rapid burst lasted less than three seconds.

Blake tried to gauge the distance. He decided the Little Bird was getting closer.

"They're gaining on us," Blake said.

"I'm pushing her as hard as I can," Griff responded. The stress now apparent in his voice. "One-hundred-seventy-six. Anymore and I'm not sure she'll hold together."

Blake slapped the trigger a few times, letting off several bursts until the magazine was empty. He reached back and felt for a new magazine. He estimated the distance again.

Haeli keyed the mic before he could. "Fifty yards."

The familiar silhouette of the black BDUs and rocket launcher appeared from the side of the Little Bird.

"Direct Fire, Direct Fire," Blake said. "RPG incoming, on my mark."

"Roger," Griff responded.

Blake locked his mic in the on position and focused on the tip of the grenade, letting the rest of it fade in the background. There was no rattling fuselage, no buffeting of the air above their heads. There was nothing but his own heartbeat, keeping perfect time.

The orange flash came, and with it the knowledge that the explosive projectile had already set its destructive trajectory.

"Now," Blake yelled.

Griff yanked the collective and slapped the stick in a combination that jerked the aircraft upward and to the left.

Blake braced for impact. It didn't hit.

The helicopter leveled out and another burst of fire came from Haeli's side. Blake's eyes followed the man's body as it tumbled, head over heels, arms and legs flailing, on the long journey from the sky to the inevitable shallow crater it would create on the desert floor.

Blake stuck his head back inside. "Tango down. Good shootin' Haeli." He released the lock on his mic.

"We are bingo fuel," Griff reported. It meant that they couldn't push it much longer and still have enough fuel to make it back to Henderson.

"No worries," Haeli said, "they're bugging out."

Blake poked his head back out to confirm. The Little Bird had stopped all forward movement and faded back in the distance. It made sense. With no weapon systems on board, and no capable help, the remaining pilot could follow, but would have no effective way of mounting a further attack.

Blake unwrapped the strap from his arm and joined Haeli, who sat quietly. The butt of her rifle rested on the floor in front of her and she gripped the barrel with two hands.

"Everybody good?" Griff asked.

"All good," Blake answered.

The statement was accurate in that neither he nor Haeli had been wounded. But Haeli was not all good. He reminded himself about what she had been through in the previous few days. The bombshells that had landed on her lap. He wanted to help. Give her insight. But such words didn't exist.

Blake shifted in the seat next to Haeli, put his hand on her back, and settled in for the long, silent flight back to Henderson.

24

From above the tarmac, Blake picked out Peter Grant by the mop of blonde hair. He appeared to be riding an oversized skateboard in a lazy zig-zag pattern. Grant had been a fearless and brutal operator. Now, he didn't seem to have a care in the world. A marked difference from his own post-retirement experience.

Beyond Grant, two men leaned against a lifted Ford F-150 with enormous tires, their arms crossed. It took Blake until the helicopter touched down onto the asphalt before he recognized them.

Before pulling off his headset, Blake keyed the mic one last time. "Looks like we're getting the band back together, Griff."

Fezz and Khat stayed put while Griff, Haeli, and Blake hopped off the helicopter and approached the welcoming party, the rotors still winding down behind them.

Grant skated toward them. He jumped off the board and kicked the back of it to flip it upward. Grant caught it by the wheel truck and caught up to the group.

"Easy peasy?" Grant asked.

"Yep," Griff said. "Easy in and out. Not a scratch on her."

"Sweet." Grant tossed the board on the ground and jumped on it.

Fezz and Khat stepped forward as the group approached. Blake and Griff moved out in front.

"Who let these cowboys in here?" Blake said.

The four men shared handshakes and the usual rough embraces.

"Couldn't let you two have all the fun," Fezz said.

"Well, you're a little late." Blake smiled.

"I see you've met Kook." Khat motioned toward Grant. "And this must be Haeli. I'm Khat. That's Fezz."

The group exchanged greetings. Grant circled them, intermittently pushing his foot along the ground to increase his waning speed.

"We've heard about you," Fezz said. "We had to come out and at least meet the woman that brought Mick back from the dead."

"Yeah. We heard you were a cyborg or something," Khat added.

"Please." Haeli feigned disgust. "I prefer you refer to me by my proper title. Cyberdyne Systems model T-102." She grinned.

Blake chuckled at Khat's failure to put Haeli on the spot.

Fezz's big shoulders bounced as he burst into laughter. "I think we're gonna get along just fine. Now, I hear we're about to mess up somebody's day."

"Slow down, killer," Blake said. "I appreciate you coming out to help, but even with the five of us—."

"Six," Grant piped in as he rolled by.

"Even with the six of us, I don't know that we're looking at a viable operation."

Grant rolled up next to Griff, pulled a roll of papers out of his back pocket, and handed it to Griff.

"What's this?" Griff asked.

"That's the stolen vehicle paperwork I was going to file if you guys got caught. Not that I didn't have faith."

"There is one thing you should know." Griff turned toward the dormant helicopter. "If I were you, I'd get new decals on her as soon as possible. We may have taken a bit of a detour over the strip and we may have drawn a bit of attention."

"Fantastic." Grant laced the word with sarcasm. "Did you at least bring my guns back?"

Griff reached in his waistband and withdrew the Kimber. He slapped it down in Grant's outstretched hand.

"And the others?" Grant asked.

"Jettisoned in pieces from here to Amargosa Valley." Blake squeezed his lips together to prevent himself from smiling.

"Aw, come on. Seriously?" Grant shook his head. "What happened to easy in, easy out?"

"Relax, Kook," Fezz said. "We've got you covered."

Fezz walked to the back of the truck, opened the tailgate, and pulled back the green canvas tarp to expose two long trunks.

"Give me a hand with these," Fezz said.

Fezz and Kook grabbed the two exposed handles of the closer crate and dragged it to the edge of the tailgate. Blake and Griff reached around to grab the other two handles. They lifted the case with a duet of grunts and eased it to the ground. Fezz popped the latched and cracked the lid to reveal a cache of small arms.

"The beauty of military flights," Khat said. "Take your pick."

A pearly white grin spread across Grant's face while his arms disappeared behind the open lid and emerged with an M107 Barrett .50 caliber sniper rifle. Grant brought the weapon to his lips and kissed it. "Forgiven."

"Mind if we leave this stuff here for a bit?" Fezz asked.

Grant whistled air through his teeth. "That's a dumb question, brah."

"Thanks."

"Let's get out of here," Khat said. "You can fill us in, and we'll figure out our next move."

"You guys know we can't go back to Vegas, right?" Haeli said.

"We've already got it covered," Fezz said. "Booked a few rooms out of town. Hop in the truck."

"Damn it." Griff groaned. "I left my laptop at the hotel."

"We've got one," Khat said.

"But there's a thumb drive—"

Haeli laid her hand on Griff's shoulder. "I've got it." She tapped her pocket as if she were confirming for herself that it was still there.

"Okay then, let's go." Blake opened the rear door of the truck and waited for Haeli to climb in. Fezz moved around to the driver's side and Khat took the front passenger seat.

"Thanks, Kook," Griff said. He pointed to the EC-130. "She's a beauty."

Grant agreed.

"We'll call you if we need you," Khat said through the open passenger side window.

"I'll be here," Grant responded.

Griff stepped up to the back seat as Blake scooted` into the middle.

"You're ridin' bitch," Griff jabbed.

"Someone's got to," Blake said. He looked around the truck and wondered how the hell he ended up there, surrounded by the people he cared about most. Why he ever thought that isolating himself would aide him in battling his demons. These people strengthened him. Emboldened him. He could feel it radiating off them. And he would never make the mistake of remaining solo again.

"Where are we headed?" Haeli asked.

"A terrible place." Khat paused, waiting for someone to take the bait. Receiving no bites, he said, "You'll see."

25

"I can't believe they changed the name," Khat said. "Terrible's Hotel and Casino was way more fitting. Truth in advertising and all that."

"Whatever you call it, I don't know how much longer I can stay in this room," Fezz said. "It smells like cat piss."

"I've stayed in worse," Haeli said. "Anyway, it was a good idea. No one will look for us out here. I'd never even heard of Jean, Nevada, until twenty minutes ago."

"Can we get this going, Mick?" Fezz clapped his hands.

"Just another minute." Blake glared. "Could you guys be any more impatient?"

Blake double checked the thermal screenshots and blueprint documents he had superimposed onto the Google Earth satellite images were oriented based on the recorded coordinated directions. Along with this work, he had been listening to the banter and agreed. The room was not the ideal location for a briefing.

"Logos would be super handy right about now," Khat said.

An understatement if Blake ever heard one. The military intelligence satellite array, code named Logos, would have provided them with a real-time high-resolution feed. The problem was access to the system had been locked down after they had discovered an inordinate amount of system allocation procured and directed over Virginia for reasons later officially deemed exploratory. Griff took the hit for it —with almost no real consequence to his own career—but the request protocol was no longer rubber stamped. Going anywhere near Logos now was off the table.

"Okay, this is the best I can make it." Blake placed the laptop on one of the two double beds. Griff, Fezz, Khat, and Haeli sat in a line on the other. Blake dropped to one knee.

He pointed out several of the blue-colored areas. "Each of these is in the corner of a room. Every lab, office, and living quarter has one, and only one. They serve as a point of air exchange, but I'm willing to bet that each is a hatch that could provide access to the compound. Problem is, I doubt any of them are accessible from the outside."

"Then how do they get in?" Fezz asked.

"Good question," Blake replied. "Do you see this section of the blueprint labeled Main Access? On the satellite image, there's nothing visible. But, if you draw a line a half mile north, you end up here." Blake tapped his finger on the screen, then put two fingers on the computer's track pad and zoomed in on the image, an overhead view of a small building positioned along a narrow access road leading toward an established state route. Next to the building was a parking lot big enough to hold twenty or thirty vehicles.

"That's the main entrance," Haeli said.

"I think so," Blake said. "There must be an underground tunnel that leads to the facility. It's the only above ground structure anywhere close to this location."

"That's a major problem," Fezz said. "If they know we're there, and they will, we'll be trapped in that tunnel."

"I agree," Haeli said. "They'll have cameras and sensors all throughout that compound. Even in the mountains. And especially on the road and at the entrance. We won't be able to drive up to the front door and expect to walk in."

"Exactly," Blake said. "We have to figure out a way to take out the cameras for a couple of minutes. And we won't be able to drive all the way in. We'll have to get close, then trek in on foot."

Griff stood up to walk away but realized there was no room for him to do so. He sat back on the bed. "I don't like it. Even if we could get in and find Dr. Becher, there's no way we're getting back out."

Blake said, "I don't like it either. They built this place to be defensible. No matter how we slice it, there's no smart play here."

"What if I go?" Haeli said. "Alone."

The room fell silent.

"I mean, what if I showed up at the front gate? They'd let me in, right? They'd have to. Then, once I get in, I prop open a hatch, giving you an in."

"Are you insane?" Blake said. "They'd kill you before you could say hello. And if not, they'd deliver you to Levi on a silver platter."

Fezz and Khat spoke up at the same time. Khat backed off. Fezz continued. "She may be onto something here, Mick. Say one of us could walk in, the right credentials, backstory, setup. Then it would be a matter of opening an access point."

The room hushed as the collective wheels turned. Blake was the first to break the silence.

"This entire valley is wide open. From the north, it's a little over a half mile. From the east or west it means navigating the mountains, and then it's still a mile out in the open. The south is wide open, past the end of this map. There's no way to get across this valley undetected. Hell, they knew we were flying over with enough lead time to deploy a helicopter to intercept us. The only way to do this is to go in fast and hard. To make the play so brazen that... Fezz, what's the one enemy that's impossible to beat?"

Haeli interjected with an answer before Fezz could respond. "The suicidal kind."

"Right." Blake pointed at Haeli with four fingers extended. "We always assume that, like us, the enemy is trying to survive. It gives us permission to eliminate certain vectors from our defensive strategy because for the enemy to attempt them, it would mean certain death."

"I don't know about you, but I'm looking to survive." Khat protested with a snicker. "No offense Haeli, I'm sure your father is a good guy, but I enjoy being alive."

"That's not what I mean, and you know it," Blake said. "I'm talking about going straight in. No quarter given. Simple, quick, and dirty. Before they even know what hit them."

"Mick." Fezz paused and took a breath. He opened his mouth as if he were going to speak but bailed out. Fezz glanced at Haeli, who waited for the rest of Fezz's sentence. An expression of realization washed over her.

"Let's take a quick break, I need to get some air," she said.

Fezz agreed. "It'll be good to let the ideas ferment for a few." He stood, as did the others. Haeli pushed by the group and exited the room as all four men watched in silence.

"Mick," Fezz said, "what are you doing?"

"Making a plan. Isn't that why you came all this way?"

"You know I will, and have, put my career, my freedom, my life on the line for you. Khat and Griff, too. We're all glad you're back from the abyss. But are you? Back? Because the Mick I know is smart and doesn't make emotional decisions. He finds the angle by pure, cold calculation."

"There isn't one," Blake said. "Not a good one, anyway. But that doesn't mean that we can look the other way. Levi needs to be stopped."

"So, this is about Levi? Or is it about Haeli?" Fezz paused. A puff of air escaped through his nose. "Or is it about Anja?"

Blake lunged toward him. "Don't you throw that back at me."

"I'm not throwing anything at you, Mick. I'm trying to make you see clearly."

"I see more clearly than I ever have. It's about right and wrong. Everything I've done, everything we've done in the last year is wrong by all societal standards. Illegal. Immoral by many doctrines. But it was right. I went to your so-called abyss to find out who I am. That is who I am. I'm the guy who makes it right when no one else is willing to."

Fezz said, "I could have told you that."

Blake plopped onto the edge of the bed and ran his hands through his hair. "If you guys want out, I understand."

"Hold up, I didn't say that. I'm not questioning whether you know what you're doing. I want to make sure you know why you're doing it."

"You know I'm with you, Mick," Khat said, breaking the tension.

Griff weighed in. "I vote we go with Mick's plan. We fight our way in."

"They'll never know what hit them." Khat added.

All eyes landed on Fezz.

"Screw 'em," Fezz said. "I'm good for at least a dozen of 'em."

HAELI STARED out toward the mountains in the distance. The dusty little town was depressing. Oppressive, even. She felt the sting of every second deposited in the place; the way she imagined the vagrants felt as they dropped their last few quarters in a slot machine inside the roadside casino. The difference was even the most destitute person could happen upon a few bucks. Buy themselves a few more spins. Time was the one thing that couldn't be earned, bought, or stolen. If her father was still alive, he was down to his last nickel.

Haeli wasn't sure how the phone ended up in her hand. She scowled at it, transferring her anger toward her own lack of willpower to it. Turning it on would jeopardize the entire team. But her daily message to her father was the only proactive option available. What if he had responded? What if she had missed it?

Her thumb tensed. The screen lit up. It was done, she told herself. Too late to prevent the device from registering with the network. She might as well send a message.

The icons appeared. A notification slid down from the top of the screen. A text message. From Dad.

GRIFF STARTLED at the explosiveness of Haeli's entrance.

"You're gonna be pissed." Haeli bent over to catch her breath. She swallowed hard. "I turned my phone on. I know I screwed up. I probably gave away our position. But before you flip out, just listen, okay? Forget the op plan. Forget Levi. My father is safe."

"What are you talking about?" Blake said. "You spoke to him?"

"He sent me a text. He finally responded." Haeli's face glowed in a way that Blake had not yet seen.

"What did he say?" Griff asked.

Haeli cleared her throat. "You were right to run. I know that now. They would have killed me. I had no choice but to flee. We can both be free to start a new life together. I hope you can forgive me. Meet me at your mother's place if you can. I'll be there at 6PM. Make sure you're not followed."

"So that's it, then. Mission accomplished," Khat said.

"Wait," Blake said. "Where's your mother's place? I thought she passed away when you were a kid."

"She did," Haeli responded. "At least that was the story they gave me. The only reason I know what she looked like was a single picture I kept next to my bed for years. She was young and beautiful. I would stare at that picture for hours, imagining what she was like. She looked so glamorous with the City of Los Angeles sprawled out in the background. When I was a teenager, I told my Dad I wanted to go to L.A. one day. I asked him where the picture was taken. He told me it was the Griffith Park Observatory. He said it was my mother's favorite place."

"You're sure that's where he's going?" Fezz asked.

"It has to be. He knew I would remember and that no one else could know what he meant."

"This is a good thing, right?" Khat asked.

Blake would have admonished him for asking such a stupid question but judging by the deflated reaction of all the men in the room, himself included, he reconsidered whether it was a stupid question at all.

"Of course. This whole thing is finally over. We will disappear.

Live on some tropical island somewhere, who knows. Techyon will be out of my life forever. Can I borrow your truck? It's after one. I need to leave now if I'm going to make it on time."

"I'm going with you," Blake said.

"Thank you. But I need to do this on my own," Haeli said.

"I know you do," Blake said, "and you will. Once we get there. But you don't get the truck unless you agree to let me get you there safely. Plus, someone's gotta drive it back here. You don't want us stranded out here in no-man's-land, do you?"

"That's okay," Griff said, "I'll Uber back to Henderson and grab my rental."

Blake lifted his hand. "Not helping, Griff."

"Fine, but can we leave right now?" Haeli's entire being oscillated like a guitar string.

"Let's go." Blake opened the door.

"Thank you all for everything you've done for me," Haeli said. "I will never forget it, or you."

"Bye, Haeli. Good luck." Griff sulked against the padded headboard.

Haeli disappeared into the daylight, leaving Blake to face the stunned crowd.

"Don't lose too much money," Blake said. "Drinks are on me when I get back."

He closed the door behind him.

26

The five-liter V8 howled, drowning out the incessant buzzing of the knobby tires, which had grated on Blake's nerves the first few hours since they left Jean.

Blake shaved off some time on the wide-open highway of the Mojave but ended up giving it back, and then some, to the bumper-to-bumper traffic around Pasadena and Glendale. Traffic was light on North Vermont Canyon Road, only a few minutes out from the observatory.

"Time check," Blake said.

"Five fifty-eight," Haeli responded.

Blake navigated the last few curves of West Observatory Drive, passed the parking area, and stopped alongside the curb at the apex of the observatory loop, bringing them as close as possible to the building.

Blake left the truck running while he got out and met Haeli on the passenger side. The two walked along the grass toward the astronomer's monument. Beyond stood the iconic three domed observatory building. The location had been featured in so many movies and television shows over the years, Blake felt as though he'd been there before. It took a moment of digging through the annals of his brain before he was confident he hadn't.

An older man, wearing a brown blazer and striped tie, stood at the top of the steps leading to the grandiose main entrance of the building. Blake saw him. Haeli didn't.

At some level, Blake already knew it was him. Doctor Benjamin Becher, as promised. He felt an overwhelming urge to wrap his arms around Haeli. To squeeze so tight she could not escape. Instead, he pointed at the staircase.

"Would that be him?" Blake asked.

"Dad!" Haeli took two steps toward her father, then stopped. She turned, walked back toward Blake and took each of his hands in hers.

"You saved me. I can't thank you enough." She leaned in and placed a tender kiss on his cheek.

Blake appreciated the theatrical parting words, but he felt it cheapened the genuine connection they shared.

"Will I ever see you again?" Blake's internal struggle with saying goodbye was a little more evident than he intended to let on.

"Honestly, I don't know." Haeli let go of Blake's hands and bowed her head. "Don't think I don't know there is something between us. And under different circumstances, I would have loved to see where it went from here. But right now I have an opportunity. A chance for the life I always wanted. To be normal. To be a family. You understand that, right?"

"I do," Blake said. "Now go get it."

Haeli smiled. She put her hand on his cheek and kissed him. A soft, longing kiss that could only exist with the benefit of knowing it was the last. Her lips tasted sweeter than anything else he could remember.

"Thank you." She sprinted off toward her own destiny.

Blake watched as Haeli and her father embraced. He returned to the truck, vowing to never look back.

Sitting at the wheel, Blake couldn't help but to acknowledge the sense of emptiness that filled him. The time had come to turn the page. To start the next chapter. Only, he had no idea what that would be. For now, he decided, the next step would be the long drive across the desert and a few too many whiskies with his knucklehead friends.

He put the truck in drive and headed down the mountain toward Los Feliz. True to his vow, he didn't look back.

HAELI LEANED on her elbows along the circular railing surrounding the pendulum that hung from the ceiling of the main rotunda. Benjamin Becher assumed a similar posture.

"I was so scared that something bad had happened to you," Haeli said. "I'm having trouble believing it's over."

"I'm glad you're all right, too."

"I saw the files, Dad. Your journal. I know what I am."

"I'm sorry, Haeli. I should have been the one to tell you. I'm sure you have questions."

"So many questions. Like, are you really my father? Was that picture really of my mother? Do I have parents at all?"

"Haeli..." Benjamin paused.

Haeli could tell that he didn't want to get into it. Not now, not here. But she wanted something. Some bit of truth to kick off their new life together. So, she waited.

"Look, I never wanted to lie to you. In many ways, I never did. My DNA is the basis for half of your genetic makeup, before the modifications, so technically I am your father, Haeli."

"And my mother?"

"The picture I gave you was Sandra Moore. She was a sculptor who lived in Los Angeles. She needed cash and, as a result, donated her eggs for use by those who could not have children on their own. Thanks to a partnership with UCLA, the lab notified us that the DNA matched the profile we were looking for. She never knew about you. Nor did she expect to."

"Is she still alive?"

"Unfortunately, no. She died of breast cancer a few years back. It was shocking to us because her DNA contained none of the markers. If it had, we never would have chosen her."

"Doctor Joseph carried you so you might say she's your mother. You were quite fond of Doctor Joseph, as I recall."

"You understand why it's a little hard to wrap my head around this, right?" She searched for a hint of understanding behind his steady gaze. "My entire life has been a complete fabrication. With everyone in it, just an actor in the grand illusion. Some twisted, fucked up version of the Truman Show."

"Haeli, listen to me. You are special. The most special person on this entire planet. And now that we're reunited, do you know what I can accomplish? What impact my research will have?"

"Research?" Haeli scoffed. "You said we were starting over. There is no research. No more manipulation. We're a family. And we're finally free of that place. We can go wherever we want. Do whatever we want."

"There's too much at stake for that, Haeli,"

"Dad?" A softball-sized pit formed in Haeli's stomach. This wasn't right. The text. The meeting. Lies. More manipulation.

"I'm sorry, Haeli, I really am." He patted her on the back and walked away.

Haeli didn't have to look behind her to know that the six black suits who had emerged from around the rotunda were surrounding her. She considered fighting. But unlike Vegas, there were no metal detectors here. The men would be armed. She wouldn't have gotten through two of them before they mortally wounded her. The most she could do was bide her time. Pick her moment.

The circle of men tightened. Haeli placed her hands behind her back and leaned over the railing. If only she hadn't let Blake go. If only she had listened to her gut. She had made the wrong choice, and it would cost her.

BLAKE PULLED over to the side of Vermont Avenue and retrieved his phone. Griff would be interested in knowing that the reunion had gone off without a hitch. He eyed the sign of the Palermo Italian restaurant. The thought of a chicken parmesan sandwich reminded his gurgling stomach that he hadn't eaten all day.

First the call. Then the chow.

The distant chopping of a low-flying helicopter grew louder. LAPD, no doubt. He'd wait for it to pass before making his call. He thought about the way his day started. The story no one would believe if he were to tell it. Even Fezz and Khat thought he was embellishing. One thing was for certain, he'd be happy never to hear or see a helicopter again.

The sound grew louder still. The paper coffee cup that he had grabbed from the lobby of the hotel on his way out rattled in the plastic cup holder.

Blake opened his window. No longer muted by the glass, the timbre of the chopping blades elevated in pitch. He stuck his head out of the window and looked up.

Little Bird.

It wasn't the type of aircraft used by the LAPD. Or any police department. And by the direction it was heading, it meant one thing.

Blake threw the truck into drive and mashed the accelerator while he turned the wheel as far as it would go to the left. Even with the monster tires, the rubber let out a squeal as the truck spun around and headed north.

He blew through the light at Franklin and at Finely, but luck was on his side and he hit the green at the next two intersections. He navigated the residential stretch of North Vermont, passing several cars on the two-lane road, once on the grass median, when a motorist refused to get out of the way.

Blake pinned the gas as the Greek Theatre streaked by to his left. He only hoped the lifted suspension didn't topple the truck when it hit the winding turns at the top.

He accelerated onto West Observatory Drive. The wheel jittered and pulled against his white-knuckled grip. As he rounded the last corner, he could already see the helicopter sitting on the ground in an empty section of the parking lot. Haeli was nowhere to be seen.

They were already onboard.

Every course of action and the expected outcomes flashed before his eyes. If he were to ram the helicopter, he might disable it and prevent it from taking off. But what about Haeli? If she were onboard, the move could leave her mortally wounded. But if they escaped with her, they could kill Haeli before Blake had any chance of getting to her.

It was no decision at all.

Blake steered the truck in a beeline for the aircraft. The off-road suspension nimbly hopped the curb, tore through the shrubs and deposited him into the parking lot on a collision course with Techyon's Little Bird.

He held steady as the skids lifted off the pavement.

Come on.

The roof of the Ford F150 passed just below the elevating skids of the MH-6.

Blake slammed on the brakes and skidded to a stop in time to avoid careering off the embankment at the edge of the lot. He jumped out of the truck and stood with his head turned to the sky.

A fire burned inside him. A raging inferno of hatred that scrawled the words in lighter fluid across the foreseeable future.

You. Will. Pay.

27

"I lost her Fezz." Blake hit the speaker-phone button and tossed the phone onto the seat next to him.

The phone crackled. "I co— —ar y—Mi—, ev——ing ok—."

"You there?" Blake said.

"I'm here." Fezz answered. The connection was strained but passable.

"I said, I lost her, Fezz. She's gone."

"I know, brother. But it's for the best. Come on back, Griff's killin' it at the craps table. We were thinking about taking a ride out to Vegas when you get here."

"Fezz, you're not listening to me." Blake white-knuckled the steering wheel. "They took her. It was a trap. I let her walk right into it."

"Wait, what? Hold on, Mick, let me step outside. Can't hear you in here."

Blake crossed into the left lane. He passed the Chevy Impala as if it were standing still and eased back over to the right. He checked the speedometer. One-hundred-six miles per hour. The speedometer dial went to one-forty but, by the feel of the steering, Blake didn't feel like he could eke much more out of it without severely reducing his chances of making it back to Jean in one piece.

"Okay, that's better," Fezz said, his voice clearer and more at the forefront. "Are you saying the drop went bad?"

"The drop? She wasn't a bag of money, Fezz. I'm saying the whole thing was a setup. She thought she was starting her new life. It turned out to be the opposite."

"Oh crap," Fezz said. "It wasn't her father that texted her?"

"No," Blake said. "It was her father. That's the problem. He was there. I saw him. It was her father that set her up."

"Unreal. Where are you, Mick?"

"I'm on fifteen. I'm coming. You need to grab Khat and Griff. Tell them to stop drinking right now."

"We're doing this, aren't we?" Fezz asked.

"I'm not gonna let this happen again," Blake said. "I don't care if I go down trying, but I'm going after her."

"We're with you, Blake, you know that. You sure they took her to the desert?"

"I'm not sure of anything." Blake tried to rationalize his logic. To connect a thread from point A to point B. But he had to admit to himself it was just a feeling. It was only his intuition that told him they took Haeli back to the underground lab. He talked through it.

"Techyon's helicopter showed up and carted her away," Blake explained. "They could have killed her, or they could have shoved her into a car if they didn't want to do it there. They put her on the helicopter because they're taking her out to the desert. They're taking her to Levi, I'd bet my life on it."

"Okay, then," Fezz said. "I'll rally the troops. Let 'em know it's still a go. I don't think they'll be upset. Do you want me to call Kook?"

Blake agreed. "We're down one. Could use all the help we can get."

"Done," Fezz said. "Meet us in Henderson. Call me when you're close. Gonna need that truck. We'll get loaded up when you get here."

"Thanks, Fezz. Call you in a few."

The phone disconnected and entered sleep mode. Blake turned up the radio to distract his mind for the next couple of hours. He couldn't get there soon enough.

28

"Move." The command came with a jab to the spine by the muzzle of an MP7 submachine gun.

Haeli recognized the voice, but she couldn't place the man. Then again, she expected this would be somewhat of a reunion, having worked with and around many of Levi's cronies for her entire adult life.

The tunnel was wider and brighter than she imagined. For the most part, the team had been accurate in their assumptions about the location and layout of the entrance.

The pilot, called Coop, touched down in the parking area next to the small building she had previously only seen from space. Up close, the structure looked more like a rustic home than a commercial building. A carved wooden sign identified it as a ranger station.

Inside, corkboards pinned with flyers warning of fire danger and low-impact camping tips verified the illusion. Paperwork was strewn about two metal desks, complete with knickknacks and family photos.

As far as Haeli could tell, the disguised guard house was manned by two men, each wearing the khaki uniform of the Nevada State

Park Ranger. Haeli wondered if either of the men would help an injured hiker or stranded motorist who wandered upon the shack, counting their prayers as being answered. She decided they would. Because she would have.

It was the same with men who trailed behind her, poking, prodding, and yelling. She had a hard time finding animosity toward them. Just a few short months prior, she could well have been part of the same welcoming party.

Sweat beaded on her forehead and dripped into her eyes. The temperature in the tunnel was stifling.

Haeli had tried to take mental pictures of her surroundings on the way in. The cabinet in the back room of the ranger station that served as the access point to the steep subterranean stairwell, the number of stairs, the number of strides from the bottom of the stairs to the end of the tunnel. It was a sound idea, but she had gotten distracted by the pain of the steel handcuffs that one of her escorts sadistically twisted on her and lost count of her steps after about an eighth of a mile. It wouldn't matter, though. She had no way of relaying any of this information to the team.

The team.

A sense of amusement swelled in her, fueled by the irony of her predicament. All because she was chasing something that wasn't real. If she were giving advice to someone else, she'd say no one ever reached their goal by looking back. For her, it had all been about family, about connection.

Haeli, you idiot.

In the short time she had known Blake and Griff, and even the other guys, they had felt more like a family than anything she had ever known. They cared for her. About her. And they truly had her back. She had found what she was looking for, too blinded by the past to see it. Now, she wondered if they would come for her at all.

"Stop here," one man said.

The tunnel ended at a concrete wall which housed a single, windowless steel door. Embedded in the wall was a thin plastic pad, typical of any office building that employed electronic access control.

A man stepped forward. She expected him to wield an access card or key fob. Instead, he swiped his hand in front of the sensor. The sensor beeped. The door swung open. A blast of cool air rushed over Haeli's glistening face, and the loose strands of hair danced against her nose. It felt good. Even in times like these, simple pleasures still applied.

The muzzle of the gun nudged her through the door. As she passed, she took another hard look at the hand of the man who had gained them entry. *Empty.* She came to the only logical conclusion. A subdermal device. Radio frequency identification chip, most likely. She added this piece of information to the list of things she wished she could tell Blake.

For the next few minutes, they led Haeli through several rooms and corridors. She counted each turn. Five, so far. Despite her heightened level of attention, she doubted that she could retrace her steps exactly.

They stopped in front of a door labelled Genetics Lab. There had been no opportunity for conversation en route, and Benjamin had separated from the group and hurried inside as soon as the helicopter touched down. But now, with another swipe of the hand and a shove from behind, Haeli stood face-to-face with the man she had called Dad for her entire life.

Two of the men in the escort group stayed in the room while the other four exited. The door clicked shut. Haeli figured they weren't going far.

"Give me the key," Benjamin said.

The younger of the two guards reached in the breast pocket of his fatigues and handed over a small silver handcuff key.

Haeli looked around the lab for something she could use as a weapon if the opportunity presented itself. There wasn't much. A small fire extinguisher hung from brackets at the far side of the room. Not incredibly useful, but maybe she could work with it.

During her visual scan, one thing stood out. Not a weapon, something better. In the corner to her left was a metal ladder that disappeared into a two-foot by two-foot opening in the ceiling.

Blake, you glorious bastard, you were right.

Benjamin walked around Haeli and freed her wrists. She resisted the urge to rub the deep depressions. She wasn't sure how much pleasure her supposed father would take in even the smallest acknowledgment of suffering.

"I'm sorry about the handcuffs, Haeli. It's barbaric, really. I told them they weren't necessary. We're all on the same team. Right?"

A cold callousness oozed from her father's voice and demeanor. It was jolting. Not because it had changed, but because it hadn't. She wondered how she could not have noticed it before. The dangers of trust.

"You can't honestly believe that," Haeli said.

"Haeli, what have I done? What have any of us done to aggrieve you in such a way?"

"I don't know, let's start with lying to me, handcuffing me, kidnapping me, and holding me at gunpoint." She glared at the two silent men flanking her father, the H&K MP7s slung on each of their shoulders pointed in her general direction.

"Yes. But all that nasty stuff was for your own good. I told Levi that you were not a liability. You're an incredible asset. For many reasons. Don't be silly, girl. You're safe now. You're home."

Haeli wanted to lash out. For the first time in her life, she wanted to hurt this man. To deliver the physical approximation of her own internal pain. But she knew it would be the wrong move. She needed to buy herself time. To see how it played out.

"Don't pretend you care about me or my feelings," Haeli said. "This is about preserving Techyon's investment. About retrieving your precious super-soldier. What I don't understand is why send someone to kill me? What, was Levi afraid someone would get ahold of his precious technology. Or was it just an 'if I can't have her, no one can' kind of thing?"

Benjamin let out an awkward laugh. "Please, child. You think this is still about building the ultimate war fighter? No. It's much, much bigger than that." He pulled a stool from where it was tucked under one of the several floating work-counters. He motioned to an identical one, a few feet away. "Please, have a seat."

"I'll stand." Her anger manifested as a throbbing in the muscles of her thighs, shoulders, and jaw.

"Suit yourself. If you read my notes, you'd already know the experiment was less successful than we had hoped. Don't get me wrong, you're an extremely capable, deadly operative. A great asset to any mission. But marginally better than those who rose to the top through, how should I say it, natural selection. But what we didn't know in those early days, what we couldn't have known, was just how resilient your body really is."

"What does that mean?" Haeli's impatience was becoming too strong to mask.

"Your cells, Haeli, I'm talking about your cells. We have been doing weekly analyses since you were born. Blood work, cheek swabs, hair samples, and, in the spirit of honesty, I will admit that we have harvested a few of your eggs."

She changed her mind. She didn't want to hurt him. She wanted to kill him with her bare hands.

"But we were looking at the wrong things. You would never lift a truck over your head or run fifty miles an hour or any of the things a comic book character might do, but you are superhuman. At the molecular level, your cells closely resemble those we might see from a teenager, not a thirty-four-year-old woman."

Haeli let go of her anger for a moment while she tried to process what her father was implying. She worked up the nerve to say the words out loud. "I'm not aging?"

"I'm saying you're aging at an incredibly slow rate. Your cells rejuvenate faster, mutate less. Wounds heal faster, muscles and bones remain stronger, even your skin has kept its elasticity. Surely you've noticed that?"

Haeli thought about it. She felt young. But she had no frame of reference to compare it to. A sudden and surprising sadness overtook her. She spoke without conscious intention. "Will I ever grow old?"

"You will. But there are still so many questions. We don't know if the aging process will speed up. Or slow down. You could live two hundred years for all we know. Or your body could fail at eighty, despite the biological advantages. That's one reason continuing with this research is so imperative. I told you, you're special. You are the only one of your kind on this earth and your very existence changes the future of humanity."

Haeli wasn't sure how to absorb this new information. How to incorporate it and remain herself. She did what most people would do. She ignored it for the time being. A reckoning would inevitably come. At some point she would be forced to face the implications of its meaning if it were true. But that time was not now.

"So that's what this is all about?" Haeli asked. "The fountain of youth? Then why is there someone trying to kill me everywhere I go. If I'm so important to the future of humanity, wouldn't I be more useful to you alive?"

"Yes, infinitely more useful. But Levi didn't take kindly to you going around marauding and pillaging or whatever you were doing, which I assumed was some kind of tantrum to get back at me. Using your unique skills to hurt innocent people crosses the line, even for Levi."

"That's a load of crap and you know it. He wanted me out of the picture. Maybe you know why, maybe you don't, but he has a reason and whatever it is, it has nothing to do with protecting the innocent."

"Maybe so, but I am the one who stood up for you, Haeli. I am the one who vouched for your character and convinced Levi to let me bring you back into the fold. And do not worry, he gave me complete assurances that you would not be harmed."

"You're not just a liar, you're a fool. You're no less of a pawn than I am. Do you really think vouching for my character made Levi Farr change his mind? Really?"

"I must admit, you may be right. He was a tad more amiable when I convinced him I'm on the verge of several major discoveries. Discoveries that will put the name Techyon in the history books for a hundred generations to come. I just had to convince him I needed more time."

"And delivering me back to Levi somehow buys you more time?"

"Precisely. Look, Haeli, I'm not a well man. I hadn't told you this because I didn't want you to worry. But I have a rare genetic condition. My heart is failing. And there's almost nothing I can do to stop it. I've tried, believe me, I've tried everything."

"*Almost* nothing?"

"Ah. You always were keen at parsing language. One treatment, a stem cell therapy, appeared to be promising at first. The problem was that my stem cells are pre-programmed with the genetic abnormality. I realized what I needed were stem cells from a healthy individual. Only they would have to come from a close relative to be useful."

"And I'm your only living relative."

"You are." Benjamin punctuated the statement with a pointed hand gesture.

"So not only can you repair your heart cells, but you—"

"—can ensure they're pumping for many, many years to come. Now you've got it."

Haeli inhaled loudly and rubbed her temples. "That's why you set me up? To get my stem cells?"

"Understand what this will mean for my work, Haeli. I will usher in a new dawn of scientific discovery. I'll be able to witness the technological advances of the next century. Think of the continuity of work. Even the most brilliant minds lose their edge. Their bodies tire, their priorities change. Look at Einstein as he grew old. I will have the time to see it through."

"You could have just asked," Haeli said. She wasn't defeated, not yet anyway, but the tone and tenor of her voice implied otherwise.

Benjamin's mouth sagged and his eyes glistened. It was subtle, but it offered some hope that a few scraps of decency may have survived, buried deep within the desperate man.

"Well," Benjamin said. "I'm asking now."

"No," Haeli said, matter-of-factly.

Benjamin's frown disappeared as he scoffed. "I'm afraid you don't have a choice. I will need to extract marrow from your femur. But I promise the procedure will be quick and painless. You'll be sedated."

"You are right about one thing," Haeli said.

"Which is?" Benjamin yawned.

"You are a sick man."

29

The dashboard clock read 9:29 PM. Blake bypassed the parking area and proceeded around to the tarmac side of the hangar building.

Henderson Executive Airport was eerily still. At ground level, the orderly patterns of red, blue, yellow, green, and white lights broke down into a jumble. Even in the sun's absence, heat rose off the blacktop. The lights shimmered and waved like paper luminaries floating along a quiet, inky river.

Blake left the truck in front of the door and let himself in. He hurried through the classroom, following the sound of voices to the maintenance hangar.

Despite his exuberant entrance, he was greeted only by the acerbic odor of petroleum and burnt metal.

"I'm here," he declared. "Are we all set to go?"

All four men remained engrossed in their various tasks. Loading magazines, oiling parts, and whatever Griff was doing, sprawled out on the floor and peering through a tripod mounted sniper rifle. Not one of the four men looked up from their work, but at least Grant went out of his way enough to acknowledge him.

"About time." Grant pulled a patch of cotton wadding through a disembodied pistol barrel, then held the barrel to the dangling fluorescent light fixture like it was a miniature telescope.

"Jump in, Mick," Fezz said. "I've got a tach vest for you right here. As far as toys go, there's plenty of stuff left to choose from."

"I was thinking about what we talked about earlier." Griff drew his legs up into a squat and then stood. "I know we're all on board with the shock and awe approach, but we should be prepared to go in as quietly as possible. The longer we can avoid bringing the whole thing down on us, the better." Despite being behind the other men and out of their line of sight, Griff shifted his eyes with unnecessary furtiveness, pinning them toward his teammates.

Blake got the message. He couldn't agree more. The trick would be to fire as few rounds as possible without bringing attention to themselves. Small caliber subsonic ammunition. If they could get close enough, a knife would do the job even better. Blake didn't relish the proposition. Close-quarter combat was messy and personal. The men who would inevitably stand in their way were doing their job. Following their own orders. He held no resentment toward them; and he'd had enough killing, period. But for Haeli, for his team, he would do anything necessary.

They don't call it wet work for nothing.

"Here." Fezz slid a Glock 17, suppressor already attached, across the stainless-steel bench.

Blake trapped the pistol with the tips of his fingers before it reached the edge. "You know me well, my friend."

The Glock 17 was Blake's go to sidearm and had been for years. All of them knew his preference just as sure as they knew his name. Except maybe Kook.

This was Blake's first experience working with Grant. It would be imprudent to add a variable to the team at the last minute for a high-risk mission, especially one falling square within the modus operandi of multiple state and federal criminal penal code definitions. It took years to build the unbreakable trust that Blake, Fezz, Khat, and Griff enjoyed. But Grant's impeccable reputation, Fezz and Khat's unwavering endorsement, and sheer necessity made it digestible, if not palatable.

"Mine's better," Fezz bragged, displaying his own Glock 18 as if he'd invented it himself.

Visually, the Glock 18 was almost identical to the Glock 17, except for the addition of a turret selector switch, which allowed the pistol to switch to fully automatic mode. Fezz had added a small buttstock for better stabilization. With the stock, the thirty-three-round magazine, and the six-inch-long suppressor attached, the pistol looked more like the submachine gun it was.

Blake dove into the crated stockpile, coming up with a desert tan colored Kriss Vector SMG. He examined the receiver. Its etched markings verified that it was chambered for 9x19mm pistol cartridges. He counted the find as a minor victory.

The futuristic looking weapon was perfect for their purposes. At twelve hundred rounds per minute, the angry little machine could mow down an entire rugby team in less than a few seconds. To add to its general nastiness, the downward reciprocating bolt design virtually eliminated recoil, making it a breeze to tame the upward creep that accompanied compact automatic platforms.

He cradled the weapon in the crook of his left elbow and dug back in the crate with his right. He located a second Kriss and rested it against the other. Two more dives in the cache yielded two more identical weapons. The fifth, however, proved fruitless.

Blake approached Grant's station and swept his forearm along the slick countertop. The meaty wiper blade moved the small horde of weapons Grant had compiled for himself. An eclectic assortment which included a Desert Eagle .50 caliber and a short-barreled 12-gauge shotgun with a pistol grip. Blake placed the Kriss Vector in the newly cleared space.

"Aw, come on," Grant said.

The team understood Blake's authority over the mission. It had always worked this way. The one with the most invested, the most passion for the cause, often took the lead. The willingness of his teammates to follow was shown not in words, but actions.

Grant was no different. Besides, Grant's short-lived protest had already given way to fixation as he caressed the Kriss, his mouth moving as if whispering sweet nothings under his breath.

Blake was never a huge fan of guns. He saw them as a tool to master, as any tradesperson might. Grant was something else entirely. And, although Blake wasn't sure how much of Grant's eccentricity was schtick, he was sure his experiences had knocked a couple of screws loose.

"You are one unique individual, Kook," Blake said.

"Thank you," Grant said, with an unabashed grin.

Blake moved on to Khat and then to Griff. Fezz had already set himself up with the Glock 18, so Blake kept the last Kriss for himself. He gathered a handful of suppressors and dropped them onto the workbench between Fezz and Grant.

The Santa Claus routine had most likely spoken for itself, but Blake felt the urge to explain.

"The Kriss Vector 9mm SMG. Compact, quiet, vicious." Blake paced along the opposite side of the bench as if he were a chemistry teacher. His four pupils, lab partners who grouped together to goof off. "But above all of that, one important distinction."

"Glock magazines," Grant said.

"Standard Glock magazines," Blake said. "We carry one kind of ammunition. We carry identical magazines. Sidearms included. As many as we can hump. If any of us runs dry, well, nobody runs dry."

Grant kicked the metal stool backward. The clang echoed off the corrugated roof. He slid the Kriss Vector toward Fezz. "Gotta grab something from my truck."

Grant jogged across the hangar to the far wall, which was bare except for a three-buttoned control panel and the conduit that fed it. With a press of a button, the twenty-one-foot-tall hangar doors parted with a squeal. Grant released the button and picked up his jog toward the three-foot gap.

"Is he wearing flip flops?" Blake asked.

Grant's choice in footwear stood out not from the setting, but from the rest of the ensemble. Half dressed, Grant wore desert camouflage cargos and kneepads, a drop holster strapped to one leg and a six-magazine pouch strapped to the other.

"Looks like it," Griff said.

"I'm getting a sense of why you call him Kook," Blake said.

"Don't let him fool you," Fezz replied, "the guy is solid. Smart as hell, too. And Kook doesn't mean what you think it means. Not in this case, anyway. It's a surfing thing."

Blake provided the obligatory follow up. "A surfing thing?"

"We were in San Diego, and Kook had taken a couple hours to go off and surf. When he got back, he was all pissed off, going on and on about how these kooks kept getting in his way or something. I guess the term means a beginner or a wannabe. Apparently, there's a hierarchy out there, an etiquette, and these so-called kooks just crap on it. Of course, after hearing that, we started calling him Kook. It got a rise out of him at first, but then it just stuck."

The clopping of Grant's flip flops preceded his return through the dark slot. He clutched an assault rifle as he ran, first to the controls, then back to the group. He placed the rifle on the bench.

"Modified Troy 9mm," he said, catching his breath. "Full auto conversion, Glock mags."

"That works," Blake said. "Now let's get moving."

"Hold up," Grant said. "I need the rundown of the place. You mind drawing me a quick sketch?"

"We've got better than that. Blueprints. Got a computer handy?"

"In the front office," Grant said. "You get that cued up, I'm gonna load some big boys onto the truck. In case we run into an ambush on the way in or out. We may need to go loud."

"Why don't the other guys take care of that while you go find your boots," Blake said.

Grant reached under the table with one hand and lifted a worn pair of size twelve Danner's. "My lucky boots brah. Don't wanna waste the juju, ya know?"

Blake did know. For the first time, Peter Grant had said something he could relate to.

❄

"THIS IS A STIMULATING CONVERSATION," Haeli said.

Since the moment her father left the lab, she had inundated the two guards with questions, anecdotes, and annoyingly chipper small talk. First to break the awkward silence, then because it was fun watching the men fight against the urge to engage. They remained stoic and undistracted.

Haeli paced in an ever-expanding pattern. What started as a tight circle around the middle of the floor had loosened to the rest of the room. She wandered toward the row of glass-doored cabinets that lined two walls.

"What's all this stuff?" she asked.

The men said nothing. They held their position a few feet in front of the door. They had moved little from the spot, letting the aim of their guns do the following.

Haeli reached for a knob. As she expected, one of the two men took a step forward. She raised her hands. "Okay, okay. No touching, got it."

The man returned to his original position.

"No need to be so jumpy. We're out in the middle of nowhere, right? Where am I going?" Haeli wandered a few feet along the back wall and rested her back against the countertop.

She studied their faces for a reaction. There was none. Exactly what she'd hoped. The aimless pacing and jabbering had muddied her intentions of ending up in that very spot. Now, on the counter behind her, sat the deadliest weapon in the room.

A phone.

Haeli was familiar with the Avaya handset. The model could be found in every office in the company's compound in Tel Aviv. Although it looked like a typical hardline, it was a network appliance. They routed outgoing phone calls through the Internet, allowing them to mask the origin of the call. Haeli did not understand how the complex routing was done, but the chances of placing a call to the outside were excellent.

"Let me ask you something," she started, putting her hands on the edge of the counter and pushing herself upward until she sat on top of it and felt the bottom edge of the plastic phone against her tailbone. "What did they tell you? To be careful of me? Not to get too close? Let me guess, did they say I could kill you with my bare hands?"

Haeli slid her right hand behind her. It went to work as she spoke.

"You don't believe any of that, do you?"

She removed the handset and placed it on the counter, then took another read of her captors' faces. Nothing. She dialed nine, relying on faith that the system worked the same way as the one she was used to. The back of her hand and fingernails brushed against the keypad, allowing her to orient herself to the location of each key. She dialed each digit of the memorized number with extreme care. Then paused for several seconds.

"How about this facility, huh? Impressive."

"Questions?" Blake asked.

"Nope. Good to go," Grant said.

Blake removed the thumb drive and stashed it in a cargo pants pocket. He slung the weighty tactical vest over his head and connected the Velcro straps. The others had already done so.

"All right boys, mount up," Fezz said.

Fezz's light-hearted bravado sent a jolt of nostalgia through Blake's spine that settled in his stomach. Here he was again, racing headfirst into impossible odds. Familiar, yet different. Like the smell of home upon returning from a long trip. It smells different, but you're still damn happy to be there.

A slow drip of adrenaline leaked into Blake's bloodstream. His mind focused and his muscles buzzed. So much that he almost missed the phone vibrating in his pocket. He fished it out and glanced at the screen.

Unknown Caller.

Blake accepted the call and held the phone to his ear. "Blake," he said.

There was a voice on the other end, but it seemed distant. Already engaged in a conversation. A pocket dial, he guessed. He raised his voice, "Hello."

"—cost a fortune to build this out here. Levi's upping his game."

Blake used his thumb to increase the volume without moving the phone away from his ear. He recognized the voice. "Haeli? Is that you?"

Haeli continued speaking without responding. It clicked. She couldn't respond. She wasn't alone. This wasn't a pocket dial. She was sending a message.

Blake turned to Grant; Blake's frantic expression so contagious it infected Grant's face. Blake pinned the phone against his head with his shoulder, held out his left palm and mimed the strokes of an imaginary pen with his right.

Grant flung open a desk drawer and slapped a pen and paper on the desk.

Blake jotted notes while he listened.

"—especially love the whole ranger station thing. That was a nice touch. Fits in perfectly. I mean, even if someone were inside, who would suspect that one of those cabinets opened to a stairway into a covert lab. I mean seriously, it's like something out of a movie. Even the two guards look like actual forest rangers."

All four guys crowded in, reading over Blake's shoulders as he wrote.

Ranger station. Two guards. Stairway in the cabinet.

Haeli hardly sounded like herself. Her phrasing, her demeanor. She seemed scattered. The opposite of reality. Her apparent rambling was contrived and discontinuous. Delivered any other way, it would have been highly suspicious. Among many other things, the woman was a master of manipulation.

"—but even if someone got down into the tunnel, it'd take a nuke to get that through that door if you didn't have a chip. Do you guys have the chip in your hands, too? Yeah, you'd have to, seems like you need that thing to go anywhere down here. We weren't that advanced in the old place, just carried around a key fob." Haeli paused.

RFID embedded in hands.

Blake listened for a response, another voice besides Haeli's. He heard nothing but dead air. Haeli's voice returned.

"As much as I enjoy hanging out with you two, even if you insist on pointing those MP7s at me, I'm getting bored. Do you know how long before Levi gets here? He's probably lost, trying to find this room. It's like a maze, right? We must have taken like five turns just to get here. Maybe Levi went to the wrong genetics lab. Where do you think we are right now? Southeast corner? I bet one of the other four guys knows. I don't suppose you wanna open the door to ask them."

For the first time, Blake heard a male voice on the other end of the line. He had wondered who she was talking to and why they were letting her drone on without being able to get a word in edge wise. He got his answer.

"Shut up," the male voice said. Though barely audible, the frustration was clear. "Another word and I cut your tongue out."

"Sorry," Haeli said, "Okay, so you don't wanna talk."

"Shut up!"

Blake heard the rattle of the receiver and the call disconnected. He scribbled a few last notes.

Genetics lab - Southeast corner. Five turns. Two tangos in lab, four outside. MP7s. Levi on premises.

Blake realized that four pairs of eyes were resting on him. He tore the top sheet of paper from the pad and said, "I'll fill you all in when we're on the road."

30

Haeli held the Sukhasana pose, one leg crossed over the other, for what she estimated to be an hour, maybe an hour and a half. The speckled epoxy floor was immaculate but did nothing to add comfort to the concrete below. Still, it was important that she conserve her energy, quiet her mind and body, for whatever came next. She knew she would need to fight. She just didn't know when.

What were they waiting for? Was Levi not yet on site? Was her father already preparing for the procedure? Or was it a misguided interrogation tactic, the way suspects are left to stew while detectives gauge their body language from behind two-way mirrors?

Interrogation wasn't likely. Here, the captors possessed the information, not the captee. Besides, if Levi had been watching, it wouldn't have been much of a show. Three people locked in a strange tableau. A freeze-framed piece of performance art entitled Yogi turns armed men to stone.

No one was on the phone with tech support complaining that the video feed had frozen. As far as Haeli could tell, there were no cameras in the genetics lab. At least none visible.

While her body had remained motionless, her mind used time to consider her options. She ran through every scenario she could imagine, some bordering on the ridiculous. Over and over, her attention returned to the ladder in the corner of the room. It beckoned her. Whispered in her ear, "Do not forget me."

Haeli was impressed with the physical stamina of her guards. It was difficult to stand in one position for a long period. She recalled her early assignments, working security details. How she would have to fight the urge to bend her legs, stretch her hip flexors, shift her weight from side to side. But it had gotten easier. These men were experienced in this task. She wouldn't have expected less. She was a high value target.

The murmur of voices coming from the hall gave Haeli enough time to get to her feet before Levi and her father entered. The two stone-faced men moved, their expressions emitting a sense of relief as if the three had been in a staring contest and she had blinked first.

"The prodigal daughter returns." Levi's words, loud and energetic, accompanied his entrance. "We were worried about you."

Haeli responded with a disapproving glare. Not at Levi, but at her father, who had slinked in on Levi's heels. He seemed so weak in Levi's wake. She almost felt bad for him.

Another man slipped into the room, his hands in his pockets. Haeli knew him. Dr. Sebastian Roberts. She wondered what he had to do with this.

Levi acknowledged Roberts with a near-imperceptible nod. Roberts took a position against the wall, as Levi had asked Roberts to be there, but he was trying to stay as far away as he could get.

"I'm glad we got this chance to chat," Levi said, "I didn't think we would—"

Haeli interrupted. "Because I'm supposed to be dead?"

"Quite." Levi paused. "I'm not here to blow smoke up your ass, Haeli. I'm here because I think you deserve an explanation. It is the least I can do."

"The very least." Haeli snarled. "You're going to explain to me why you're spinning lies about me going rogue?"

"Sure. That. But also, the real reason you must go, Haeli. I'm going to tell you the truth before I end your life. Not a courtesy often extended, wouldn't you agree?"

The callousness and utter confidence of the statement sent a shiver through her spine. It was a rare peek inside the man and, she realized, the first time she had ever heard him speak the truth.

"End her life?" Benjamin interjected. "You said she would be unharmed. You promised me."

"Ben," Levi said, "don't be so naïve. And don't worry, I will reward your loyalty."

Haeli examined her father's face. He didn't know. He had lapped up Levi's lies and licked the bowl clean.

Levi turned back to Haeli, dismissing any forthcoming rebuttals. "Haeli, I see what a waste it is. You are special. A marvel of modern science. And you're worth a lot of money to me."

"You're not making your case." Haeli had been listening to Levi, but half her mind was preoccupied with her own survival. The fight was coming sooner than later. She wanted to make sure she didn't miss that perfect moment. The instant all circumstances aligned for the best outcome. It didn't mean she'd win, but at least she wouldn't leave any chance to do so on the table.

"I tried to sell you. Rather, the *idea* of you. The promise of a longer, healthier life. I figured one of the drug companies would bite. Come up with a way to package and sell the technology your father stumbled upon. I was only asking a hundred billion, a rather good deal if you ask me."

"They shot you down," Haeli said.

"On the contrary. Not only did one of them bite, they all did. At first, they were at each other's throats, jockeying to be the one who landed the deal. But then, as they each did their due diligence, as the actuarial studies came back, they each realized that the ability to slow the aging process, whoever owned it, would sink them. At best, they estimated it would take twenty years before they were looking at bankruptcy. At worst, ten. They ran the numbers over and over and none of them could find a way to monetize the technology to surpass the losses they would take to their existing products."

"Because young people don't get sick," Haeli said.

"It would push off many of the conditions that come with aging for a few extra decades. Who knows, maybe more? Sure, it would eventually catch up again, years down the road. But by then, big pharma would already have been ruined. When you think about it, it would affect many industries, not just pharmaceuticals. It could, theoretically, tank the economy. You understand the concern?"

"So, your plan is to save the world by getting rid of me?"

Levi chortled. "I don't care about the world. They're paying me a lot of money."

"Ah, there it is," Haeli said. "It's always about money, isn't it?"

"Yes and no. It's about domination. Which takes money. And it's worth a half a trillion dollars to them to have this entire project go away. Sure, they could have stopped at destroying the research, but that's not really what they're paying for. Having you in the wind is a liability. In the right hands, it's possible that your genetic code can be reverse engineered. Your mere existence threatens them."

Since learning of her unnatural origin, Haeli worried people would see her as something other than human. For maybe the first time in her life, she had been self-conscious, even embarrassed. But now, as she stared into the manifestation of her biggest fear, there existed more sinister implications than hurt pride. Levi saw her not as a person but as intellectual property. It allowed him to divorce himself from any semblance of morality or human decency. She decided she would appeal to his better nature, even if there was no sign that he had one.

Haeli's voice softened. "I've known you my whole life, Levi. I've bled for you. I've sacrificed for you. My father told me you followed my progress. Visited me almost every day. You cared about me. Is my life really nothing more than a business transaction to you now?"

Levi's shoulders sagged and his eyes widened. Had she hit a nerve? Had the simple statement cracked the icy exterior?

"I'm so glad you understand, Haeli," Levi said. "Very well put. A business transaction. Nothing personal. And just in time, too. I was becoming concerned that I'd be showing up to the meeting tomorrow with some explaining to do. Instead, I'll be delivering on my promise, and they'll be delivering everything I need to decimate the competition."

Levi remained unaffected. Haeli could not say the same about her father. Tears welled in his eyes. His once undying loyalty and obedience was now too fragile to prevent his thoughts from escaping. His voice trembled. "My life's work? You want to destroy everything I have worked for?"

Levi cocked his head. He spoke in a patronizing tone. "I already have. All of it wiped clean. But it's not all gone, is it? There's plenty of information locked in that big, beautiful brain of yours, isn't there?"

Haeli cringed at the degradation her father must have felt as Levi poked his index finger against her father's forehead. Instead of seeing embarrassment wash over him, she saw revelation. It wasn't just Haeli that was to be eradicated. Wentz had been right. Her father was in danger all along. Only kept alive long enough to help draw her in. She hated him for what he had done, but she couldn't let it happen to him either. If she was getting out of there alive, her father was coming with her.

Benjamin turned to Roberts. "You knew about this?"

Roberts's chin remained pinned to his chest while his eyes shifted upward to meet her father's gaze. The sanpaku effect made him look more deranged than guilty, but Haeli sensed the latter.

"Questions? Or should I just get down to it?" Levi asked.

Haeli shifted gears. She needed to gain the upper hand, or at least take control of the conversation.

"You will not kill me." Haeli stared menacingly into Levi's eyes. "All this stalling. All this talk. You don't have the stomach to do it yourself."

Levi laughed. Not an evil genius, take-over-the-world laugh. It was hardy. Infectious.

He turned to the younger of the two guards.

"Brant," Levi said. "What is your first directive?"

"No one touches the girl but you, sir."

Levi's hand was a blur as it dove beneath his lapel. The pistol appeared as if out of thin air. Haeli had miscalculated. They were not moving her to another location. There would be no procession, procedure, or further delay. No moment she could seize or misstep she could exploit. Levi was going to kill her now. His finger bore down on the trigger before a single instruction made it from her brain to her muscles.

Then, something else she hadn't calculated. Dr. Benjamin Becher, a prominent scientist and consummate pacifist, threw himself desperately in front of the gun, his arms raised above his head. His hands clasped together.

Haeli watched, helpless, as each millisecond brought her father's double fist down toward the outstretched pistol. The events of the last fraction of a second were sickeningly out of order. The bang came first, then the strike, then the sound of the pistol bouncing off the epoxied floor and skittering toward her.

As she dove for the pistol, she saw the crimson bloom expanding from the center of her father's back. Levi's feet streaked by her head as she closed her grip around the handle of the pistol. Haeli flipped onto her back in time to see the last sliver of Levi's body disappearing down the hall. She swung the pistol and fired twice, striking the first guard in the head and then the second in one continuous motion. Had Levi's directive caused them to hesitate an extra second, or had it just been the shock of the unexpected turn of events? Either way, she considered herself lucky they hadn't been quicker on the trigger.

She trained her sights on the door and fired at the first glimpse of a gun barrel. The muzzle disappeared and she could hear the men clamoring for cover.

It was a good bet that Levi had rescinded his little directive on his way out. Regardless of if he had or not, Haeli posed a big problem that these men would be forced to deal with.

The warning shot had bought her a minute or two. The men on the other side of the door understood the predicament they were in. Every cop and soldier did. The fatal funnel, they called it. A universal truth that the person in the room always had the drop on the person entering the room. The doorway was a funnel, delivering victims into her waiting sights.

Haeli also knew how to overcome the problem. In a moment, the men would stack up and flood the room, branching out in different directions. In theory, it was a numbers game. She would have to take each of them out before one of them could land a shot. It wasn't a game she would win.

Haeli trained the pistol on the door while she moved to her father, almost losing her footing on the slick puddle that continued to creep out from under him. She tugged at his shirtsleeve, flipping him over onto his back. All color had drained from his face. His chest was still. He was gone.

She had expected nothing different. Based on the location of the exit wound, Haeli figured the bullet had passed straight through his heart before ending up in the wall a few inches from her head. It was a sad irony. The very heart that turned him against her had saved her. A heart that had more capacity for love and sacrifice than she believed. She would mourn. She would break down and cry.

But not now.

A flash of movement caught her eye. She snapped her head around to find one eye peeking around the edge of a cabinet. Roberts.

He was a coward and a snake, that much was clear, but he posed no threat to her. She gave him no further thought.

Haeli heard the whisper of the metal ladder. The men would assault the room any second. And she wouldn't be there when they did.

31

The F150 bounced in a front-to-back oscillating pattern, the enhanced suspension forced to its limits by the rough terrain. The truck's off-road capabilities weren't designed with speed in mind, but he continued to hammer the accelerator.

It had been several hours since they'd left Henderson. With each passing minute, Blake had become more impatient. Thoughts of finding Haeli's mutilated body crept up on him like waking nightmares. Worst case scenarios replaced the monotony of the dark desert road.

The decision to take the truck instead of Grant's helicopter had been a difficult one. Grant had offered, but flying would have meant either losing the element of surprise or tacking on a few hours to hike in, defeating the purpose. The truck would let them get close and now, minutes away from their target, Blake knew it was the right choice.

Lit up by the screen of his phone, Fezz's face broke through the pitch darkness of the cab like a character in an Alfred Hitchcock movie. "This is good. The access road should be right over that hill." Then, with a click of a button, he withdrew to the darkness.

Boots were on the ground before the truck rolled to a complete stop. Blake killed the engine and gathered his weapons. He pushed off the running board and met the ground a few feet away.

The density and height of the vegetation surprised Blake. He had turned the headlights off when they left the road. Blind, his two-part navigation strategy comprised a wing and a prayer. Within a minute or two, his eyes had adjusted enough to make out some features, but the scratching of the wiry branches on the truck's undercarriage remained the sole sign of life.

Blake took the lead up the steep hill, dropping to his stomach when he reached the top. The rest filed in next to him, the five foreheads protruding like spines on the sloped back of a stegosaurus.

Fifty yards to the southeast and ninety degrees from their position, the creatively disguised guardhouse nestled itself in the mouth of the valley. The hills, which flanked the building, morphed into mountain peaks in the distance.

Blake counted four vehicles in the parking lot. Five if he included the Little Bird helicopter that sat within the white painted circle to the east side of the lot.

"Bring back poor memories, Griff?" Khat jabbed his elbow into what would have been Griff's rib cage if it wasn't buried under a half an inch of Kevlar. "Any way we can disable that thing?"

Blake understood Khat's concern, and he agreed. It was a long drive out of there. The last thing they needed was an air assault. A good idea in theory, it was imprudent. There had been no time to work out a way to disable the cameras and sensors like Blake had originally planned. The lack of preparation would have to be compensated by sheer speed, skill, and luck.

"It's too risky. We have no idea where the cameras are, how many there are. If we tip them off, give them even a few seconds lead time, we're screwed." Blake pointed toward the northwestern corner of the ranger station. "No, we go straight along this angle. Once we leave this spot, we don't stop 'til we're inside. Fezz, you take the door and then hang back. I'm in first. There shouldn't be much risk of anyone hearing us up here, so spray and pray boys." He patted Fezz on the back. "Ready?"

The big man said, "Born ready."

"See you on the other side." It was something Blake always said in the last calm moment before the storm. Something he was compelled to say. And, man, did he feel good saying it.

Fezz bolted, then Blake, then the others. They reached the wooden door of the station before Blake had started breathing heavily.

Fezz's foot slammed against the door, just above the handle. It swung open with mild protest.

Blake crashed through the opening, mashing the trigger at the first glimpse of movement. Twenty bullets went down range, at least ten of them fatally striking his target. The man in the khaki uniform slumped over the desk, his rifle leaning uselessly against the wall a few feet away.

Khat, Griff, and Grant pushed into the back room. Fezz joined Blake, keeping his attention on the front entryway.

Blake performed a combat reload, replacing the half-depleted magazine with a fresh one. He had expected to hear additional shots as the team moved to the second room. There were none.

Blake joined the rest of the team in time to see Grant press his index finger to his lips and point to a piece of wood attached to a lone interior door. Cursive letters were burned into the plank with a soldering iron and read: Water Closet.

Grant pointed the Kriss Vector at the door and let off a flurry of rounds. A smattering of jagged, splintering holes appeared. They listened. Apart from the ticking of a vintage Smokey the Bear clock, there was only silence.

Khat planted a knee at a forty-five-degree angle to the bathroom door, the weapon seated on his shoulder and his index finger taking up the slack of the trigger. Grant snapped the door open. Khat held.

A khaki mound of a man laid in a heap, a pistol still clutched in his hand. Grant drove the heel of his boot down into the man's limp hand, then reached down and removed the pistol. Judging by the lack of even the slightest flinch, it was a safe assumption that the man would not be mounting a counterattack.

Griff opened one of the four cabinets. Paper goods. He opened a second. "Bingo."

The green glow of fluorescent lights rose from the bottom of the concrete stairs and illuminated the inside edges of the cabinet.

Khat pushed past Griff and started down the stairs. "Let's go."

"Khat, wait." Blake let his weapon hang from its sling. He moved to the bathroom, grabbed the dead man's ankles, and dragged him into the room. Stepping on the man's feet, he pulled his arms, hoisting him upright into a ghoulish ballroom dance. Finally, he dipped down and flung the limp body over his shoulders in a fire-man's carry.

With his cargo securely fastened, Blake took a few labored steps toward the cabinet, then stopped to look around the room. "Where's Kook?"

Grant emerged from the front room. A bloody combat knife in one hand, a gory microchip pinched between the fingers of his other. "Is this what you're after?"

Blake sloughed the body off his shoulders. It hit the ground with a thud. "Better idea."

"Now, can we go?" Khat didn't wait for the answer before he was once again descending the stairs.

Step two, underway.

The team grouped at the bottom and moved as a unit through the wide tunnel. Dead straight and level, they could see its termination in the distance. It was helpful, but they would not be covered should someone appear. The faster they could get to the end and out of the death zone, the better.

This time, Blake found his breath labored by the time they finished traversing the half mile stretch. Grant waved the chip in front of the sensor to pop the latch. He cracked the door a half inch and held it there until the team stacked up behind him.

Once inside, they would face two corridors. One that led straight ahead and one that branched off to the right.

Blake had taken several photos of Grant's computer monitor and texted them to the others. During the drive, the four others studied the blueprints and took turns testing each other. Other than Blake, Grant had seemed to have the best recollection despite not having seen the plans until just before they hit the road.

The exercise had devolved into something akin to bar trivia night. The penalty for a wrong answer was relentless ridicule. The prize for a perfect score would be revealed in the next few minutes.

Last they knew, Haeli was being held in the genetics laboratory. Although the plans showed multiple laboratories, only one sat in the southeast corner of the structure. From where they stood, it was in front of them. Only the hallway they were about to enter did not lead there. Not directly. The layout of the facility comprised a series of snaking and branching corridors.

Griff had been the one to boil down the shortest path into a mnemonic. Some Rottweiler Let Loose on the Red Rug. Straight, Right, Left, Left, Right, Right. As ridiculous as it sounded, Blake couldn't have forgotten it if he tried. Six simple instructions that would lead them to Haeli.

With a tap on his shoulder, Grant swung the door wide and burst into the underground compound and peeled right. Blake pushed forward and held. The others split between the two options.

"It's a ghost town," Griff whispered.

"It's three o'clock in the morning," Khat replied.

"Hopefully, it stays this way. Keep moving. Fezz, you're with me on point," Blake said.

The five men fell into formation and moved as a group. Blake and Fezz led, directing their weapons ahead. Griff took the left and Khat took the right, ready to react should anyone emerge from one of the closed doors along both sides of the corridor. Grant took the rear, shuffling backward to address any threat that might appear from behind. To avoid taking their eyes off the prospective targets, each of the men always kept a shoulder or hip in contact with another man.

Reaching the first corridor on the right, Blake raised the back of his left hand to Fezz's chest. The group stopped. Griff and Khat each shifted to a forty-five-degree angle, covering the rooms they had already passed.

The sound of shuffling feet pierced the baseline silence of the whirring air exchangers. Not close, but close enough. Blake held his breath to eliminate the sound of air passing through his nostrils, then listened. Metallic jingling. A small, muted sleighbell. He tried to clear the absurd first impression from his mind and replace it with something more feasible. He waited. The sound came again, and with it the same mental image of a sleighbell being squeezed tightly and shaken. The footsteps grew closer.

Blake weighed the benefit of visually assessing the approaching person with the risk of alerting the person, or persons, to the group's presence. Was there only one, as it sounded, or were there more? An unassuming scientist, or one of Levi's mercenaries? He decided it was worth the risk.

Pressing his body against the wall, Blake peeked down the hallway. The vantage point offered a profile view of a single male, late twenties or early thirties, wearing the familiar Techyon black fatigues. The man jiggled the handle to a room. The source of the metallic clicking sound became obvious in retrospect. Blake retreated behind the corner.

A non-combatant would have been preferable but, all things considered, it wasn't the worst-case scenario. There was only one, and he appeared to be engaged in a routine task that had nothing to do with him or his team. If he kept on his current trajectory, they were going to become well acquainted.

The man was not an issue. It wasn't even the MP7 that hung from his shoulder and bounced against his kidney that concerned Blake. Against his alabaster skin, a slender microphone jutted from his ear across his cheekbone and looked like a deep facial gash. The deadliest weapon in the place.

The group waited for the results of the momentary reconnaissance. Blake would relay them in five simple gestures. First, he pointed his index finger in the threat's direction. Second, he held up the same finger to signify that there was only one man. Third, he flipped his hand over and pointed at his gun to relay that the man was armed.

Fourth, he added his middle finger, flicking the two fingers like two tiny legs walking through the air. Last, he turned his back to the wall and chopped his bladed hand in the direction the man was moving.

Because the group broke the formation and lined up, backs against the wall, the message had been fully received.

Fezz had filed in next to Blake. He withdrew his combat knife. Blake reached over and pushed Fezz's forearm downward. Fezz nodded and re-sheathed the blade.

Blake tapped Fezz's vest and grabbed his attention for a second silent message. He paused for a moment while he contemplated how to best convey the desired course of action without words. He settled on something, then executed it.

Blake held his finger to his lips, snapped his hands outward in a grasping motion, and twisted his fists toward the ground. Snatch and contain.

Footsteps drew closer. In what seemed like the blink of an eye, the man was upon them.

Fezz lunged forward, smashing his right hand into the mouth and nose of the unprepared opponent. Fezz's left hand hooked around the back of the man's head. The man's eyelids opened so wide it looked like his eyeballs would fall out.

Blake ripped the radio from the man's hip, snapping the plastic clip that fastened it. The earpiece popped out and lodged against his collar. Blake yanked downward in three violent motions until the plastic microphone snapped and sent the remaining portion of the device down his back and out the bottom of his shirt.

Fezz kicked his foot behind the man and swept it back, knocking both his legs out from under him. He hit the ground in a seated position, legs extended straight in front of him, head still trapped in the vice.

Khat leaned in and jammed the business end of the suppressor into the man's forehead. There was no resistance. The man's hands remained glued to the floor where he had planted them to break his fall.

Grant sauntered around the man and removed the sling from his shoulder. The MP7 came with it.

Blake peered down the corridor from which the man had come. There was no one else in sight. He decided it was safe to communicate verbally. He motioned to the closest door and whispered, "Get him inside."

Fezz spun the man around, maintaining his grip. He dragged the man along the floor by his head until reaching the door. Griff grabbed the man's right wrist and torqued it upward toward the access control sensor. The latch clicked.

The lights switched on upon entering, revealing a small sea of cubicles. Blake looked around for something substantial to bind the man to. The only option appeared to be the two structural columns that divided the room.

Several pairs of flex cuffs dangled from the webbing of Blake's tactical vest. The same was true for all of them. Blake would have liked to have strung a few of the oversized zip ties together to secure the man to a column, but they had already been formed in a handcuff shape and there was no way to release them once they were engaged. Blake moved on to the second option.

"Hold him tight." Blake unlaced the man's boots and removed them. He flexed the man's feet and worked a pair of the plastic cuffs over the man's heels and on his ankles.

"Give me your hands," Blake said.

The man lifted his arms.

Blake cinched a cuff around one wrist then reached under the leg shackles to grab his other.

At the prospect of being hobbled by having his hands bound on either side of his leg restraints, the man pulled his arm away and squirmed. Although Fezz's hand covered much of the man's face, his muffled protests were heard.

"Khat," Blake said.

Khat again jammed the muzzle of his gun into the man's forehead, off-center from the round red mark that still lingered from the last time.

A muted stutter came from the man. Blake wasn't sure if it was a nervous laugh or a cry. Maybe both. Either way, he relented.

As the last zip tie ratcheted, Fezz let go of the man's mouth.

"What do you want?" the man asked.

"What's your name?" Blake countered.

"Bobby," the man answered. He paused a moment, then dropped his head. "Dempsey."

"Listen up, Bobby Dempsey," Blake continued, "if you answer our questions, the worst of it is behind you. If not, well, I'm sure I don't have to tell you what happens."

Griff jumped in, skipping the theatrics, and getting right to the point. "Where's Haeli?"

Dempsey craned his neck to look over his shoulder at Griff, then turned back to Blake. "I don't know. I know nothing about it."

Blake shook his head. "Twist his head off."

Fezz scooped his hand under the man's chin.

"Wait. I know who you're talking about. The girl. Who used to work for us. There was a big meeting tonight, I know that. I heard some guys talking about it. But I don't know what it's about. I just started here three months ago. Whatever it's about, it's above my pay grade. I don't ask questions."

"Did you see her?" Blake asked.

"No. The meeting was already over by the time I got here tonight. I don't think it went well, though."

"Why do you say that?" Blake asked.

"Because when I arrived, Mr. Farr was getting into one of the Tahoes. I said hello, but he didn't respond. He looked upset. Then he peeled out, leaving the lot."

Blake caught Grant's eyes. Their blue intensity said what no one dared verbalize.

They might be too late.

"Stay quiet and you live," Blake said.

Dempsey swallowed hard and nodded.

Grant cracked the door. He looked and listened. Dempsey didn't say a word.

"All clear," Grant said.

The team moved out to the hallway and resumed their formation. Some Rottweiler Let Loose on the Red Rug.

They moved quickly, increasing speed as they rounded each corner. Left. Left. Right Right.

As they rounded the last, they could see the square splotch of light spilling onto the hallway floor through the open door of the genetics lab.

They pushed ahead, breaching the entryway without hesitation.

Blake sucked in a gulp of air, unable to catch a breath. For an instant, it was as if all the oxygen in the room had been used up. On first sight of the pool of blood, Blake's brain had jumped to conclusions. He was sure that he would find her there, lying on the floor, drained of life. But he was wrong. Wonderfully wrong.

There were three bodies in the room. All men. Two wore the telltale black uniform of the Techyon henchman. Although Blake had only seen Benjamin Becher for a few moments on the steps of the Griffith Observatory, he recognized the gray, mottled face of the third.

Who he couldn't place was the living man that knelt beside Dr. Becher. Hands and knees covered in blood. His face red and swollen from crying.

"Who are you?" Blake asked.

"Dr. Roberts," he choked out. A band of mucus strung from his nose over his lips, stretching like an elastic band when he spoke.

Blake bent into a crouch. "Where's Haeli?"

Roberts said nothing. He lifted his arm and pointed to the ladder in the room's corner.

Griff and Grant darted up the ladder and disappeared.

"What happened?" Blake asked.

Roberts opened his mouth to speak, then took a moment to clear his throat and collect himself.

"Levi shot him," He started sobbing again.

Blake shot Fezz a look. He knew what little use Fezz had for men who couldn't pull themselves together. The same went for all of them. But the fact was, they had a use for this one. They needed answers, and something told him Roberts could provide them.

"Dr. Roberts, I'm sorry for your loss." Blake intended for the statement to calm Roberts, but it only reminded Blake of Haeli and what she had lost. Benjamin Becher had been the only family she had ever known. She had been willing to risk everything. To sacrifice herself to save him.

The deep sadness Blake felt for her was not because her father's death had taken away her chance of normal life. Her father had done that the moment he betrayed her. It was because Blake knew the pain and guilt that comes with failing to protect someone you love. He did not wish that upon anyone, especially not her.

"Is she alright? Is she wounded?" Blake asked.

Roberts shook his head. "No. I don't think so." He glanced at the bodies of the two guards. "She shot them and then escaped through the hatch. It all happened so fast."

Vibrations emanated from the corner. Clang. Clang. Clang.

"We found a bunch of footprints," Griff announced as he reached the bottom of the ladder. "Looks like they're all going south."

"The men went after her," Roberts said.

Blake had figured as much. "How long ago?"

Robert shrugged. "A few hours."

Fezz tapped Blake on the shoulder and gave a brief cock of his head. Blake knew what it meant. Fezz wanted a sidebar. Blake stood and moved a few feet away from Roberts.

"It was a hundred and twelve degrees yesterday," Fezz said. "If she's stranded out there at sunup, she's going to be in serious trouble. I doubt she has any water with her. It's a day's hike to the closest town, and that's if you know where you're going. We've got to go after her, now."

A defensiveness bubbled up in Blake. How dare Fezz insinuate that he would even consider not going after her? The misdirected anger subsided as fast as it appeared. Fezz didn't know the scope of it. He didn't understand the deep connection with Haeli burrowed in

Blake's guts and coursing through his veins. He hardly understood it himself.

"Fezz, I swear to you. I will bring her home." Blake thought about rephrasing his statement. He unintentionally used the word home. Unconsciously, at least. Haeli didn't have a home. Her life all but revolved around that premise. But she did, if she wanted it. With him. With them.

"What about Levi?" Griff asked. "Should we split up? Go after him?"

"He took off a few hours ago. Could be anywhere by now," Khat said. And he was correct. They had lost him. And they had more pressing issues now.

"I could help with that," Roberts said.

The conversation suspended at the unexpected offer. All eyes shifted to the slight man.

Roberts continued. "I don't know where he is now. But I know where he's going to be. I'll tell you everything you need to know. Consider it my resignation letter."

Blake smiled.

Grant climbed down a few rungs, then jumped to the floor.

"Do we know what kind of head start they have?" Grant asked.

"A few hours." The group spoke in near unison. Even Roberts.

Grant offered his palms. "Jeez, just asking."

"Kook, come here," Blake said. "I have a plan."

32

A hint of light blue touched the eastern sky and spread like a drop of dish detergent in a Caribbean oil spill. With it came the orange tinge rimming the underside of the few clouds. It was a welcomed sight.

Since the painted white circle receded beneath Blake's boots and faded into the blackness, he had been willing the sun to appear sooner than scheduled. It only made it seem longer.

The goal had been to use the million-candle handheld searchlight to scour the valley floor and find Haeli. Not long after takeoff, it became clear how difficult the task would be. Positioned on the platform attached to the right side of the commandeered Little Bird helicopter, Blake would have had an expansive view of the area. In the darkness, he may as well have been looking through a pinhole.

Khat had taken up his position on the left side platform, not that he was going to see anything. He chose it for comfort. Unlike Grant's Eurocopter, the small MH-6 didn't have six seats in the rear compartment. In fact, it didn't have any.

Even the cockpit of the Little Bird was cramped in comparison. Fezz had wedged himself in the front to help Griff with navigation. He tried to calculate how far Haeli would have gotten based on time and conditions. The resulting area was a band of probability, shaped like a carpenter's staple. If she had stayed on a southerly track, she would have made up more ground. The further she veered toward the rocky slopes, the less distance away she would have travelled.

For the last couple of hours, Griff had zigzagged above these areas, pushing further south after each circuit. It was an exercise in futility. Haeli could have been standing in the middle of the valley, waving her arms, the beam of Blake's spotlight passing within feet of her.

Grant had left with Sebastian Roberts the same time as they did. Blake had watched the Ford's headlights trailing off to the north toward the State road for several minutes after they took to the air. By now, he had already made it to the agreed upon rendezvous point to their southwest.

Blake placed the light on the deck and slid it further inside. He dragged the Kriss Vector toward him by its stock, then grasped its handle. He looked down at the emerging desert. It was amazing how the human eye could capitalize on even the smallest amount of light. And under the predawn sky, it may as well have been noon.

"Drop a bit," Blake said.

Griff's affirmative response came, not through his headset, but through the slight negative G-force.

Now that both he and Khat could survey wide swaths of land, Blake felt a glimmer of hope returning. He shifted his eyes along the ground like a cathode-ray tube.

Then he saw something. A lot of somethings.

"I've got eyes," Blake said. "Fifteen to twenty Techyon men about a half a click to the south. Widely spaced out."

Griff spun the aircraft. The ground picked up speed beneath them. In a matter of minutes, they would pass directly over the armed squad.

"Get ready for some action, Khat."

Khat gave an enthusiastic thumbs up.

In that moment, Blake regretted the oversight that put them in the air without first trekking out to the truck to pick up a few longer-range weapons. The 9mm submachine guns, while perfect for their purposes inside the compound, would be ineffective from that distance. They would have to be accurate to hit the men on the ground. The men on the ground had to hit the proverbial broad side of the bus. They were, without a doubt, at a disadvantage.

As they passed over the first of the men, Blake noticed little reaction. Apart from one man who appeared to glance upward and give a quick, half-hearted wave.

"They think we're with them," Blake said.

It made sense. Over the past couple of hours, they had been weaving and hovering overhead. The men assumed that it was their own people, aiding in the search. Levi had been so secretive that most of the employees, like the man they left hog-tied on the floor of someone's office, didn't even know any of this was going on. The ones who had set out on foot did so before Blake and his team had even arrived. Blake took back his original assessment. They had the advantage after all.

Fezz set about recalculating. Haeli had left a few minutes before her pursuers. Unlike the men wearing tactical gear and carrying weapons, she wore regular street clothing. Likely the jeans and tank-top she had been wearing when Blake dropped her off. The men were fanned out, performing a line search. This extra care would slow them down further. On top of all of that, Haeli was just faster.

"At a minimum," Fezz said, "she would have put a few miles between herself and these guys. With them behind her, I don't think she would try to hunker down or risk the terrain heading up to the mountains. She'd want to put as much distance between her and Techyon as possible."

Blake agreed. Although Haeli would have known that heading south would only further strand her in some of the most inhospitable landscape in North America, he also knew that she would have no qualms about taking such a risk. Because he would do the same. In a choice between battling against exhaustion, heat-stroke, and dehydration, and an incoming wall of bullets, the choice was more than obvious.

Upon reaching the starting point that Fezz had chosen, Griff resumed the zigzag search pattern. Blake let his eyes relax, hoping to pick up any slight movement in his peripheral vision. It was a tactic he learned years prior. As a vestige of the past. When people were more prey than predator, the human brain was wired to detect movement more acutely from the sides. The problem at this moment was that he didn't detect motion from anywhere.

HAELI PULLED her knees in close to her chest, wrapping herself up into the smallest package she could manage. The small grouping of chaparral didn't provide much cover. She hoped it would be enough.

The Little Bird helicopter hovered almost directly over her now. She could feel the downdraft ruffling the back of her shirt, pushing it halfway up her back.

The ache in her knee was more pronounced in that bent position. She suppressed the urge to rub it. After tripping while in a full sprint and landing knee first on a rock, she had tried to use a little more caution. But she needed to keep moving at all costs. It was the crux of the dilemma she found herself in.

If they detected her from the air, it was over. There would be no way to outrun the helicopter, and there was nowhere to take cover from an air assault. If she stayed hidden, she would likely avoid detection, but the men pursuing her would make up any distance she had put between them. They already drew closer.

In the dark it had been easier. As the helicopter weaved this way and that, the probing light had made it a simple task to keep track of its path. She had only needed to curl up in a ball twice, and only for a few seconds at a time.

Now, in the daylight, she had to use a different strategy. Whenever the aircraft moved closer to her position, she would lie low. Whenever it turned away, she'd run. Simple in theory, not so much in practice. Because of the repeating diagonal pattern, the helicopter was never coming or going. She'd have to make a judgement call. Be ready to take an opportunity when it presented itself.

The opportunity arrived sooner than she had expected. As the helicopter swooped around and back over her, she got ready to bolt.

Wait. Wait. Now.

Haeli unfolded herself and reached top speed in a matter of seconds. She struggled to keep her balance, along with her maximum speed, as she kept her head turned and eyes on the movements of the Little Bird.

Conservatively, she traversed a quarter mile of land before the helicopter made its turn. Without hesitation, she dove into whatever scraps of vegetation were available and squeezed herself into obscurity. A pixel on a giant screen.

The Little Bird roared overhead. In a minute or two or three, it would pass over again, and she would be off.

"WE'RE LOW ON FUEL," Griff said. "This is going to have to be the last pass if we're going to make it to the rendezvous."

"We're not leaving her, Griff. You can put me down right here. I'll go alone."

"Whoa, brother, no one said anything about leaving her," Griff replied. "I'm just saying, we're going critical here. We can take more passes, but we won't be able to get out. We can put her down and search on foot, then at least we'd still have a ride. That's if we can get back without running into a small army."

It was a tough decision. Blake didn't like the odds of finding her on foot. The Techyon men could all attest to that. Then again, if they spent all their fuel finding her, or not, they'd be in the same position she was. But if she had been willing to take that risk, he was more than willing to take it with her.

"Do another pass," Blake said.

"Roger," Griff said.

The helicopter turned, inching its way further to the south. Nothing.

Even in the stream of thrusting air from above, Blake could feel the heat rising.

In the scheme of things, Nevada was nothing compared to some places he had been. Iraq stood out amongst them. Parts of Africa. The Himalayas at the other extreme. Blake had always been prepared. He hated the thought of Haeli being out there. Alone. Exposed. Under attack. No matter how capable she might be.

Blake directed his unfocused stare to the ether once more. The muted browns blended. And then, out of the corner of his right eye, he caught it. Movement. To his distant right, about twenty degrees off the back of the tail, a stick figure. Arms pumping, black hair flowing.

"Got her!" Blake yelled. "Turn southwest so I can keep a visual."

Griff did. As they made the turn, she vanished. Blake struggled to keep his eyes on the exact spot that he had last seen her. A spot that looked like every other in the entire valley.

"A little further," Blake said. The helicopter moved; his eyes remained fixed. "Ok, cut it dead west."

A half mile later, they approached the spot that Blake had picked out. At least, they'd be close.

"Put her down, Griff. Right here."

Blake inched further from the fuselage with each foot they descended until he was connected to the helicopter by only the toes of his left foot and the fingers of his outstretched left hand. He waited until they were within four feet before he let go and dropped to the ground.

Boots planted, he swiveled his head. Had he been seeing things? A kind of mirage brought on by his own desperation?

She wasn't there now. But a small, dark-colored mound mixed in between the dull greens of the sparse desert foliage. He would not have given it another thought if he hadn't seen Haeli fit into that towel cart at the motel.

Could it be her?

Blake inched closer but only made it a third of the way before the peculiar little lump bloomed into a full-grown human being. One that was already in mid-stride, heading away from him.

"Haeli!" Blake yelled as loud as he could. Barely loud enough to overcome the drone of the helicopter.

Haeli looked over her shoulder. She slowed to a stop, long enough to reverse directions. In a blink, she was running toward him. With each bounding stride, her glistening eyes and expanding smile came more in focus. She was radiant.

In Haeli fashion, she left her feet before she even reached him. Throwing herself into his arms and wrapping her legs around the back of his thighs, she kissed him. A deep, passionate kiss filled with need and relief and possibility. Blake's hands, fingers spread along her back, pulled her close with no intention of ever letting go.

Haeli dropped to her feet. Their lips parted. They lingered in each other's eyes.

Although they said nothing, it was as if a full conversation had taken place. The apologies for the mistakes that were made. The fear of having lost out on a chance at something real. The acknowledgement of the pain and baggage that had emotionally paralyzed both of them. All wrapped up in one perfect moment.

Haeli turned her head to find the smiling faces of Khat and Fezz staring back at her. Khat waved. Haeli laughed. Although the sound of it was drowned out, it was infectious.

Blake had seen her face in his mind's eye a thousand times in the last twelve hours. In his vision, she wore an expression of alarm. Despair. Now, she stood before him, her face glowing. Beaming from ear to ear. But it wouldn't last long.

The corners of her mouth turned down, pulling her smile with it. Her thin eyebrows pitched in toward the bridge of her nose. Her gaze left his and drifted off over his shoulder, and her mouth moved as if she was speaking.

They're here.

Blake spun around to see the line of men approaching, no further than a football field away. He placed his hand on Haeli's back and pushed her toward the Little Bird. Haeli broke into a run. Blake followed, watching as the muzzle flashes popped like a string of fire-crackers in the distance.

Khat hopped to the ground and sprayed a barrage of bullets downrange.

Haeli threw herself inside and Blake stepped up on the personnel platform, pausing for long enough to empty his own magazine toward the advancing men. He hoped at least one round had found a victim.

Blake hung on tight as the pitch of the engine cried out and the skids teetered.

More rounds came, clinking and clattering off the Little Bird's skin.

Blake reloaded. Haeli, taking up Griff's unused weapon, laid on her belly and scooted herself out onto the platform by Blake's feet.

They took turns sending full magazines raining down on their adversaries. Haeli, then Khat, then Blake. Fezz, one-handing his weapon around the A-pillar, fired haphazardly over the nose.

They ascended smoothly. One hundred feet. Two hundred feet.

The helicopter shuttered and bobbed, then spun a hundred eighty degrees.

Blake feared the worst. They had hit a critical piece of the aircraft. It turned out not to be the case, exactly. But a round had hit the most critical component of the machine.

The pilot.

The bullet had torn through Griff's left bicep. Blake had a clear view of Griff's left side from the outside. He tried to assess the damage.

The bullet passed straight through, high on the bicep, before being stopped by Griff's vest. It missed the humerus and brachial artery. The absence of any arterial spurting was a promising sign.

Blake leaned within an inch of Griff's ear and hollered, "You're lucky. It's only a flesh wound. Can you get us out of here?"

Griff nodded.

Blake would have told him it was a flesh wound even if his arm had fallen off. Hundreds of feet in the air with the only guy who knows how to fly a helicopter wounded, was no time for honesty.

The Little Bird spun, the nose dipped, and they were en route.

As the black fatigues and muzzle flashes receded into the distance, Blake couldn't help but think about what would happen now. For him. For Haeli. For all of them. He really didn't know. But tomorrow was going to be a hell of a lot better than today.

33

Levi dabbed the handkerchief against his forehead. There was an adage in business, he thought. Never let them see you sweat. This was true about the people he was about to meet. The heads of the world's biggest pharmaceutical companies practically fed on it.

It crossed Levi's mind that was the reason they had left him sitting by himself at the boardroom table for the last half hour. To make him sweat it. They knew that he would deliver bad news.

For a while, Levi had considered lying. Buying himself some more time to make it right. But then he decided against it. They possessed the power to destroy him and his company. If Haeli could somehow continue eluding him, and the secret was to get out after they had paid him, it would be all over.

No, he would put the deal off. Petition them for more time. It was in their best interest to let him fix the problem once and for all. Deadline be damned.

Initially, he hoped things would still work out on schedule. Once he had escaped and made it to his jet at Fresno Yosemite International Airport, he received word that his men had tracked Haeli to the desert and were closing in on her. Levi learned the truth upon landing in New York yesterday morning. Haeli had been rescued. And he knew exactly by whom.

All of that aside, Levi remained confident that his firm had the resources to track her down. She was a loner. A wanderer. And while she had help now, that wouldn't always be the case. One night, Haeli would return to her room at some roadside motel and he would be there to greet her.

Levi checked his watch.

Let's get on with this already.

He hadn't heard the creak of the door behind him or the shuffling of feet, but he felt the blade of the knife pressed against his throat. A hand squeezed his collar bone.

They were going to do him like this? Before he had time to explain?

"Long time, Levi" the voice said.

Levi recognized it. It wasn't Big Pharma's hitmen rubbing him out. This was personal.

"Brier?"

BLAKE APPLIED MORE PRESSURE, pressing straight in, not to the side. He didn't want to draw blood, not here. He wanted to deliver a message.

"What do you want?" Levi asked.

"You know what I want."

"Haeli?"

Blake brought his cheek in close to Levi's head. "Haeli is dead. Gone. You no longer need to concern yourself with her. And that's exactly what you are going to tell the men who come through that door. You will take your money. You will take your win. But you will never speak her name again."

"And if I don't agree?"

"You will. Because you know that if I can get to you here, I can get to you anywhere. You can't hide from me. Tell me you know that."

Levi's breathing quickened. "I do."

Blake pressed harder. "I should kill you right here."

"No, please," Levi muttered.

Blake tightened his grip on Levi's shoulder. "You saved my life once. This is me saving yours." Blake withdrew the knife from Levi's neck and tucked it in his suit jacket. "Now we're even."

Levi let out a sigh, rubbed his throat, and then looked down at his hand. He looked relieved. Relieved to be alive and relieved to have an excuse to accept the money. But, by doing so, Levi would be in a compromising position. And that's exactly where Blake wanted him.

A gaggle of suits poured into the room. Blake walked past them toward the exit as though he belonged.

"My attorney," Levi explained, "he has to excuse himself. Pressing matters, you know. But Gentlemen, I have good news..."

Blake walked away, leaving Levi Farr to do the thing he did best. Lie through his teeth.

34

One point two seconds. The average time it takes to spot Fezz across a crowded bar. On this night, it might have been less. But instead of rushing over, Blake lingered for a moment, taking the scene in from afar. Fezz, Khat, Griff, and now Haeli, sharing a drink and a few laughs. They were rowdy, sure. But they were good people. The best people.

Blake's people.

He watched as Haeli hopped off her stool, moved around Griff, and stole Khat's ball cap off his head. She put it on and strutted around in what Blake decided was a good impression of Khat. The routine seemed to kill. At least, Fezz and Griff got a hardy laugh out of it. And Khat couldn't seem to help but smile.

Blake, standing there on the fringe, felt like he was standing out in the snow, looking in the window of a baker's shop. Fire blazing, the smell of pies wafting through the air. It was inviting. So much warmer on the inside.

Blake removed his jacket, draped it over his arm, and set off to join his merry band of misfits.

Haeli was the first to notice him.

"Mick, you're back!"

Blake had called to fill everyone in as soon as he left Levi. They were ecstatic it had worked. Levi had made his deal, and Haeli was free to live her life as she saw fit. They planned the evening as a celebration of their victory.

"Good to be back in Virginia." Blake placed his hand on Griff's good arm. The other was tied up in a sling. "How's the arm?"

"Hurts like hell," Griff said.

Blake laughed. "Hey, you wanted to be part of the action."

Haeli handed Blake a glass of whiskey. He didn't need to ask what kind it was.

"Gentlemen, and lady," Blake said, his glass held at eye level, "a toast to my man Apollo. MVP." The group offered a few hoots and hollers. Blake took a sip. "Seriously, I love you, brother. All of you. And I'd even extend that to Kook if he were here."

"Well, you're in luck." Khat motioned to the happy-go-lucky thatch of blonde hair emerging from the restroom. The California Dream himself.

Blake offered his hand as Grant approached. Grant skipped the handshake and went straight for the hug.

"This is a surprise," Blake said. "What are you doing in these parts?"

"I heard there was a celebration happening and, seeing as though I was instrumental in the mission's success, I figured you'd need me here to sing my praises." He slapped Blake on the shoulder. "And it's been a while since I'd been back. I figured I'd visit my sister while I'm here."

"Glad you're here," Blake said.

Khat removed his cap from Haeli's head, then reseated it onto his own. "I wish I was there to see the look on that cretin's face when you showed up."

Blake laughed. "Let's just say, he may have needed to change his skivvies afterward."

"What irks me is Levi got exactly what he wanted." Fezz lamented.

"You'd hope he'd learned his lesson," Griff said. "Use that money to do something worth doing."

"I wouldn't count on Levi to learn anything," Blake said. "But as long as Haeli's safe and we never have to see his smug face again, I'm good."

Fezz pointed at Blake. "That's the part I wouldn't count on. I just have this feeling Levi's not going away."

"Time will tell," Blake offered. "What else did I miss in the last day?"

"Not much," Fezz said. "Once we left you, we got Haeli and Roberts squared away at the airport, arranged a flight for ourselves out of Henderson, got the equipment back, and set up Haeli in a safe house nearby for a few days so she can get situated. Guess we did quite a bit. Oh, and Griff had surgery."

"Thanks for remembering," Griff said.

"What happened to Roberts?" Blake asked.

"Illinois," Haeli responded. "He said that's where he was from. I sat down with him for a couple of hours at the airport. Asked him a million questions."

"And? How are you feeling?"

A word formed on her lips but receded before it could escape. Her bottom lip quivered. She gained control of it by pursing her lips and forcing a breath of air through them. "I don't know. Hasn't set in yet, I suppose. What really sucks is that I won't know what happened to my father's body."

Blake wrapped his arms around Haeli. She nestled her face into his shoulder and spoke into his chest.

"I still really haven't come to terms with what I am. Who I am. Or what I'm going to do now. I'm a little screwed up in the head." She lifted her cheek from Blake's chest. "And I'm pretty sure there aren't any shrinks who specialize in treating ex-science experiments."

Blake chuckled. "Probably not. But at least you seem to have conquered your heights thing."

"Yeah, don't remind me." Haeli's cheery smile relaxed again into contemplation. She reached out, placed her hand along the side of

Blake's face and stroked her thumb against his cheek. "Don't worry about me. I'll work through it. I'll find my purpose."

"That reminds me of something a wise Sherpa once told me." Blake paused at Haeli's distrusting expression, as if she were already waiting for the punchline. "No joke, he's a real guy. His name was Tashi. A Buddhist monk believe it or not. He told me, 'Your purpose in life is to find your purpose and give your whole heart and soul to it.'"

Haeli squinted, processing the ancient wisdom. "No idea what that means."

Blake laughed. "You will in a minute." He shifted to face the entire group. "Listen up. Since we're all here, let me float something by you all. I know we've joked about it in the past, but I'm being serious right now. Hear me out for a minute."

He had their attention.

"What if we worked together again?"

"You wanna come back?" Fezz asked.

"No, definitely not. I mean the other way around. What if we went private? Small scale, completely off the radar. I know you'd be leaving pension money on the table by quitting the Agency, but do you want to stay until you're fifty? Financially, jumping over to the private sector is a sound move. Look at Kook. Look at me. We'd be doing what we do best. And money aside, we can make a difference."

"How would that work?" Fezz asked.

"Word of mouth, mostly. Connections. It would be slow at first. But we can do things the government can't, which makes us valuable."

Grant bobbed his head. "Right, like vigilantes."

"Not exactly." Blake paused. "Look, I don't want to get cheesy, but think about it. The thing we all have in common, besides our skill, our training, our experience and all of that, is we see something that's wrong and we make it right. Haeli, what Tashi said about purpose. This is our purpose. Every single one of us. Am I wrong about that?"

The group looked around at each other's faces. No one seemed to disagree.

"We'd be losing the resources we currently have," Griff said. "Apart from a favor here and there. It would take a pretty good chunk of change to get up and running."

"I've got a few bucks stashed away," Grant said.

"I'd be willing to fund it myself," Blake said. "But I don't think it will be necessary. I know a guy. Greyson Whitby's his name. Filthy rich. Terrible climber. Got a feeling he'd be willing to bankroll us for a percentage. And he owes me a favor."

"There's something else to consider," Khat said. "I know we've gotten away with a lot, but we have to remember we aren't above the law. The last few days, we've really pushed our luck. You especially, Mick. That stunt above the Palazzo. It's a matter of time before we all find ourselves in jail. You really wanna risk it?"

Blake agreed. He had looked over his shoulder, wondering if his sins would finally catch up to him. But it was about more than self-preservation. Like Haeli, he faced an existential crisis of his own. It forced him to ask himself the hard questions. What separated him from a common criminal? Was he becoming a monster? He had taken lives. Men who were guilty only by association. He had done bad things for good reasons, or so he told himself, but he wondered if the scales balanced out.

"You are one hundred percent right, Khat. If we do this, we do it by the book. We hold ourselves accountable."

"This is a big ask, Mick," Fezz said.

"I know. I'm not looking for anyone to decide tonight. Just think about it. That's all."

"Well, I'm in." Haeli broke the tension. "But only if I get an ultra-cool nickname like the rest of you."

Blake wrapped his arm around her. "How about Pegasus?"

"Gross."

Blake chuckled. "Yeah, I didn't think so."

"Bartender," Khat announced in an inexplicable and inaccurate British accent. "Libations all around."

The oddest family that ever existed drank and laughed and hurled their best insults at one another. But Blake noticed the subtle change in the mood, each of them trailing off from the conversation to lose themselves in thought. A few seconds here, a few seconds there. His proposal had already burrowed deep in their brains. The seed had sprouted, and it would continue to grow. Like the pre-dawn glow over the distant mountains of Nevada, it took the tiniest bit of light to open one's perspective.

"Mick, come here," Haeli said. She pressed against him. Her plush lips brushed against his ear. "You wanna go someplace else?"

He smiled.

"Gentlemen, it's been fun, but I'll leave you to it. Haeli and I have a lot to talk about."

The expected childish heckling gave way to handshakes and a couple of gruff embraces.

As Blake and Haeli departed, he stopped. He took two hurried steps back and then rapped his knuckles against the hardwood bar top.

For luck.

Because, well, it never hurts.

***

Blake Brier returns in Uncharted, available for pre-order now!
https://www.amazon.com/dp/B08RRZ2YKP/
Turn the page to read a sample of Uncharted.

UNCHARTED

BLAKE BRIER BOOK THREE

by L.T. Ryan & Gregory Scott

UNCHARTED CHAPTER 1

Saturday, May 29th. Afternoon.

Jason wiped the sunscreen-laced bead of sweat from the corner of his eye before it had the chance to infiltrate under the lid. He opened his eyes as much as the beating afternoon sun would allow. Satisfied that he thwarted the eyeball-stinging scourge of the SPF 15, he closed his eyes and sunk back into his thoughts.

Stretched out across the V-shaped cushions of his parent's twenty-two-foot bowrider, Jason had but one concern. Properly maintaining his tan.

"That's a hot look," Brian said over the cracking of another can of Miller Lite.

"Shush. You're interrupting my work." Jason formed the words by utilizing as few facial muscles as possible. He knew what his best friend was referring to and had expected the ridicule. With the legs of his palm tree patterned swim trunks hiked up to his groin, it probably looked like he was wearing some kind of Hawaiian Sumo diaper. *Better than pasty white thighs*, he thought.

"Your girlfriend's getting jealous over here," Brian joked. "She won't say it, but she's worried you're gonna be prettier than her."

Shelly giggled. It was a running joke that her boyfriend was obsessed with himself. It wasn't entirely untrue, but she had to admit that he doted on her more than himself, which was all she cared about.

"Aren't you gonna have a beer, Jason?" Emma asked.

Jason sat up with a groan and adjusted his trunks. The answer was no. Although he had experience operating the boat, it still made him uneasy to be wholly responsible for it. If he had learned anything about boating, it was that whatever can go wrong *will* go wrong. Even in the relatively tame waters of the Narragansett Bay.

"Jay doesn't drink when he's driving the boat," Shelly said.

"Ironic, right?" Jason pointed out as he moved aft to join his friends. "Since I'm the only one who's legal."

"Oh yeah, you're way cooler than any of us 'cause you turned twenty-one first. Even though I'm like three months behind you."

"Still, I have to look out for you young kids." Jason plopped down next to Shelly, put his arm around her shoulder and kissed her on the side of the head.

"Okay, Boomer." Brian shot a proud smirk.

Jason clasped his hands behind his head and kicked his leg out, crossing his ankles on top of his best friend's knee. "Tell me this isn't the life."

Brian shoved Jason's feet to the side, causing them to flop to the fiberglass floor.

"Let's get a group shot," Emma suggested. "I've gotta post this on Insta."

The group sputtered half-hearted protests while obediently squeezing together. Emma crouched on the floor in between the bench seats and extended her arm as far as she could.

"Jason, you're blocking the bridge," Emma said.

Using the preview on the screen of Emma's outstretched smartphone as a guide, Jason repositioned himself so that the visible portion of the Jamestown Verrazano bridge, some two miles in the distance, was in the frame. He tightened his abs, chest and biceps and pasted on his prepackaged social media smile.

The screen flashed. Emma slid onto her seat and began pawing at the screen.

"Ya get it? How do I look?" Jason asked.

Emma shrugged and handed him the phone.

"Oh, yeah. Post that," Jason said. "I look fine as hell."

Emma snatched the phone. "I don't. I look like a hot mess." She stood up and gazed out to the west. "Anyways, I wanted to get more of the background. Like, look at this place."

Jason glanced over his shoulder to take in the view. The scene had been the backdrop of his whole life. So common that he rarely noticed it.

Anchored only a hundred feet offshore in a protected corner of the bay at the mouth of Zeek's creek, the ripples of the calm shallow water smoothed out to a glassy sheen in the distance. Beyond the bobbing sailboats anchored in the harbor was Dutch Island, an uninhabited mound of dense foliage rising from the center of the West Passage. Along the shore, to their south, stood a row of quiet houses. Each of them a better example of old Rhode Island architecture than the next. In a way, Emma's enthusiasm had breathed new life into all of it.

"I can't believe y'all grew up here," Emma said. "It's awesome. God, I would never want to leave if I lived here."

Originally from Fort Worth, Texas, Emma met Brian at the University of Notre Dame. The two had been dating for the past two years, but this was the first time she visited Rhode Island. Not to mention the first time that Jason and Shelly had the chance to set eyes on her.

Since their early teens, Brian and Jason had rated the girls they met on a number scale. One being the most undesirable and ten being, well, impossible. Jason had to admit, Emma far exceeded his expectations. In his estimation, she was a solid eight and Brian should have felt lucky to land a five.

"Don't you think so?" Emma asked.

"Yeah, I mean, I do," Shelly said. "I never really thought so when I was growing up. Just took it for granted I guess."

"Well, I think this is paradise." Emma sprawled out across the cushions of the port side bench seat. She rested her head on Brian's lap.

"If you're visiting, maybe." Brian brushed a loose strand of hair from Emma's cheek. "Me, I couldn't wait to go to school. Trust me when I tell you nothing interesting ever happens here."

"Oh, come on," Shelly said. "We had fun growing up. Remember? We'd ride our bikes everywhere as kids. Body surf at Mackerel Cove. Play hide and seek in the tunnels at Fort Wetherill. Before they buried most of it."

"You mean that time you kissed me?" Brian asked. "She left out that part, Em. We were hiding in the fort and it was dark and, all the sudden, Shelly just plants one on me. Tongue and everything."

"We were twelve." Shelly shook her head as if to force the blood away from her reddening cheeks. "Don't let them fool you Emma, there are so many great memories. Just take this one spot. See that opening to the marsh right there? When the tide goes out, that whole marsh drains back into the bay through that spot. Before low tide, it's like a moving river. We used to hang out on that beach for hours, waiting for the perfect conditions. Then, we'd walk up a ways, float on our backs and ride the current back into the bay. Over and over."

"I wanna do it." Emma said.

"Too late," Jason said, "the tide's almost out."

"There were tons of other things going on. The Fool's Regatta. The Tall Ships. Even movies being filmed. Look, ya see that house there?" Shelly pointed out a large rustic cottage clad in weathered cedar clapboards, a stone's throw from where they floated. "It's called Riven Rock. Steve Carell filmed a movie in that house."

"Really," Emma said, "what movie?"

"I don't remember the name. We were like, I don't know, seven. I didn't know who Steve Carell was at the time, but I thought it was cool that there was a real movie star here."

"Jim Carrey made a movie here too," Brian said.

"Yeah, before you were born," Jason said.

Emma sat up, pulled her hair into a ponytail and secured it with an elastic band that she had stored around her wrist. "What's that over there?"

Jason followed Emma's pointed finger and made a guess as to what she was looking at. "In the water? Those are oyster beds."

"Oh my god, I've never had oysters. Can we try 'em?" Emma asked.

"Sure. We'll grab some at dinner. Every restaurant has a raw bar around here."

"No, I mean like right here." Emma said. "Can't we just go over there and grab a bunch?"

"Girl, are you crazy?" Shelly said.

Jason chuckled. "What Shelly means is that's like a cardinal sin around here. Worse than murder. Oyster beds and lobster pots. Don't even think about it."

"The last person that got caught trying to poach oysters got put in the stockade in the center of the village and the townsfolk stoned them to death with live steamers," Brian said.

Jason tried to hold in the laughter but the frightened look on Emma's face made it a futile effort.

"That's not true," Shelly said. "Stop messing with her. We'll find you some oysters. I was thinking we should go over to Newport tonight, anyway. We can eat there and then do a little bar hopping."

"I'm into that," Jason said.

"Definitely," Brian said. "We can hit the Landing. That was the first place I ever used my fake ID. It'd be funny if it was the last, too."

"Cool, it settled then. You're gonna love Newport, Emma." Shelly finished the last swig of her beer, opened the cooler and tossed the empty can inside.

"Well, if we're going out, we should probably head back and get cleaned up," Jason suggested. He picked up a couple of cans that Brian left rolling around the floor of the cockpit and added them to the cooler. "You ready?"

"I'm good," Shelly said, maneuvering her way into her tank top.

"Brian, help me pull the anchor," Jason said.

Brian moved through the gap in the center of the windshield and took his position on the bow.

Jason spun the wheel, straightening the big outboard, and turned the ignition key. The motor fired up with a plum of white smoke.

"Let me get you some slack," Jason said. He pushed the throttle forward slightly. The motor clicked as the prop engaged, then shuttered and let out a squeal before stalling.

"Damn it. Do you have tension on that line, Brian?"

Jason was fairly sure he knew what happened. The anchor had likely dislodged, and the line had drifted near the back of the boat. If the anchor rode had fouled the propeller, he hoped it didn't cause any permanent damage.

"I've got tension, Jay. The anchor's seated."

Shelly moved to the stern, rested her hands on the cowling and strained to get a look at the prop. "I think there might be something wrapped around it, like a piece of clothing. Raise it up a bit."

Jason pressed the trim button on the throttle and the motor began to tilt with a mechanical whine.

The ear-splitting scream that erupted from Shelly's lungs sent Jason's heart rate skyrocketing. "What happened?" he yelped.

The response came as a duet of ear-piercing screams, followed by a splash as Emma dove into the water and began swimming toward shore.

Jason leapt up and bound to the stern, almost crashing into Brian, who had also reflexively began barreling toward the back of the boat.

"Are you ok?" Jason grabbed Shelly and hugged her tight. As she buried her face into his shoulder, her screams morphed into muffled ramblings. Jason leaned over and immediately saw the source of her terror.

"Holy shit, holy shit."

"No way, dude, I think it's a girl," Brian said. "Is she dead?"

"What do you mean is she dead?" Jason's body trembled. "She's got no face!"

Brian's eyes twitched, as if catching quick glimpses of the body without the commitment of actually facing it. "She must've swam into the prop. Oh god, this can't be happening."

The blood curdling shriek resumed as Shelly pushed off Jason and, without warning, launched herself into the water.

"Shelly, wait... What are we going to do?" Jason asked himself as much as Brain.

"Dude," Brian said, "this is messed up. I can't. I just can't."

Before Jason could respond, Brian was in the water, his arms flailing in an overhand stroke. Within a few seconds he caught up to Shelly, who, herself, was halfway to shore.

On the beach in front of Riven Rock, Emma stood, with her back to the cove and her head in her hands.

Alone, Jason remained frozen, shivering under the oppressive afternoon sun. His neck tensed as he forced himself to look at the sickening scene once more. He struggled to make sense of any of it. *Who was she? Where did she come from? What was going to happen to him now?* He couldn't begin to answer most of the infinite number of questions that swirled in his overloaded brain.

But there were two things that had solidified themselves as facts. This girl— if it was, in fact, a girl— was dead. And he had most definitely killed her.

UNCHARTED CHAPTER 2

Saturday, May 29th. Afternoon.

Blake stared at the red and yellow splotches of acrylic paint that coated the stretched canvas, fully expecting to find order in the seemingly haphazard pattern.

A fat fish. No. A slice of bread.

The inner door of the waiting room swung open and Dr. Maritza Perez appeared, accompanied by an attenuated but welcoming smile.

"Ready, Mr. Brier?"

Her voice was melodic, which, among other things, served to soften her sharp appearance. Dressed in a gray business suit and high heels, the ensemble would have predicted corporate attorney more than therapist.

Perez was attractive and, Blake guessed, older than she appeared. The clues were subtle but conclusive. Plump lips that moved in a slightly unnatural way. Eyelids that seemed to be pinned at the outer corners. The work was good. Almost imperceptible, if not for the discrepancy between her face and neck. The neck always gave it away.

Blake stood up and took a step toward Perez. He paused in front of the mounted artwork and squinted at it. "A horse, right?" Blake's hand hovered an inch from the surface. "The eyes. Here and here. The nose. And this is the mane."

Perez's smile grew less subdued. "If you say so."

"Am I at least close?"

"It can be whatever you want it to be. But it's not a Rorschach test, Mr. Brier."

Blake shrugged it off, walked into the office and headed directly for the couch. Perez closed the door before taking up her own seat in the opposite high-backed leather chair.

The room was sparsely decorated but achieved a sense of warmth, nonetheless. There were two doors. The one he entered through, and the one he was to exit by. The purpose of the forced traffic pattern was obvious. He appreciated Perez's respect for her patients' privacy.

"If you want to know the truth, a couple of months ago I went to a winery with a few girlfriends. They happened to be putting on a painting event. The theme was *Abstract* something or other. Basically, there was an actual painter demonstrating and the rest of us were supposed to copy what she did. Turns out, I wasn't very good at it. But it was fun. Plus, the colors worked nicely in the waiting room, so I hung it up. I never thought it would end up being so thought-provoking."

"Maybe you have more talent than you think."

Blake may have been a perpetual schmoozer, but in this instance, it was part of the game. During his first visit, Blake was struck by how similar a therapy session was to an interrogation. While he had no experience with the former, he was an expert at the latter.

The first step in any interrogation is the rapport building phase. In it, the interrogator shares an innocuous story, usually fabricated, with the purpose of establishing a conversational tone. An interpersonal connection. Dr. Perez's use of similar tactics was not lost on him.

"I must tell you, knowing your reluctance to all of this during our first session, I wasn't sure if you'd show up today," Perez started.

"Like I said before, I made a promise to Haeli. I'm not in the habit of breaking promises."

"That's admirable. But could it also be that you found some value in our previous conversation, apart from appeasing Haeli?"

He considered it. While he couldn't say he was counting the days until his next visit, he did find himself looking forward to it in some respects.

Blake had never been under any delusions that he was a well-adjusted individual. Even beyond his idiosyncrasies, he carried a hefty share of baggage. But then, so did everyone else he knew. The solution, for all of them, had always been one of compartmentalization. As far as he was aware, he was the first of them to find himself in these circumstances.

"Look, Doc. I hope I didn't come across as rude when we last met. I'm fully aware that I've got my issues. As much as Haeli does. Probably more so. But I have a hard time buying into the huggy-feely stuff."

"Is that what you think this is all about? Some kind of love fest, where we cry it out?" Perez laughed. "Well, I hate to disappoint you but if that's the case, you're way off. I'm going to ask you hard questions and you're going to be expected to provide even harder answers. It'll be contentious, at times. But my job is to hold your feet to the fire. So, to answer your question, no, you were not rude. You were honest. And if you can be that, I believe this can be of some benefit to you. Whether *you* believe it or not."

At some point, the soothing timbre of Perez's voice evaporated, leaving only it's raw mechanics. Blake figured she had hoped to hit a nerve and, he had to admit, it had been effective. Blake could subscribe to this version of psychotherapy. No indulgence. No excuses. She had pivoted in her approach. Parried his attack. He would have done the same.

"Honesty I can do," Blake said. "What do you want to know?"

"Why don't we pick up where we left off." Perez flipped to the previous page of her notepad. After a quick glance, she flipped the page back and looked him in the eyes. "Last we spoke, Haeli had brought up the idea of the two of you moving in together. You believed your hesitancy was causing a strain on the relationship. Have you spoken to her about your concerns, as we discussed?"

"No. She hasn't brought it up again, so I left it alone."

"Then things have improved?"

"Things are fine. I mean, they were never bad. But..."

"But?"

"Ever since she brought it up, she seems off. We still spend a lot of time together and we have a good time, but I can tell she's not right."

"Do you think it could be that she feels hurt? Hurt that you're not willing to take the next step. To show her that you're committed. Can you understand why she might feel that way?"

"Of course, I can. The thing is, I don't know what's wrong with me. It's not that I don't love her. I do. She's an amazing person on many levels. And it's not that I'm not committed to her. I really am, even if it doesn't seem that way. The weird thing is that she stays at my place almost every night and it's great. But when I think about her moving in, I have a physical reaction. It's like I'm in fight-or-flight mode. It's ridiculous."

"Good. You recognize the trigger and the response. That shows an adequate level of self-awareness. It seems you have an aversion to the idea of cohabitation that may even be unrelated to Haeli. The type of reaction you are describing is often indicative of past trauma. Can you identify a past experience that you would consider traumatizing?"

Blake laughed.

Perez's neutral expression remained unchanged.

"We're going to need a lot more than an hour and a half," Blake said.

"I see." Perez scratched at the pad notepad, then paused. Her brow tensed as if saddened or, more likely, concerned. "Did you serve?"

"I did."

"Tell me about that."

"I won't lie to you," Blake said, "there's a lot I can't tell you. Most of it, actually. But I can say that I've seen many terrible things. And I'll admit that I've had to do terrible things."

"That must have been difficult for you."

"That's part of the problem, I think. Being in the thick of it, life or death situations, dangerous situations, is when I feel most at peace. The hard part is fitting into regular life, as crazy as that sounds. When I'm set into action, so to speak, I'm like a totally different person. A better person. It's like I have a split personality."

"Well, you don't," Perez assured. "That's called Dissociative Identity Disorder, and it's very rare. It's characterized by completely separate personality states, almost as if more than one person is inhabiting one body. What you're describing is something that is much more common, even expected, for a man with your experience."

Blake knew what she was alluding to. He had known for many years. "Post-Traumatic Stress Disorder," he said.

"Yes. Exactly. PTSD manifests itself in a number of ways, at different levels of intensity."

"I know. Too well, unfortunately. I've known more than a few good men who have lost their battle with it. It's the reason I'm here in the first place. Or it's the reason Haeli felt the need to seek professional help. Then convinced me to do it with her."

"Here's where I ask a tough question, Mr. Brier."

"Please, you can call me Blake."

"Thank you, Blake. What I want to ask is if you have experienced extreme depression. Suicidal thoughts, suicide attempts, self-mutilation?"

"No, never. Just the opposite. I want to live *more*. Bigger. With a purpose. I'm going stir crazy right now. That's the real diagnosis."

"Many in your position, typically task-oriented individuals, struggle with feelings that they are no longer useful. You mentioned that you are retired. Have you considered some part-time work? Maybe join an organization or get involved in community service. Something to focus your energy on."

"Yes. In fact, it's in the works. A few old friends and I have been considering starting a new venture."

"That sounds excellent, Blake." The injection of enthusiasm was jarring. Almost patronizing, however unintentional. "What type of venture?"

Blake weighed his words. "The details are being finalized, but it's mission will be to help those in need."

"That sounds worthy, indeed."

A loud electronic chirping cut through the relative quiet. Blake admonished himself for forgetting to shut his ringer off as he reached into his pocket to retrieve the device. "Sorry about that."

"No worries."

Blake pressed the button on the side to silence the sound and, before stowing the phone into his pocket, glanced at the screen.

Andrew Harrison.

It was the last name he'd expected to see. Especially after so much time had passed. The last time he had spoken to Anja's partner was around the time of her death.

"What I would like to do," Perez continued, "is dig into some of these events. You may leave out whatever details you feel necessary. The important thing is the impact they may have had on you. Now, I want you to recall an event that affected you. The first thing that pops into your mind, okay?"

Blake was aware that a question had been posed to him, but his mind was preoccupied with questions of his own. *Why would Harrison be calling him? Had there been new information? Something to do with Anja? What could possibly cause him to reach out after all this time?*

He touched his phone through the coarse fabric of his jeans. The mystery of what words would have been spoken from the other end of the call tugged at him.

Even though Blake hardly knew the man, he felt they shared a bond. A bond forged by mutual suffering. He recalled the pain on Harrison's face when they met at the cemetery, as clear as if the man were standing in front of him.

A surge of grief overwhelmed him. Anja's delicate face permeated his thoughts. A mixture of deep longing and outrage hijacked his rational brain. Tears welled in his eyes.

"Blake?"

He swallowed hard, then cleared his throat.

"Anja," he said.

"Okay, good. Who's Anja?"

Who's Anja? Blake was struck by the absurdity of the question. Not on Perez's part, but his own. The death of his beloved Anja defined him. Near crippling flashbacks snuck up on him on a regular basis, becoming more frequent, the more time that passed. Yet, he had not mentioned her to Perez.

"Someone I loved very much," Blake said. "She was murdered."

"I'm sorry to hear that."

Blake took a breath and tried to slow his pulse. He reached into his pocket and brought his phone to his lap. He stared at the missed call notification for a moment, then thrust himself to his feet.

"I'm sorry, Doc," he said, "something has come up. We're going to have to cut this session short."

"Blake, we've touched on something that I think is extremely important we talk about."

"You're right. And I promise we will. Next time."

Perez stood as Blake made his way to the exit.

"I wish you'd stay," Perez said.

"If it's any consolation, you were right. It never had anything to do with Haeli."

Blake tapped the notification, causing the phone to redial Harrison's number, and held the phone to his ear.

"Next time," he said and disappeared through the door.

UNCHARTED CHAPTER 3

Saturday, May 29th. Evening.

The tires of Tom Hopkins's Chevy Impala crunched along the substrate of crushed seashells as it approached the end of the pier. He scanned the landing for an open parking spot.

With boating season in full swing, parking at the West Ferry was notoriously hard to come by. And with the overflow of vehicles stretching several blocks up Narragansett Avenue, he hadn't been optimistic.

As Jamestown's Chief of Police, he would have had the latitude to wedge himself in somewhere. Possibly along the small area set aside for picnic tables or up against the small out-building that housed the bathroom. But it would have been obnoxious, and the last thing Hopkins needed was another complaint.

Instead, he lingered a minute while a stout man loaded three fishing poles into the back of a minivan. Inside, his two young boys bounced back and forth between the second-row seats.

After the man hopped into the driver's seat and presumably persuaded the children to buckle themselves in, the illumination of a single working reverse light signified that it was worth the wait. He slid into the vacant spot as the minivan pulled away.

Hopkins walked to the edge of the pier and down a metal gangway that led to the dingy dock. Despite posted signs that the dock was reserved for those utilizing the services of the Dutch Harbor marina, Hopkins found the dock occupied by two local teenage girls. Wearing what he considered to be age-inappropriate bikinis, they were performing a choreographed dance to a cell phone they had propped on the shorter of two adjacent pilings.

Upon noticing his presence, the startled girls grabbed their towels, scooped up the phone and scurried up the gangway. Having changed from his uniform into civilian clothing, Hopkins figured they probably didn't know who he was. They had hurried off, not because they thought they would be in trouble, but because they were embarrassed. Or, more likely, creeped out.

At least they have some common sense.

Hopkins held his bladed hand to his brow to block the glare from the low hanging sun. He quickly located what he was looking for.

About a quarter mile in the distance, the twenty-five-foot rigid inflatable boat, easily identifiable by the words *Jamestown Police* scrawled along the side in block letters, had already turned out of the channel and was moving through the mooring field toward his position.

As the boat drew closer, Hopkins could make out Lieutenant Charlie Fuller's enthusiastic wave. Although not close enough to see the details of his face, he imagined the exaggerated motion was being accompanied by an equally cheesy grin.

A life-long Jamestown resident, Charlie Fuller was among the nicest people that Hopkins had ever met. So much so that when Hopkins retired from the Providence Police Department and took the job in Jamestown, he distrusted Fuller more than anyone else. In his experience, at a place where even the new recruits are jaded, anyone who was that friendly, that happy, or that helpful was full of crap and likely angling for something.

Eventually, Fuller's relentlessly positivity won him over. Before long, Hopkins had taken the young officer under his wing, even helping him prepare for the Sergeant's exam and then the Lieutenant's exam, a year later. Ultimately, it turned out that Fuller was only competing with himself for the Lieutenant position because the other Sergeants, mostly older guys who had retired from other places, didn't want anything to do with the added responsibility. But he did well, nonetheless.

Unlike Providence, the fifteen-man police department had no need for a deep cadre of supervisors. There were no Deputy Chiefs or Captains, which made thirty-one-year-old Charlie Fuller second in command. Technically.

As Fuller approached the dock, he cut the wheel, allowing the starboard edge to kiss the dock. Hopkins stepped in with one foot while kicking off with the other in a single motion.

"Were you waiting long?" Fuller asked.

"Not at all. But we'd better get moving. We're losing daylight."

Fuller had made good time, thanks to favorable conditions. Jamestown's only police boat was docked at the Conanicut marina, located at the East Ferry on the opposite side of the island. Connected by the one-mile-long Narragansett Avenue, travel between the two by points by vehicle took a few minutes. By boat, the journey was considerably less convenient. It required one to first travel south through the east passage into open water, then west around the southernmost point of the island, known as Beavertail, and, finally, north through the west passage toward Dutch Harbor.

It was for this reason that Hopkins had twice proposed funding for a second police boat and dockage at Dutch Harbor. Unfortunately, the line item was shot down by the council on both occasions.

Fuller steered the boat north through the moorings, taking care not to kick up too much of a wake. Many of the boaters were on deck, enjoying a cocktail or a meal. As was the custom, they returned each friendly wave in a repetitious pattern.

"I called everyone like you asked," Fuller said. "Mostly everyone's already here except for Bobby and Allison. Both said they were out of town."

"I'm aware," Hopkins said.

Robert "Bobby" Berret was the department's only Detective. It was ironic that Berret was absent from the first investigation in two years that involved more than petty theft or mischief, but there was little Hopkins could say about it. After all, it was a Saturday and Barrett's regular day off. On top of that, Berret had put in for a few vacation days to extend the weekend. He said he was visiting family in Maine, but Hopkins knew it was a lie. He and Officer Allison Konesky had been carrying on for some time and, although they went to great lengths to keep it a secret, Hopkins was well aware. In fact, after approving Berret's leave, he penciled in Konesky's coinciding vacation before she submitted the request.

"Did you read the statements from the kids that were on the boat?" Fuller asked.

"I did."

"The way they described it, it sounds like this is gonna be gnarly."

"Most boating accidents are," Hopkins said.

"Do you think they're telling the truth? I mean, all of their stories match and everything, but it seems like they gotta be leaving something out, right?"

"It's possible," Hopkins said. "They did have time to agree on a story before they were separated. But even the smallest details matched. That's the stuff you've got to focus on, Charlie. The things that otherwise seem insignificant. I've never seen a group of career criminals that could put together a story that tight, let alone a bunch of scared college kids. As it is right now, I think we have to assume they're telling the truth."

Through the swaying masts of the last few sailboats, the flickering strobes of two identical Coast Guard RBS-II response boats marked the outer perimeter of the scene. Positioned at the mouth of what was essentially a cove formed by a V-shaped recess in the coastline, the two crews could easily cordon off the area by intercepting any approaching vessels.

"Hook up with them for a minute," Hopkins directed.

Fuller nodded. Having cleared the harbor, Fuller jammed the

throttle forward. The bow of the small RIB lifted and planed over the rollers, slapping the crest of each tiny wave in a hypnotic rhythm.

As they closed in on the nearest of the two Coast Guard vessels, Fuller cut back on the throttle. Hopkins grabbed hold of one of the canopy stanchions to steady himself as Fuller swerved hard to the left, then again to the right. The wide S-turn maneuver brought them parallel and about four feet off the port side of the orange and white craft.

A young man with jet black hair and a broad, hairless chest was stepping into the second leg of a wetsuit. His name was Paul Russo. Both Hopkins and Fuller had crossed paths with the guardsman many times, but neither could say they liked him much.

"Feeling better, Tom?" Russo asked. "'Cause you look like hell."

Hopkins never ceased to be amazed at how fast gossip travelled. It was bad enough he had to deal with the local residents. But if Paul knew about his recent issues, that meant that half of Newport knew, or would soon enough.

Hopkins had a few words he wanted to throw back at Paul Russo, but he decided not to give him the satisfaction. He tried to force a smile but, apparently, couldn't quite pull it off.

"Come on, Tom. Just foolin' with ya. We ready or what?"

"Give me a few minutes," Hopkins said. "We've gotta take some shots. Charlie, grab the camera. I'll take the helm."

Fuller stepped away and Hopkins grabbed the wheel. "Hang here Paul, I'll flag you down when we're ready."

Hopkins didn't wait for a response before he goosed the throttle, leaving Russo in his literal wake.

Ahead, the small abandoned bowrider bobbed and tugged at its anchor. Beyond it was Zeek's creek. Hopkins immediately noticed that several cars had stopped on the edge of the roadway that crossed over the marsh. Several motorists gathered outside of their vehicles, no doubt drawn by the Coast Guard's display of flashing blue and red lights. That kind of attention is exactly what he was trying to avoid.

Hopkins keyed his handheld radio. "Alpha Two."

"Alpha Two," came the reply.

"Swing over to North Road. I've got a bunch of onlookers impeding traffic. Then standby there and make sure no one else congregates."

"Roger. En route."

Hopkins tossed the radio onto the seat and slowed the boat to a comfortable speed.

"Charlie," Hopkins said.

Fuller, with the strap of the bulky DSLR camera slung over his neck, came closer.

"I'm going to make the largest circle I can around the scene," Hopkins explained. "Think of it like a clock. I want you to take a shot at every hour mark. Center the boat in the frame on each shot. Then, we'll get in closer and I'll do another circle. We'll do that three or four times, okay?"

"Got it," Fuller said.

As patronizing as the basic instructions would have sounded to a third party, Hopkins knew that Fuller needed clear and thorough instructions. It put Fuller at ease to know exactly what was expected of him and it was a time-saver for Hopkins, avoiding the barrage of questions that would inevitably follow a vague direction.

Hopkins started his circuitous route. Face pressed against the camera, Fuller snapped away. Hopkins struck up a one-sided conversation.

"One of the things I learned early on," Hopkins said, projecting over the wind and churning motor, "is to document the crap out of the crime scene. Even in the case of an accident. You never know where it'll go. I'll share a cautionary tale with you. When I was new to the Detective Bureau, we had a suicide. My partner and I went out to the scene. Just like Patrol reported, the guy had offed himself with a forty-five. Gun was still in his hand with an empty magazine and there was one spent cartridge on the floor a few feet away. Cut and dry. We decided not to call in the Crime Scene Unit. We did take a couple of pictures, but not before we manhandled the body. Then we left it to Patrol to release the body to the medical examiner, in time to make it to lunch. See where this is going?"

Fuller continued squinting into the viewfinder. "It wasn't a suicide?"

"Nope. The gun and the shell were sent to the State Lab for ballistics as a matter of policy. Turns out, the spent cartridge wasn't from the gun that was on scene. And, to make matters worse, the old forty-five wasn't even capable of firing a shot."

Fuller dropped the camera a few inches and turned to face Hopkins. "What happened?"

"We botched a murder scene is what happened. No search, no fingerprints, no anything. My partner got the brunt of it because he was the veteran guy."

"But did you end up catching the killer?" Fuller stared like a child waiting for the dramatic conclusion to a bed-time story.

"No. Never did. Now, pay attention to what you're doing."

Fuller jerked the camera to eye level.

"The point is, you can never go back once you've disturbed the scene. If a case ends up going to the jury, all they have to work with is what you documented. The goal of these photographs is to let them see what you saw."

Of course, Fuller knew all of this. It had been in every book that he was required to read for his promotional exams. But Hopkins couldn't help but use the real-world scenario as a teaching aid. Things like this didn't happen often and, accident or not, it would likely be the most useful experience Fuller will have had to date.

Hopkins completed several circles with the final lap being only fifteen feet from the bowrider. He slowed the boat to a crawl. As they passed the back, they got their first close-up look at the deceased.

"Aw, that's sick," Fuller said. "What a horrible way to die."

Hopkins couldn't think of a truer statement. The damage to the poor girl's face was catastrophic. A blade of the propeller was buried deep into her skull where her nose and eyes would have been. The motor, when tilted, had lifted her body halfway out of the water and her thin, delicate arms dangled as if she were pushing herself up by an imaginary ledge, hidden below the waterline.

Hopkins completed the circle, then came around to the port side.

He tossed a line to Fuller, who lashed the police boat to the side of the bowrider, such that the back of the RIB jutted out ten feet past the transom of its counterpart.

"Take some pictures of the interior from here," Hopkins instructed. "Then jump on and take more. Be careful not to disturb anything. And get a picture of the inside of that cooler. I'll raise Paul and let him know we're ready for him."

Fuller set out to complete his task as Hopkins retrieved his radio. Before he could call, he noticed that Russo was already motoring toward him. He crouched down and leaned over, getting as close as he could to the victim without falling in.

"What were you doing here?" Hopkins whispered.

Based on her petite frame, long hair and feminine clothing, it was clear that the victim was a female. How old she was, that was another story. The natural postmortem processes had modeled her skin and she had already begun to bloat. More so than he would have expected. Hopkins wondered if being half submerged in water had somehow accelerated decomposition.

The Coast Guard vessel arrived and set up in the opposite configuration. The three boats tied together created an open-ended box around the victim. Hopkins was satisfied that the configuration would provide some shielding from the nosy residents that had come out of their homes along the shore to gawk.

Russo zipped up his wetsuit and slid into the water. He was able to stand on the bottom with his head and a sliver of his shoulders above the water.

"Ready for me to pull her loose?" Russo said.

"Yeah, go ahead. Then Charlie and I will help you pull her up here." Hopkins waved to Fuller. "Charlie, get some shots while he frees her from the prop."

Russo moved in close, with a pair of neoprene diving gloves, he grasped the girl's head on either side and pulled.

"She's stuck," Russo said. "Her hair is all wrapped around the prop. I'm going to have to cut it free. Frank, grab me a pair of scissors."

One of the other two guardsman handed Russo the scissors. He cut away a clump and held it out toward Hopkins.

"Charlie," Hopkins said, "grab a bunch of paper bags from under the seat. And a sharpie if we have one. I want to bag each one of these clumps individually. Number the bags sequentially and put the time on them."

"On it," Fuller said.

Hopkins pulled two pairs of rubber gloves from one of his pants' cargo pockets. He put on a pair and tossed the other to Fuller.

Fuller put on the gloves, reached over and took the first clump of hair from Russo, who's slack facial expression gave away his impatience.

Russo continued cutting. On the fourth cut, before anyone was prepared for it, the weight of the body pulled itself free with a grotesque suction sound and a splash.

"Okay, see if you can lift her up a bit. Charlie, give me a hand."

Russo reached under the girl and lifted her as if performing a military press. Hopkins and Fuller guided her into the boat and laid her on her back.

"Oh my god." Fuller blurted.

"This was no accident," Hopkins said.

The thin fabric of the girl's shirt was torn and tattered, exposing most of her chest, including one of her breasts. A dozen half-inch long stab wounds dotted her torso. Stranger still, the fingers of her right hand appeared to be missing, and the portion of her hand that remained was tightly bandaged.

"Looks like you got yourself a murder," Paul said. "You up for this?"

Hopkins was in no mood, especially not now. "Thanks for your help Paul, we've got it from here."

"Always glad to help," Russo hoisted himself out of the water and unzipped his suit.

"If you guys don't mind holding the perimeter until we can collect the evidence off of the boat and get Sea Tow out here, I'd appreciate it," Hopkins said.

"Sure thing." Russo untied and the crew set off to join their colleagues.

"I had a feeling this girl was in the water for more than just a couple of hours," Hopkins said. "She didn't swim into the prop; she was dumped somewhere else and washed up here. Those kids will be relieved. As much as you can be about someone being stabbed to death."

Fuller grabbed the camera and snapped a few shots of the body. Hopkins lifted the seat and pulled out a small flexible ruler. "When you take closeups of the wounds, make sure you put the scale in the picture. Closeups can be deceiving without a reference." He laid the piece of plastic on the victim's chest, next to the top-most wound.

"What do you think she was stabbed with? It looks like something real thin. Almost like a screwdriver, or something like that," Fuller said.

"Not necessarily. When someone's stabbed, the skin stretches and then closes back up. The wound always looks smaller than the instrument that caused it." Hopkins said.

"Ah, ya learn something new every day. So, what do we do now? If this girl has been dead for a little while, someone would have reported her missing. And we did get that missing— "

"I know, Charlie. I was thinking the same thing."

***

Pre-order your copy of Uncharted now!

https://www.amazon.com/dp/B08RRZ2YKP/

ALSO BY L.T. RYAN

Visit https://ltryan.com/pb for paperback purchasing information.

The Jack Noble Series

The Recruit (Short Story)

The First Deception (Prequel 1)

Noble Beginnings (Jack Noble #1)

A Deadly Distance (Jack Noble #2)

Thin Line (Jack Noble #3)

Noble Intentions (Jack Noble #4)

When Dead in Greece (Jack Noble #5)

Noble Retribution (Jack Noble #6)

Noble Betrayal (Jack Noble #7)

Never Go Home (Jack Noble #8)

Beyond Betrayal (Clarissa Abbot)

Noble Judgment (Jack Noble #9)

Never Cry Mercy (Jack Noble #10)

Deadline (Jack Noble #11)

End Game (Jack Noble #12)

Noble Ultimatum (Jack Noble #13) - Spring 2021

Bear Logan Series

Ripple Effect

Blowback

Take Down

Deep State

Rachel Hatch Series

Drift

Downburst

Fever Burn

Smoke Signal

Firewalk - December 2020

Whitewater - March 2021

Mitch Tanner Series

The Depth of Darkness

Into The Darkness

Deliver Us From Darkness - coming Summer 2021

Cassie Quinn Series

Path of Bones

Untitled - February, 2021

Blake Brier Series

Unmasked

Unleashed

Uncharted - April, 2021

Affliction Z Series

Affliction Z: Patient Zero

Affliction Z: Abandoned Hope

Affliction Z: Descended in Blood

Affliction Z: Fractured (Part 1)

Affliction Z: Fractured (Part 2) - October, 2021

ABOUT THE AUTHOR

L.T. Ryan is a *USA Today* and international bestselling author. The new age of publishing offered L.T. the opportunity to blend his passions for creating, marketing, and technology to reach audiences with his popular Jack Noble series.

Living in central Virginia with his wife, the youngest of his three daughters, and their three dogs, L.T. enjoys staring out his window at the trees and mountains while he should be writing, as well as reading, hiking, running, and playing with gadgets. See what he's up to at http://ltryan.com.

Social Medial Links:

- Facebook (L.T. Ryan): https://www.facebook.com/LTRyanAuthor

- Facebook (Jack Noble Page): https://www.facebook.com/JackNobleBooks/

- Twitter: https://twitter.com/LTRyanWrites

- Goodreads: http://www.goodreads.com/author/show/6151659.L_T_Ryan

Made in the USA
Coppell, TX
02 December 2022